Obscure Intentions

A Geneviève Benoit Novel

Anthony J. Harrison

Published by Anthony J. Harrison

Copyright© 2018 Anthony J. Harrison

ISBN: 978-0-4632933-3-1 (ebook version)

ISBN: 978-1-7324081-3-5 (print version)

License Note

Cover design by Damonza
http://www.damonza.com

Editing Services provided by
Cecily Tartaglione at Red Pen Editor
http://redpeneditor.weebly.com

<u>This book is dedicated to:</u>

All the women in the world who are brave enough to overcome their fears and past traumas, becoming stronger and more self-aware of their strengths. They are the ones who will shape the future for others to follow, breaking down the barriers of injustice through-out the world.

Table of Contents

Table of Contents (con't)

Chapter One

A prickly burlap blanket slid off the shoulders of the solitary figure lying on the cell floor. Hakim Talib opened his eyes to see a pitch-black void. Propping himself up against the wall, he shook the cobwebs of sleep from his thoughts. What day is it? How long have I been down here? He reached his arms out in front of his body, but he couldn't see his stiff and bloody scab-covered fingertips that were courtesy of the sandstone chiseled hewn walls and floor. The former dungeon he was occupying was obscure as the desert on a moonless night.

Outside, waves of radiant heat rippled off the stone walls of the fifteenth-century prison as the late summer sun beat down upon it. Hakim didn't feel the heat, insulated from the elements by massive stones used to build the once mighty citadel; instead he was surrounded by the cold dampness that hung in the air of his windowless room.

Hakim's captors knew how many days had passed since his return to Marseille by the Algerian State Police. After being checked by a police department physician, Hakim was sedated and moved from the Police Municipale jail to one with the specific purpose of disorienting and isolating suspects.

As he entered his third week of isolation in the basement of Chateau Il d'If, the Algerian was being kept away from prying eyes roaming the streets of Marseille. At the same time, members of the DJSE continued their preparations to raid the drug processing facility he spoke of during chemically enhanced interrogations. Utilizing the former citadel, the French had established a means to conduct questioning of prisoners with anonymity.

Hakim heard heavy boots crunching along the gravel, echoing off the walls and interrupting his thoughts, the only discernible sound he heard twice a day. The scraping of the key sliding into the lock told him it was once again feeding time.

The glow from a single lightbulb hanging in the corridor lit up the room as the door swung open. Hakim shielded his eyes from the sudden light surrounding the silhouetted figure. "Tell me where I'm being kept." It was the same demand he'd been asking of his faceless captors for days as he stood away from the door.

Holding the tray out, as if calling a bowl of tepid fish-head soup and crusty bread a proper meal, the officer, clad in black, said nothing. Each day the scene was played on video screens in a control room located a hundred meters above the basement. Activity was observed by a senior police psychologist, and today by Detective Geneviève Benoit and Detective (Captain) Claude Lemieux.

As he studied the silhouette holding out his ration of food, Hakim sought to gauge the size of his captor as he took the tray. Unlike members of the military who might have been exposed to some level of survival training, he had nothing to call upon except his own wits.

The 3-meter square room he was kept in, with a thread-barren blanket and small bucket to relieve himself in, did little to keep his physical and mental acuity. A soldier would try to maintain their physical prowess by exercising and mentally focus on trying to formulate an escape plan.

Watching the display provided by the low-light and infrared cameras positioned throughout the room, Benoit and Lemieux could see both the guard and Hakim moving without the aid of lights. With this setup, the doctor and his staff could closely monitor the patients' activities, like consuming food that had been laced with a potent derivative of sodium pentothal. This had likewise led to a continuing discussion by the female staff commenting on the drug's side effect: causing Hakim to fondle himself while sleeping.

"We've been able to record pretty much everything he's said based on the questions you wanted us to ask," the physician said to the two police officers. "And he doesn't even recall he's done it."

"All the information you've gathered was done while he was sleeping?" Detective Geneviève Benoit asked.

"Yes. With the right combination of drugs and the subliminal messaging we've played, he 'sang like a canary,' as the actor James Cagney would say."

"Amazing," Detective (Captain) Claude Lemieux said, shaking his head. "And Nadine used to say all I needed was a bottle of good Bordeaux," alluding to his deceased wife.

Glancing at the clock, Geneviève saw their scheduled departure time was fast approaching for the ferry returning to the city. "Claude, we need to make our way to the dock if we're going to join the raiding party," she reminded.

"Going so soon?" the physician asked.

"Yes, we need to see if the information you recorded has proven fruitful," Claude said, placing his aviator sunglasses over his eyes. "We can't do our police work here watching someone stumbling in the dark."

After a circuitous walk through the hidden passageways of the fortress, the two detectives soon headed towards the single dock and the vessel returning to the city. As both officers stood along the rail of the ferry, the cool breeze refreshing their senses, they watched the city of Marseille grow closer. Tourists bustled about the deck in vain attempts to capture views of the city on their cell phones as the vessel approached the docks.

"After three weeks of 'immersion interrogation,' we've learned that drugs the British are focused on are arriving here from somewhere in North Africa, and then being shipped elsewhere," Claude said. "But no names other than what we previously had."

"But since our suspect has given us this information, we can now direct our attention to Algiers and Omar Khalid as one of the potential sources, right?" Geneviève asked, her untethered hair swirling in the breeze.

Tilting his sunglasses down the bridge of his nose, Claude said, "Your days of travel are over, especially to Algeria."

As she turned to look at her partner, Geneviève knew from his gaze he was making his statement based on a genuine concern for her. Even though her last trip to Algiers resulted in the capture of Hakim Talib, it likewise came with a failed attack on her by Khalid's men. If not for her training, the outcome might have been different.

"The nice thing about going back to Algiers would be in knowing I wouldn't be alone; you'd be there too." Her innocent smile beamed back at him. "Not to mention having the services of Inspector Haddad and his police force."

"Geneviève, stop giving me those looks. I'm too old," Claude said, fighting back the grin he wanted to display at her comment.

"Please stand back from the exits until the gangway has been secured. Thank you," came the announcement from the ferry operator's first officer, noting their proximity to the docks.

Starting his way down the stairs to the main deck, Claude said, "Come on, we've got work to do."

***

Across the Mediterranean Sea, 1,400 kilometers from the dungeon holding Hakim, his cousin was in the middle of his own brand of torture.

8

In the sweltering heat inside a warehouse, two men worked to complete their task. Large beads of sweat formed on their brows and rolled down the faces behind the protective masks, stinging the eyes trying to blink through the discomfort. The once light blue fabric of the hazardous material suit Nazim Aziz and his helper, Malik, were wearing now showed darkened patches of sweat soaking through the material.

"This is the last one," Malik said from behind his mask, pouring the warm liquid from the cooking pot into the glass bottles on the table.

"Make sure all the pots are thoroughly cleaned after the bottles are sealed," Nazim instructed the young Algerian. "Let no one disrobe until done, you understand?"

"Of course, I understand completely."

Nazim didn't consider the environment the men would work in after moving the drug processing work from Marseille to the abandoned warehouse outside the capital city of Algeria. His estranged partner, Gregory Arsenault, had chosen the warehouse in Marseille, which included air-conditioning. This was something he'd taken for granted, but he now understood the importance of having the luxury of the cooler air.

Walking outside the packaging section, Nazim pulled the mask from his face and wiped his sweat with a clean towel. Tearing off the damp, clinging suit, he rolled it up before placing it in a bin with others, which would be taken to a local incinerator and burned.

Nazim produced a liter of water to the drug dealer while Omar Khalid asked, "Is it always necessary to wear the mask and suit?"

"Yes," Nazim answered, taking a drink from the bottle. "Your chemist warned Gregory and me about the residual effects of the drug and said our best protection should not differ from what he and his staff wear."

Omar Khalid had never seen this part of the preparation to move the illicit drugs from North Africa. His exposure to drug trafficking, even early in his criminal past, amounted to handling bundles of marijuana strapped to camels making their way across the desert from Morocco. He was beginning to understand his apprentices' earlier reluctance to include his men working with Gregory in Marseille, knowing exposure to the drug could lead to lethal consequences.

"Now, since we're essentially ready to ship, have you heard from your acquaintance in Tangiers?" Nazim asked, wiping himself down with a damp towel.

Glancing back at Nazim, Omar contemplated telling him the truth. *Youssef wants too much in return for helping ship the drugs*, he remembered, recounting the discussion he had with the Moroccan gang leader about finding a freighter to move the drugs to Marseille.

"He, um, shall we say, still wants to negotiate," Omar said.

"There's nothing to negotiate." Nazim pulled on a pair of clean trousers. "All we're asking him to do is find a ship captain willing to look the other way who sails between here and Marseille."

"You see it in simple terms, my young friend, he sees it as his reputation being at stake," the older Algerian explained, sipping his Perrier. "Anyhow, aren't you likewise waiting to find out from your former partner about moving the drugs beyond France?"

Buttoning his shirt, Nazim looked at his mentor. *How do I tell him Gregory's shipping partners want double the fee to move the drugs?* He too recalled earlier discussions centering on their drug trafficking.

"The shipper, Papillion Transport has requested twice the fee," Nazim said, conceding to tell Omar about the rising cost. "It suggests, after Gregory and I parted company, the shipping firm was advised that they're being compelled to gouge me for more money."

"This Papillion Transport does business across the Mediterranean, does it not?" Omar asked.

"Yes. I recall Gregory mentioning on several occasions about the vessel movements: making stops in Athens, Naples, Barcelona, Istanbul, Tangiers, and including here," Nazim said, lacing up his boots. "I never paid close attention at the time, which in hindsight is my fault."

"When in business, it's not always possible for the leader to be all knowledgeable," Omar replied as he dropped the empty Perrier bottle in the trash. "But, if what you say is true, then I might be able to call upon another associate to help," he said, alluding to his connections with a Mafioso don in Naples.

"Is this the same one who is helping apprehend the policewoman?" Nazim asked before drinking down the liter of water. *Three weeks, three long weeks, and still no mention of Hakim or plan to steal away the policewoman.* He conceded he relied on Gregory for information of police activities.

"I will not dictate to Alberto on how to formulate his plans, nor will I give him an unrealistic 'deadline' for delivering the woman," Omar said. "I trust he'll carry out the task in due time."

"And what of your plans to locate Hakim?" Nazim asked, alluding to his cousin, spirited away from Algiers and yet to be seen in Marseille. "For the number of dinars spent 'greasing' the palms of the police commissioners, you've no information beyond he was placed on an airplane."

"Not once have I forgotten about your cousin," Omar assured Nazim, turning to face him. "And I've been working closely with the police commissioner loyal to me to discern where he's being held." He voiced his concern with a touch of anger, feeling the loss of his nephew.

"My apologies Omar; I'm just concerned for his well-being."

"I understand your frustration, but together we'll find him and bring him back," the older Algerian said. "We still have favorable connections with several Maghrebi groups in Marseille and Nice we can call for help."

Chapter Two

"Two minutes to action." The SWAT team commander's announcement crackled through the earpieces worn by the teams. Two white panel vans maneuvered through traffic as they approached the gate outside an abandoned appliance warehouse, followed closely by two unmarked cars.

Glancing at the other seven officers in the van, Geneviève felt out of place as the only woman taking part in the raid. Beneath a black Nomex jumpsuit and a black balaclava covering her face, the only clue to her gender was her auburn ponytail hanging out from below the riot helmet. With her pistol secured to her hip, her nervousness caused Geneviève to grip and re-grip the MP5 submachine gun strapped to her chest.

"Stand by to exit," Captain Georges, the overall team leader, directed as the vans came to a halt outside the warehouse. Being the first in the van as part of Team Two, Geneviève would be the last one out, responsible for getting into position before hearing the next command.

Detective (Captain) Claude Lemieux looked on through the binoculars hanging from his chest as he waited in one of the unmarked cars outside the gate. Moments after stopping outside the building, the van doors swung open, discharging the assault teams, each moving in a deliberate pattern practiced over the days leading up to this evening's raid.

"Can you see her?" Detective Nicolas Berger asked the senior officer sitting next to him, showing concern for his co-worker. With the first female officer assigned to their department, he and his partner Masson had taken to Benoit quickly, treating her like a little sister needing protection at every turn.

"No, they all look the same," Claude replied as he scanned the scene, unable to decide which figure was his partner. "With all the gear on, you can't tell who has tits or a shapely ass."

"Stand by main entrance; Team Two, are you in position?" the commander queried over the radio.

"Team Two is in position," the senior member answered, seeing six men and one woman poised along the wall. The explosives handler for each team placed shaped charges against the hinges of each entry door, preparing them for detonation at the signal given by the commander.

"Entry in three, two, and one," the commander said.

As the senior officer uttered 'one,' charges were activated, and with muffled explosions, the doors to the warehouse were rendered useless as members pulled the remains away from the building. Arriving in a choreographed ballet, each SWAT team swept through the spaces. Beams of light danced across the walls, as each pair conducted their search, shouting out their locations for anyone who might have been inside and hiding.

As she moved through the building behind her assigned teammate, Geneviève's pulse quickened, and her breath came in short gasps. Swinging her weapon back and forth to cover her partner, she thought, I haven't felt this excited since taking part in urban assault training in February.

She found a small open box in the corner of the warehouse and applied the muzzle of her machine gun to move the cardboard flaps on the top. All that was in there were blue suits wrapped in plastic bags. "Clear," she said exiting the room. As she turned to join her partner she noticed several empty bottles lined up along a wooden crate. "I've got something," she said, sounding nervous over the radio.

"Stand by Benoit!" She heard the voices of Captain Georges and her team leader through the speaker at the same time.

Stepping towards her, they both saw the crate and bottles sitting on the floor. "Officer Cormier," the commander started into the radio, "I need you in the back of the building."

Soon, a robust outline of a man stood next to the commander, looking at the bottles and crate. "Make sure they have no surprises, Gaston," the officer asked of his explosives technician.

"Oui, Captain," the technician replied, pulling a pouch to his side and removing several tools to begin his work on the crate.

"Captain Georges, the building is clear, there's no one here," a junior member informed, walking up to the officer who'd earlier taken off his Kevlar helmet and balaclava mask. Rubbing his gloved hand over his close-cropped hair damp with sweat, the senior officer felt the adrenaline of the raid subside.

"Very well," he said. Turning to Geneviève, he added, "Detective Benoit, you and Captain Lemieux might need to explain why we prepared two weeks to raid an empty building." She pulled off her own helmet and mask.

"Captain, there's no visible sign the bottles or this crate are rigged with explosives, but there is a substance in the bottom of several bottles," the technician answered, placing his tools back in his pouch.

"We'll need to get those off to the lab," Geneviève said, noticing her partner Claude walking towards them from the front of the building. "There's a good chance we can obtain fingerprints off those."

"Officer, is there any chance it could be a type of plastic explosives?" Claude asked, looking over the technician's shoulder.

"I don't have the means to test it here. The lab would need to prepare a sample to make sure it's not, though," the technician explained as he moved to stand next to his commander. "But it essentially looks like a syrup." He held up one of the bottles so everyone could see.

Captain Georges looked at Claude and then Geneviève before speaking. "Are you saying we were sent into the building and you knew of the possibility of explosives present, Lemieux?"

"We had no such information," Claude defended. "We were told this building was used to handle narcotics. But if the process was significant enough," he continued, "who's saying the cartel using it didn't try 'protecting its assets' so to speak?" He waved his hands across the open space. "Our information was reliable enough to get us this far. But it still might be meant by the Corsican or Maghrebi criminal elements to test us, who knows."

"Well, the space is now yours to handle," the SWAT commander cleared. "All team members muster at the vehicles," he said over the radio. He turned to Geneviève. "We'll debrief the raid at the trucks, afterward you're welcome to stay with Captain Lemieux or you can return to headquarters with us."

"I'll be back in a few minutes," she said to Claude, following behind the commander who walked towards the front of the building.

Standing amongst the SWAT team members, a strange sense of calm and confidence came over Geneviève. She glanced at the small table on which a floor-plan of the building was taped, while several flashlights illuminating it in the growing dark.

Members gave a critique of what they thought worked well and what needed improvement, the discussion centering on the team's ability to work as a cohesive unit. Comments were given and accepted, assaulting no one on a personal level.

"Entry into the building was accomplished according to the plan, and dispersion of the team took place without issue," the Team Two commander said to everyone. "Penetrating the back room, Detective Benoit, did you consider the box to be booby-trapped?" her team leader asked, looking at her.

"No, I saw a cardboard box which had not been shut," she said, a shudder ebbing down her back as she realized she could have set off a bomb.

"In the future, if you are given the opportunity take part in another raid with us, always, always consider everything as a potential hazard," Captain Georges warned. "It doesn't take much explosive with a handful of nails or broken glass to make you or your team members casualties. But, even though you were not properly trained as part of the team, you did well."

"I'll keep it in mind and thank you for allowing me to play a small part in the activities today," Geneviève said.

"Does anyone have any further feedback?" Georges asked, looking at the team gathered around him. "Detective Benoit, you're welcome to return to the station with us or join Captain Lemieux," he said as the team members loaded their gear into the vans.

"Thank you, Captain. I'll stay with my partner," she said, nodding towards where Claude stood outside the warehouse with the other detectives.

***

As the afternoon faded into early evening, business was picking up at a local restaurant in Toulon. The air was heavy with the smell of roasted garlic and various herbs inside the small pizzeria. Italian folk songs emanated from the wall speakers, over the conversations of patrons sitting and enjoying their evening. The few tables situated inside the café all had patrons seated at them as a young Frenchwoman slid between several chairs to deliver a meal to one guest. "Here is your order, sir," Sophia said.

"Thank you," Alberto said, looking over the linguini and clams, the pungent odor of fresh basil and garlic wafting upward from the plate. Giuseppe has done well here, he thought as he looked over the clientele. Sticking his fork through the pasta, he swirled it on a spoon before taking his first bite, just as the owner Giuseppe 'Geno' Ricci walked up to him.

"I hope you find the meal to your liking," Geno said to the don.

He finished swallowing the pasta with a drink of wine before speaking. "I'm sure the recipe came from your family; it is superb," Alberto said.

"It was my grandfather's favorite," the young Italian replied before taking a seat at the table.

"So, tell me, how was Angelo found out so soon?" Alberto asked, alluding to one of his members' arrest in Marseille two weeks earlier.

"My sources tell me he got careless," Geno explained. "He was not discreet like he should have been. The first bits of information he provided appeared to be useful, but I believe he allowed his assignment to get the better of him."

"You mean his playboy attitude?"

"Yes, precisely. He moved from doing surveillance and planning to one of a voyeur," Geno said. "Accepting the opportunity to photograph the woman to please himself, just like he did in Malta."

"Can we use the information he provided to continue?" Alberto asked. There should be a way to deliver the policewoman to Omar and collect the bounty, he thought. "From what you told me earlier, she sounds vulnerable most evenings, not to mention walking from the bus stop to her residence."

"There are always moments one is more defenseless than other times," Geno said. "It always comes down to timing and opportunity."

"So, it does," Alberto agreed. "Have you been able to learn anything about the Algerian being spirited away from the Algiers jail?"

"No, it's really a mystery," Geno sighed, leaning back in the chair and closing his eyes. "The last time anyone saw him was the day he arrived at the airport and was placed in the police van. Since then, no one I trust has any idea where he is. I assume your friend in Algiers can't offer any more information from the police to find where he was taken."

Alberto Scuderi looked at his young friend across the table, not seeing him but trying to envision how the police could make a criminal disappear without a trace. "No, I've not heard from my friend. He's as much in the dark as we are. Though I'm surprised someone in their police force couldn't be bribed for the information. Knowing my friend is offering such a handsome reward for our help, we need to do our best to produce results."

Chapter Three

As he stood in the midst of the unused room, Gregory studied the emptiness, envisioning the chairs, desks, and cabinets his cadre would occupy as Papillion Transport. "Do you think we can manage with half the office personnel?" he asked, glancing at his colleague and friend Louis Clement. "After the police finished interviewing them, some appear uncertain of staying on."

"It comes down to having someone like Claudette to deal with the calls, one or two people dealing with the manifests such as Francine and Marco, and our bookkeeper, Pierre, handling the cash," Louis said, moving his arm in the sling Julien insisted he wore. "Since we won't have Nazim or Hakim sniffing around, we could work on the same floor, which will help decrease traffic."

"The sooner we reestablish partnerships, those not interfering with Nazim or Omar Khalid, the further off we'll be," Gregory said leaning against a pillar. "We need to avoid any semblance of operation involving the Maghrebi gangs. I don't trust them."

"And what of the two captains in the North Sea?" Louis asked, alluding to the Scotsmen, Dillan McKenzie and Bernard McIntosh. "At one point, we owed them a debt; do you think they've forgotten about their time in the Amazon?"

"No, I don't think they have." Gregory recalled the first meeting with the two British commandos. Shutting his eyes, his mind flashed back to the training mission twelve years ago. Gregory could almost feel the sticky heat of the jungle crawling across his skin again. His heartbeat quickened at the memory of the swift boats used by the British commandos, skimming across the water, carrying his eight-man team deeper into the rainforest. Two team members had been gay lovers, going against the Legionnaires' code of conduct and for which their team leader would dispense with their disciplining.

Gregory and Louis were to carry out the disciplining of the two men under the disguise of a training mission. They recognized they could fabricate any story to explain their actions as they saw fit. Arranging the site where the killings would take place beforehand, he and Louis struck a deal with British commandos operating the boats. For a sum, they secured their silence to the event soon to take place. At the agreed-upon site, the team disembarked the swift boats and made their way into the jungle.

Emilio Carbone and Arnaud Guerini never suspected they would soon be the victims of violent and bloody deaths, accomplished at the hands of fellow Frenchmen. Assigned to lead the patrol, the two Legionnaires soon came upon an area Gregory and Louis had prepared to look like a drug processing site. As each member moved throughout the perimeter of the site, Emilio became the first to suffer the trap set by Gregory.

Rushing across the trip wire, Emilio was jerked skyward, propelling him through the jungle trees. Several of the branches were sharpened and laced with poison. The Legionnaire traveled through the air until impacting the thick trunk of a mahogany tree. Hanging upside down, Emilio glimpsed his partner moving in the distance.

Upon hearing his lover's screams, Arnaud moved towards him encountering the improvised trap. This one, a shallow ditch, caused the Legionnaire to fall face-first onto a series of sharpened sticks. One of the longer ones plunged through his eye and out the back of his skull.

As the poison took effect, Emilio saw his lover's death in slow and agonizing clarity. But what was more unnerving being the sight of the four men standing over Arnaud, watching his life end, without offering help. Gregory walked to the tree where Emilio hung and was soon standing just below him. Emilio stared at him as he heard him say, "Your uncle Albert would approve of this outcome for your shameful behavior." Emilio tried to comprehend the statement just as his heart took its last beat, his last breath but a faint moan.

Gregory stared at Louis, Julien, and Hector standing above the corpse that was once Arnaud Guerini, before speaking. "As soon as he's dead, get them both wrapped up and then contact the boats," he ordered, slinging his weapon over his shoulder. "Hector, once they're ready, call in their status." Turning away from the bodies, he walked back to the river's edge and the rendezvous site to wait for the return of the speedboats.

"Gregory, what about the phone lines?" he heard Louis asked.

Gregory came out of the jungles of South America and back to the office in Marseille. "I'm sorry, Louis. I was just thinking back to Cayenne. What were you asking?"

"The phone lines; we'll need to have two accounts if we plan on separate numbers being used."

"That's a small detail we can discuss next week," Gregory said, walking over to the window overlooking the harbor. In the distance, the rocky outcrop holding the 15th-century fortress of Chateau Il d'If was visible on the horizon. "Our first order of business is to get a crew to build the spaces. We still must have a secure room or two to conduct our meetings."

***

As she stepped into the elevator, Detective Benoit selected the button for the basement to meet her partner Claude Lemieux in the forensics lab. As the numbers flashed for each floor, she recalled the raid from the earlier day. Always consider everything as a hazard. She'd been repeating what Captain Georges said during the debriefing in her head over and over. So, is the substance in the bottle a hazard too? she thought as she pushed open the lab door.

"I'm glad we didn't keep you waiting, Detective Benoit."

"A woman needs to do what a woman needs to do," she replied, alluding to her monthly curse.

"Remind me not to aggravate you then," he answered, turning back to the lab technician. "So, Jaime, what has your analysis told you about the substance found during the raid?"

Taking in the verbal jabs between Claude and Geneviève, the technician smiled before speaking. "Well Captain, the chemical makeup is nearly the same to the hashish found with the boyfriend from the Bakker suicide."

"Nearly the same you say...which means something's different?" Geneviève asked. "Hashish is hashish, isn't it?"

"Not the one contributing to Ms. Bakker's death, it looks like," the technician replied. "The makeup included a modified measure of cannabis resin."

"I don't understand...how?" Claude asked.

"It's very subtle," the technician explained. "A psychotic chemical, one I've still to detect but that may be associated to a hallucinogenic, was added. It was then mixed with the resin. If I can find which substance, then we'll learn why a young woman in her twenties dove off the balcony of an eight-story hotel."

"Did we ever ask Scotland Yard for their toxicology report?" Claude asked his partner.

"No, we didn't have a reason to consider the makeup of the narcotics until the Bakker case," Geneviève said before turning to the technician. "Can you have a copy of the report prepared please?"

"I'll have it for you in a moment," Jaime said returning to his desk.

***

Gazing out over the marina, Gregory sat at the open-air café, pondering his next course of action and the future the Papillion Transport organization. At some point, we'll cross paths with Khalid again, he told himself sipping his coffee. He opened his portfolio and jotted down the contacts he had trusted relationships with and those he had concerns with.

The shrill buzzing of his phone broke through his thoughts. He noticed the call was originating from Toulon. "Hello?"

"Monsieur Arsenault, it's Phillip," the young Frenchman said.

"Good morning, Phillip. How are you doing?"

"I'm doing well. I apologize for calling, but I thought it best pass along something I overheard and saw the other day."

Gregory sat more upright in his chair as Phillip's tone carried a hint of concern. He recalled asking the young man to keep an eye on Sophia while in Toulon, but that was the only issue he could consider for getting a call from Phillip. "What seems to be the problem?" he asked.

"Monsieur Ricci had a meeting with another gentleman who I'd not seen before last night. They were discussing another man spying on a policewoman in Marseille. Seems their man was arrested since he got careless with his assignment," Phillip explained.

"And what made you think it's important for me to hear this, then?"

"They likewise discussed the disappearance of the Algerian, Hakim Talib. You know, the one related to your partner always working with François."

"And what did they say about him?" Gregory asked, his attention now focused.

"They mentioned he was last seen being flown from Algiers and handed over to the police in Marseille. But their sources in the department do not know where he's being held now."

"You did well to let me know, Phillip. I want you to be careful now; don't let Giuseppe know you've heard their conversation," he warned.

"I'll make sure not to raise any suspicions," the young man replied. "For all he knows, I'm a just a dishwasher with a wandering eye for the new waitress."

"Since you brought up her name, how are things with you and Sophia?"

"Ah, well, things are pleasant," the younger man answered. "She's very busy working for your friend Geno so we don't spend too much time together except when working the same shifts. But I'm doing my best to make sure nothing happens to her like you asked."

Gregory's mind shifted between seeing the two young people embraced like lovers to siblings who could barely tolerate each other's presence. "I appreciate the effort you are undertaking Phillip. Is there anything I can do for you?"

"No, Monsieur Arsenault. Nothing comes to mind. But thank you for asking."

Before Gregory could ask another question, one of his trusted friends, Julien LeBlanc, walked up to the table.

"Thank you for letting me know how things are, Phillip. I'll call you in a few days," Gregory said, ending their conversation. Turning to look at Julien, he asked, "What is it?"

"Louis just took a call from Pierre," the former medic answered. "It seems he wants a raise in his monthly pay to continue working with us."

"Really, he wants a raise now? Did he mention how much?" Gregory recognized the banker was important to Papillion Transport and its clandestine payments for shipping indiscriminate goods throughout the Mediterranean.

"No, Louis didn't mention an amount, but after hanging up, he looked rather frustrated with what he heard."

"I'll have a talk with him as soon as I get back to the office," Gregory promised.

"So, how is young Phillip handling things in Toulon?" Julien asked, alluding to the earlier phone conversation.

"He says all is well. But he mentioned the Italians are considering the activities of a policewoman here in Marseille," Gregory responded before finishing the last of his coffee.

"And why do we care about a policewoman here in Marseille?"

"Phillip was bringing it to our attention since it included talk of Nazim's cousin and his disappearance from the police." Gregory tossed a few francs on the table before walking away from the café, Julien following behind him.

***

Following up on a lead provided by both German and Spanish authorities about a wanted drug smuggler, Detectives Nicolas Berger and Guy Masson strolled through crowds of tourists milling near the entrances for the cruise ship terminal. Each one was scanning the crowd for a glimpse of the suspect matching the drawing submitted by the Spanish Guardia Civil.

As he watched a group walk off the large Prevost tour bus, the detective turned to his partner. "Any luck?" Guy asked.

"Not yet. Who realized we'd have trouble finding a Spaniard with black curly hair and dark complexion?" Nicolas replied, looking over a group from Estonia. "Especially amongst all these fair-skinned tourists."

"Do you think the Spanish got their description wrong?"

"It's not possible. The sketch and the photo they provided from their surveillance were almost spot on."

"Look over at the group near the entrance. Someone looks out of place," Guy said suddenly, describing a person in the crowd.

Standing amongst businessmen and their wives from Cologne, Germany, wearing gray sports coat and slacks, Guillermo Ochoa didn't stand out because he didn't try. The biggest issue was not having Nordic or Slavic features that allowed him to blend in with the crowds. His complexion and coal black hair were not altered.

Just six months earlier, Ochoa was masquerading as a ship's engineer from a freighter docked in Marseille. Using his undercover identity, he plied the waterfront cementing his role as a petty drug dealer amongst the tourists. The last time I was here I was trying to make a sale, he thought while pulling his passport out.

Since they'd spotted their suspect in the crowd, the French detectives moved along the outskirts of the crowds. Nicolas walked along the fence line towards the terminal gates while Guy moved forward along the street.

As the groups were moving closer to the customs entrance, a woman bumped Guillermo, causing him to drop his passport on the ground. Crouching over to pick it up, Nicolas saw his chance to advance on the suspect without being noticed. He passed through the crowds in a matter of seconds, and soon stood over the Spanish drug dealer.

Guillermo noticed the feet of the detective come into view and glanced up. "Can I help you?"

"Monsieur Ochoa, I've got a few questions for you," Detective Berger said, holding his credentials out.

"You must be mistaking me for someone else, officer. My name is Javier Gomez, not Ochoa," Guillermo replied, showing Nicholas his fake identification for review.

As Nicolas was confronting the Spaniard, Detective Masson had walked up from behind, standing ready to help his partner.

Nicholas scanned over the passport issued by the government of Paraguay, noting the name and picture. "Monsieur Gomez, how did you enter Germany from Paraguay?"

"I don't understand the relevance of the questioning, officer," Guillermo asked, confusion edged on his face.

"You are traveling from Cologne but carrying a new passport. It doesn't show you entering Germany from your homeland."

"I was issued a new one last year since my earlier one expired," the Spaniard said, telling the well-rehearsed lie behind his fake document. "The staff at the embassy has the authority to do so."

Detective Masson stood quiet, shaking his head to let his partner know things didn't sound right. "You'll be coming with us so we can verify your claim," Guy said, grasping the arm of Guillermo.

As all this took place, tourists milled about, talking amongst themselves while they shuffled towards the customs entrance and their vacation on the cruise ship. From across the street, one man took special care watching the detectives escort the Spaniard away from the docks and toward their police car.

Chapter Four

With a copy of the artist's sketch in his hand, Captain Julien Duval peered through the two-way glass into the interrogation room. "He fits the description all right," he replied, gesturing to the three officers next to him. "But according to the consulate staff in Paris, his visa is legitimate. The document was supplied by government services in Asuncion to them late last year."

"So, just having a valid passport establishes him as a lawful resident of a foreign country?" Detective Guy Masson asked.

"No, it means if he's the suspect the Spanish say he is, we have two options," the senior detective replied. "We can turn him over to the Guardia Civil and be done with him or we can keep him to see if he can present us with information about the increasing drug traffic problems here in Marseille."

"And what charges are we supposed to file against him so we can buy ourselves time during the investigation?" Detective Masson asked.

"Suspicion of drug trafficking, of course," Captain Duval offered. "Has he consented to give his fingerprints?"

"No, he has not. But if we file at least one charge against him, getting them won't be a problem," Detective Lemieux answered. "At the moment, Detective Benoit is down in the lab hoping the technicians can pull something from his passport. If we could get them, we might link him to something serious. Right now, we have nothing. The tour sponsor is cooperating, but even their documents prove him meeting the group in Cologne."

Prowling about the cramped room, Captain Duval considered his choices. He rubbed the palm of his hand over his eyes and let out a groan. "Have we heard from the point of contact with the Guardia Civil yet?"

It was Detective Berger's turn to respond to his boss. "Once we had the suspect in custody, we telephoned them last night. However, according to the watch-captain, the officer in charge of the investigation in Madrid left for the evening. I'm just waiting for him to call me back. But since we appear to have a few minutes, I'll see if any messages were left with the Central operators," he mentioned, leaving the room.

"Detective Masson, do we have locations where the cruise ship was slated to dock?" Captain Duval asked.

Pulling out his pad, Guy turned a few pages before reading. "Yes, he was listed on an Italian liner, the MCS Concerto originating in Barcelona. After stopping here, it was bound for Genoa, Naples, and later Malta. The last stop on the itinerary was its return to Barcelona."

Captain Duval turned to Claude. "See if the tour group can produce a list of activities he might have registered for. I want to see if this gentleman might have had intentions to leave the tour along the way."

***

As she snooped over the shoulder of the lab technician, Geneviève tried to guess the significance behind the swirls and curls the fingerprint image represented. With the ability of a plastic surgeon, the forensics technician was able to remove a complete fingerprint image from the photograph on Guillermo Ochoa's passport. Employing a special cellophane tape and a nimble hand, she'd pulled the image without tearing the picture. Setting the tape on a slide, then under her microscope, the picture was accessible on the monitor for the police officers' viewing.

"You are a genius, Francine," Geneviève complimented.

"It's not very tough. All you need is a steady hand."

"So, is the image suitable to pass through the computer?"

"On just this single print alone?" she inquired. "It'll take a while if you hope to receive any results from an individual fingerprint," the woman answered, pulling off her latex gloves.

"Sometimes something is better than nothing, right?" Geneviève said.

"You better run to the lunchroom and grab us both something to eat then," Francine powered up the computer to examine the fingerprint. Transcribing in a few directions, the computer started the inquiry based on the picture, delving into the numerous law-enforcement databases.

***

Benito Russo placed the packet of linguine in his basket as he wandered through the market. Since arriving in Marseille three days ago, he'd used too much money eating at the various cafés seeking to track his mark. Thank the Madonna mother taught me how to cook, he thought, placing a bundle of tomatoes in his basket next to a baguette. Reaching the counter, he glanced at what he was picking up and consider how he'd need to patronize the store.

"Did you find everything you needed?" the cashier inquired.

"Yes, I did," he replied. "But I'm new in the city and was wondering if you could suggest a convenient market for meats and poultries."

"Oh, you need to go to Marcel Roy's market," the cashier responded. "It's only two blocks from here. Just go to the intersection and head towards the marina and his store is on the right side. You'll find he's got a splendid selection of meats."

"Thank you. I'll make it a point to visit later today," Benito said, getting out cash to pay. He took up the sacks of groceries, before strolling out of the little market and wandering to the intersection to orient himself. Peering down the lane, he spotted the city bus parked a few hundred meters away. "Perfect, near the market and the bus stops close by," he announced to himself.

Benito put away the items he bought at the market as he walked through the door of his leased flat. Relaxing at the table against the window overlooking a small park, he opened his laptop computer to jot down his observations. Next, he opened a file with a timeline associated with his target. At 0600, leaves the residence to jog; 0715, come back to the flat; 0830, grabs the bus; 0845, enters the building, reading the entry. "The target has performed this two of the three days I've been here," he stated to the vacant room.

He'd yet to capture the target returning to the flat at a steady time each morning. "Well, she is a law enforcement officer; can't demand her to have a typical nine-to-five schedule, can I?" Closing the computer, he snatched his jacket and left the residence. Once again, he roamed the narrow streets, scrutinizing his plan to seize the woman worth one hundred thousand euros to him.

***

The awkward silence gnawed at the young lab technician sitting at her desk. Mustering up some courage, Francine finally asked her lunchtime companion the question she yearned to have answered. "So, what can you tell me about Detective Berger?" she asked Geneviève between bites of her sandwich.

"Well, he's rather handsome, as I'm sure you've noticed," Geneviève answered. "Over the last four weeks of working with him, I've learned in the few conversations we've had that he's not seeing anyone serious. Oh, and let see, he regards himself very athletic. Says he spends his free time running the boardwalk quite often," she added. "Perhaps showing off his physique to the tourists, I imagine. And just the other day, he mentioned trying his hand at windsurfing in Nice for the first time."

"So, no one special," the technician said, more a statement than a query to the police officer.

"He has mentioned no one by name. He's not even mentioned going on a date recently," Geneviève responded before finishing her soup and tossing the dish in the trash. "Francine, he's not the timid type; you should go up and chat with him."

"Are you saying that's how you and your Monsieur Dupont met?"

"What… no," she replied, shaking her head. "We met as part of an investigation. It has been all business since the beginning," Geneviève said. "You just need to be yourself with Nicolas. That's all I'm saying."

"It's easy for you to mention being myself. He might find it simple talking in public, but I'm not comfortable around men. I mean, at least when it comes to starting a conversation." Francine squinted over the detective's shoulder at the computer, reading the flashing dialogue box. "Looks like our fingerprint got flagged," she announced, wheeling her chair in front of the console.

Spinning around, Geneviève saw the flashing notice, but couldn't make out the printing. "What does it say?"

"It seems the gentleman's print has flagged a file at INTERPOL. The message reads 'Priority status confirmation needed for access,'" she explained, referring to the screen.

"INTERPOL? As in the international police agency?"

"Yes, that one; unless you know of another," the technician answered. "And I'm sorry to say I can't do anything past this point without having the access code," Francine sighed pushing her glasses back.

"Can you print the message from the screen? I need to take it to Claude and Captain Duval," Geneviève requested. "Oh, don't forget and store the fingerprint image to the file on the suspect; we may need it again."

"Give me a minute and you'll have your printout," Francine said, keying in the command. Pacing around the workshop apparatus, Geneviève looked over the figure of the lab technician, sizing her up for her colleague. She's got a nice figure, good complexion. Looks like she keeps herself in decent shape, and nothing is out of the ordinary the way she dresses. Just means Nicolas would enjoy having his hands on her, she thought.

"Here you go, and I saved the print image to the files." Francine proudly handed over the screenshot.

"Thank you, Francine," the detective replied. "Oh, and I'll give you call when you can 'bump into' Detective Berger." She smiled at Francine as she left the room.

***

Going to the café near the bank where Pierre Segal worked would have taken just minutes for Gregory Arsenault, but he preferred to discuss matters with Louis first. Making his way up the stairs to the second-floor suite of Papillion Transport, Gregory caught Hector walking out of the room.

"Gregory, I'm glad you're back," he stated.

"Why, did I miss something?" Gregory asked, walking past Hector and into the room.

"I was leaving the old offices near the waterfront and I swear I caught a glimpse of Ochoa. He was lining up at the customs entrance for the cruise lines with a bunch of tourists."

The name of the former ship engineer caused Gregory to stop in his tracks. "You saw the Spaniard here in Marseille?" he asked. "Are you sure it was him?"

"Yes, he was being escorted by police away from the cruise ship terminal," Hector said. "He was well dressed, like a businessman. The people with the tour group he was traveling with said he joined them in Cologne."

Gregory looked at his friend and fellow Legionnaire. "Anton will be happy to learn he's alive," His heavy dose of sarcasm did not go unnoticed. After the first officer of Joan of Arc learned of the Spaniards' arrest in Hamburg, he swore he'd make Ochoa pay for their problems with the German authorities.

"Why do you think he returned?"

"I'm not sure. It would be nice to find out though. But I was hoping not to use my contact for a few months," Gregory said as he headed into his private office that overlooked the harbor. As he was sitting down, his friend and partner in business came limping into the office to sit across from him.

"Did you tell him?" Louis turned to Hector and inquired.

"You mean about Ochoa?" Gregory answered. "Yes, Hector told me."

"And how do you propose to handle him?"

28

"Why should I worry about handling Ochoa?" Gregory asked. "For the moment, he's not our problem. But, like Francois trying to run his own drugs, this Spaniard will learn there's more to pilfering a kilo and making a sale for a few extra euros."

Louis continued. "And if he talks about his time on the Joan of Arc and her operations, then what?"

"Then we'll take the necessary steps to protect ourselves," Gregory explained simply, looking out across the marina, the masts of sailboats swaying on the tide. "We may have a more important item to consider, though. Phillip Gaston called yesterday and mentioned the Italians are looking for a policewoman with connections to Nazim Aziz."

"Nothing more was mentioned?" Louis asked.

"Phillip also heard them discussing Nazim's cousin. Seems he was last seen at the airport in police custody. Now, he can't be accounted for by anyone. It was all he heard of their conversation," Gregory replied. "Still, I'm curious though. I'd like to know more about this discussion Giuseppe had, and who it was with. I don't like the idea he's playing both sides of the field." He wrote a quick note on his tablet. "Who knows? Information from their talk might be something we can use against Nazim."

Turning his chair to face his partner, he continued voicing his nervousness with the situation. "My other concern is Claire. She's provided us with valuable information on police activities affecting our operations over the last three years. I want to make sure she's protected," he said, alluding to his brother's wife. "Depending what we learn from the Italians, we might use Hakim's past affair with the socialite from Nice to our advantage against them."

"Ok, but can we get back to our current business?" Louis asked.

"You mean Pierre's demand for more money?"

"Yes. We can't afford to lose him and his position in the bank. It took over a year of negotiating with him to open the ghost accounts. And another six months to deposit our money from off-shore," Louis pointed out. "We've been very fortunate. Papillion Transport is being accepted as a legitimate business in the eyes of banks and businesses here in France; we don't want to jeopardize it over one man."

Gregory picked up his cup and stared into the bottom. "You're correct on all accounts mon ami, but we need to make sure Pierre understands we are the one in control, not him. How much more is he demanding?"

"He wants twenty-five hundred more euros a month," Louis said.

"I'll inform him we intend to increase his 'salary' by a thousand euros over the next four months beginning in September. And then we'll add one more thousand beginning in January," Gregory said. "While we appease him, we'll look for another suitor. Banque Palatine may be the oldest in the Mediterranean region, but it doesn't mean it's the safest."

"And whom do you plan on approaching? Catching Pierre having an affair with the harbor master's wife was pure luck, you know?"

"I'm fully aware how we conned him, but I'm sure we can find someone else with a few skeletons. Maybe we should try bribing a woman this time," Gregory said with a chuckle.

"Oh, and who do you plan to use for the recruiting effort?" Louis asked.

"Since you brought it up, I was considering Julien. I've never seen him hurting when it comes to the ladies. He might just swoon over a lonely bank executive enough to learn of her past," Gregory suggested. "Besides, we've contrived issues in the past; we can do so again. Now, if there's nothing else, I need to plan to see Claire and discuss this meeting Phillip mentioned and let her know Sophia is doing well in Toulon."

Chapter Five

Just as the elevator doors slid open, Geneviève stepped out nearly running headlong into her colleague Nicolas Berger, who was sauntering down the hall from the interrogation rooms. The brief physical contact confirmed what she said earlier while talking with Francine; Nicolas kept himself in shape, feeling the firmness of his chest and arms.

"Whoa there Geneviève. What's the rush?"

"I'm sorry, Nic," she replied, blushing at the experience. "I have something for Claude and Captain Duval to look at." She held the printout Francine provided. "It seems your suspect has someone at INTERPOL's interest, not just the Spanish police. So, if you'll excuse me…" she started, brushing past him and towards the interrogation room.

Opening the control room door, she found Captain Duval, and her fellow detectives, Claude and Guy, in conversation. Through the two-way mirror, she could see the suspect, Guillermo Ochoa, pacing back and forth in the isolation room like an animal on display.

"It's about time, young lady," Claude admonished the young detective with a brief smile.

"You can't rush progress, Captain Lemieux," she replied. She turned to Captain Duval and handed over the printout. "Seems the suspect is also on a watch list at INTERPOL."

"I would think he is, given the German and Spanish police agencies are tracking him. It says the information can only be provided via an access code," he confirmed, finishing his scan of the paper. "I'll have to run this up to Superintendent Chevalier. With any luck, he can get a response today and we can build our case against our guest." He absentmindedly waved his hand at the glass. "Let's move him into a single cell so we don't have to worry about escorts to the men's room," he added before walking out the door.

"You heard the good captain," Claude said, motioning to Guy and Geneviève. "I'll call the attending officer to get the cell number."

Guillermo was speaking as soon as the detectives entered the interrogation room. "You need to release me. I'm going to miss my cruise."

The two officers looked at each other before Guy spoke. "You're our guest for a little longer, I'm afraid, Monsieur Gomez," he answered, using the alias on Guillermo Ochoa's passport.

"But I've done nothing wrong. I mean, you haven't even charged me with a crime. You can't keep me here," Guillermo rebutted, trying not to sound panicked. "I wish to see my representative from the consulate." If the ship sails, I might never find my target again, considering the outcome of being in lockup.

"Well, it seems your passport has raised a few questions still needing to be answered, such as your proper name for one. Now, if you'll follow this nice young woman, we'll show you to your new accommodations," he said.

Geneviève stepped out of the interrogation room and headed towards the holding cells, with Guillermo and her partner, Guy, following behind. Within a few moments, she stopped in front of the watch officers' station, "You've got an opening for our guest?" she asked.

The police sergeant staffing the desk looked up from his work to answer., "To the right; we've reserved lucky number 13 for him, Detective Benoit." Pushing a binder through the window, he added, "Just sign the entry log admitting your 'guest' and we'll see room service is made available," the officer joked.

"Of course," she agreed, filling in the empty spaces. After signing her name with a flourish, she slid it back across the counter. "And there you are, sergeant."

Walking away from the window, she started down the corridor towards the vacant cell Guillermo, however, hesitated.

"Come now Monsieur Gomez. You're not concerned about your living arrangements, are you?" Guy asked, grasping Guillermo's forearm while ushering him after Geneviève who stood in front of the open cell, holding the door open. "I admit it's not the suite onboard the cruise ship, but it is much easier on your wallet." With a firm nudge, Detective Masson escorted the former seaman into the cell. "I'll let the officers know to be civil with you. Oh, and I'll discuss your appeal for counsel with my captain."

Closing the door, Geneviève waited to hear the security bolt latch before releasing the handle and turning to her colleague. "You will really tell Claude the suspect wants to see someone from the consulate?" she asked, wandering back to the elevators.

"Of course. At some point in time, I'm sure it will come up in conversation," the officer said with a crooked grin on his face.

***

Detective Berger approached the communications office hoping to have at least one message from his Spanish counterpart. Wandering through the doorway, he caught Sergeant Claire Dubois from the Detainee Processing office by surprise as she reached for the door.

"I'm so sorry," he said, catching the officer before she fell to the floor.

"It's not your fault, detective. I should have been more careful," Claire said. "It seems we're getting a greater number of detainees since your departments' investigation began." She held up a list of suspects being processed for their initial court appearance to prove her point. "There were seven new arrests in the last two weeks specific to drug sales along the waterfront alone."

"Well, it is what we police officers are paid to accomplish," he said, stepping to the counter.

"Can I help you, detective?" the communications supervisor asked.

"Yes, I was wondering if there was a communique from Captain Garcia of the Guardia Civil office in Madrid."

"Just a moment and I'll check." Walking over and grabbing a clipboard from the wall, the supervisor scanned the first two pages for the name Detective Berger provided. "Sorry, but nothing's come in over the last twenty-four hours."

"Thank you, I appreciate you checking," he said.

The detective made his way back to his office catching Detective Lemieux reviewing a document. The report turned out to be the situation report submitted by the SWAT commander, Captain Pierre Georges, stemming from the raid on a drug processing facility. Though there were no glaring accusations of poor communication, the SWAT commander cited the lack of foresight by him and Detective Benoit about the possibility of explosives being present.

"You look mildly upset, Claude," the detective noticed, closing the door. "Something not to your liking in the report?"

"Oh, it's nothing serious. The good captain noted in his report that Benoit, and I didn't consider the building being booby-trapped," Claude said. "But on the bright side, he mentioned how well she performed on such short order with his team. Seems Captain Georges even included an open invitation for Benoit to be added as time allows in future activities."

"Seems she's made a friend, then," Nicolas said, pulling the file on Guillermo Ochoa from the desk drawer and grabbing the phone. "By the way, the Spanish didn't leave a message overnight, so I'll be giving them a courtesy call."

"Don't let them know we've detained him, just mention he's under surveillance," Claude warned.

"Why should we keep this from them?"

"I believe he may know something which could help our investigation into Papillion Transport and their activities," he replied. "The Scotland Yard inspectors mentioned a crewman from a French vessel being suspected in one of their homicide investigations in Portsmouth. And we found out from the British the vessel in question is owned by Papillion."

"Fair enough. We are keeping him then," the detective said as he dialed the number.

***

The hum of a ceiling fan pushing the stagnant air was the only sound occupying the veranda of the Moroccan crime boss. With a view of the pool, Youssef Raif was waiting for his visitor to arrive. "Have you heard from our driver?" he asked his aide, Imad Chakir.

"Yes, both he and your guest are on their way," the aide responded. Peering at his wristwatch, he added, "They should be here in less than thirty minutes."

The lean tanned figure of Youssef's other guest came ascended the steps and sat at the table, pouring a glass of water. "How much longer must I wait?" The lack of patience was clear in his question.

"Our guest will be here shortly captain," Youssef answered.

"Youssef, I've but a day to see my cargo loaded before leaving Tangiers. Missing this departure time is not an option," the captain of the Southern Warrior, Adem Coetzee said. "At this time of the year, I don't want to deal with the storms building off the coast of Senegal. Last year I lost four containers due to a rogue wave and the insurance companies in Cape Town took their loss from my profits."

"Captain Coetzee, I don't expect you to be unduly delayed," the Moroccan replied. "My guest wants to make sure you're willing and able to undertake his shipping requests. And if all goes as we discussed last month, you'll have 100,000 euros added to your account for a single voyage."

Youssef didn't tell the captain he and Omar Khalid had earlier negotiated a fee of a quarter-million euros for moving drugs between North Africa and France. The part of the transaction worrying him the most was exposing the financial facet of his clandestine operations to both Omar and the South African captain.

The sound of padded footsteps on the mahogany flooring alerted the men sitting on the veranda that Omar Khalid was joining them. Both men turned as the screen door creaked while Imad was escorting Omar to the table.

"Good day, my friend," the Algerian said, greeting Youssef with a handshake instead of the traditional kiss on each cheek.

"It's a pleasure to see you again," the Moroccan replied. "May I introduce you to Captain Adem Coetzee?" He motioned to the South African merchantman.

"A pleasure to meet you, Captain," Omar said, shaking hands with the seaman.

"Yes, it is," Adem replied defensively.

While the members of the meeting were exchanging pleasantries, their table was prepared. Imad was already refreshing the drinks for Youssef and Adem while preparing one for Omar as the three men took their seats. He also oversaw the house staff as they brought out a platter of fruits and sweetbreads and laid them on the table.

"I don't wish to be rude, but my time is valuable, as you might expect," Adem started, setting the tone. "Our guest has told me you wish to contract my ship for a transaction... is this true?"

Omar looked across the table at the South African, picking up his glass of water and letting the cool liquid moisten his throat before speaking. "Yes, I've got a shipment I wish to schedule for movement ever three months. It would originate in Algiers and end with delivery in Marseille."

"A single shipment, just one container is all?"

"At this time, yes. With the possibility of added containers on future dates," Omar explained.

"To undertake this task, my ship would burn over 200 barrels of fuel, costing at least 75,000 euros," Adem figured. "If you want my ship to move your single container, the fee is 200,000 euros. Unless you can increase the number of containers to make the voyage worth the effort, my price is non-negotiable."

Youssef fought hard to stay quiet as he listened to the exchange between Omar and Adem. Sensing a lull in the conversation, he soon added his opinion. "If I add, let us say, three containers to the shipment to Marseille, would you be willing to negotiate a lesser fee?"

Omar looked at the Moroccan crime boss, wondering what he could move to Marseille and how it might influence his and Nazim's drug smuggling efforts. "Captain Coetzee, I understand your reluctance in moving just one container, but I hope you realize the cargo you would handle is unique," he pleaded. "My associates in France and I are a fledgling enterprise and moving with caution as we attempt to grow our business venture. I'm sure you understand that we can't flood the market with goods too soon."

Youssef was listening in the hopes his negotiations with the captain were not being wasted over the number of shipping containers between ports.

Pulling out a cigarette, the freighter captain lit it without concern of the others. "Gentlemen, if each of you can guarantee five containers to be shipped each quarter, I'll consider your offer of 200,000 euros for both transactions," Adem said. He let his offer hang in the air, just like the smoke from his cigarette.

Youssef looked over at Omar, whose expression was neutral, but he sensed his mind was digesting the offer presented to him. "Omar, I believe this to be a fair demand by the captain," he said. "You and I can discuss the details and allow the captain to return to his ship."

For what seemed to be the first time in 30 minutes, Omar blinked while holding his sights on the South African captain. "You're absolutely right, my friend," he said. Pushing up to his feet, Omar extended his hand to the captain. "I believe we have a deal, Captain Coetzee."

The captain responded, shaking hands with Omar. "Yes, I believe we do. I'd appreciate seeing your schedule for picking up the containers by the end of next week. Youssef has the means for contacting me." Turning to Youssef he said, "Goodbye, my friend," shaking hands while Imad stood to see him to a waiting car.

"Goodbye, my friend," Youssef echoed. "And may Allah grant a safe journey for you and your crew." As he followed his aide escort the seaman through the house, he turned to Omar. "Can you have two containers ready in the coming weeks?" he inquired, drawing the conversation back to business.

"I would be lying to you if I said yes. But it's not impossible for my partners and me to complete," Omar responded before turning to Youssef to make his own concerns known. "And you, can you have three containers of goods ready for shipment to France as well?"

Youssef thought for a moment before responding. "Yes, I can. But, what would you say to collaborating our efforts for the sake of business?"

Omar was stunned at the offer. He knew Youssef was remarkably shrewd when dealing with his illegal activities, certainly much like himself. Omar's contacts in both Tangiers and Casablanca had yet to find the extent of Youssef's illegal operations outside Morocco. He knew of Youssef having an informant boiled in hot oil for jeopardizing his operations in trafficking slaves between Africa and South America. Nevertheless, the Youssef never confided in him on operations outside the country.

"I'd like a day or so to discuss your offer with my colleague in Algiers," Omar replied, knowing Nazim should have a say in their discussion. "Producing enough product for a second container poses a greater risk to several of the men. And I don't want to speak too soon on their behalf," he said before finishing his water.

"I understand, my friend," Youssef replied. He waved his hand at the waiting food lay before them. "Stay and eat. It would be a waste not to enjoy all of this."

Glancing at his timepiece, Omar knew he had time before his return flight to partake of his guest's offering. "You're a generous host. I'd be honored to stay and eat with you."

Chapter Six

Detectives Benoit and Masson came through door into the office like two college students, haggling for space, each one trying to walk through the entrance at the same time. "Guy, you need to show some manners," Geneviève scolded him. "Didn't your mother teach you how to treat a lady?"

"You may be a woman, but I've seen you kick ass, and it's not how a 'lady' acts," the burly detective replied, nudging her aside.

"Both of you need to behave yourselves," Claude said, ending their fun. "Did you get our suspect settled down?"

"Yes, we did," Geneviève answered. "He's presently in lock-up as Captain Julien directed. Moreover, I believe he made a request to Detective Masson before we left. Didn't he, Guy?"

Glancing at the woman, Guy was ready to say something rude and unprofessional, but chose otherwise. "Yes, seems the gentleman wishes to converse with his consulate," he said. "I was going to finish preparing his custody paperwork before I called them, though."

Claude shook his head. "We haven't charged him with any crimes yet. What are you going to put down on the arrest report? Jaywalking? Poor posture?"

Snickering at her desk, Geneviève feigned a slight cough before coming to her colleagues' defense. "Can't we at least detain him? We have probable cause, don't we?" she asked. "We've got the notifications from the Spanish and the Germans about his suspicious activities. It's no different from how we handled the young man in the hospital, what's his name…?"

"I don't recall, and I don't care about him," Claude argued. "We've still not determined how our arrest reports were altered in his case. And this one with Monsieur Gomez, or Ochoa, depending on which name is genuine, has diplomatic consequences to it."

"Then how are we going to justify keeping him?" Detective Masson asked.

Running his hand through his greying hair, Claude realized he needed to decide, without the aid of calling his captain and friend, Julien Duval. "Note on your report 'probable cause in drug trafficking' just like Benoit mentioned," he decided. "Cite the Spanish communique as a reference. Now which one of you is buying the coffee?" he asked, holding up his empty cup.

***

Gregory Arsenault moved amongst the mingling tourists who crowded the marina promenade on most occasions, and this day was no different. Strolling between shops and stopping every so often to glance at a postcard, he took his time before entering the local bistro.

Inside, he soon saw his sister-in-law sitting by herself in the corner. Attired in a casual floral summer dress, she was showing calmness contrary to her work demeanor as a senior police officer. He dodged several patrons and a waiter with a full tray of water before he was soon standing in front of her. "How wonderful to see you, Claire," he said, placing a kiss on each cheek.

"And how are you, Gregory?" she asked, returning the greeting and the sign of affection.

"I'm doing well these days," he replied taking a seat. The waiter stepped to their table, pad at the ready. "A coffee and apple pastry, please," Gregory said. "And something for you, Claire? I'm buying."

"I'll have the same, thank you."

As the waiter left, Claire returned her attention to Gregory. "Now, you were telling me how you're doing, weren't you?"

"I had a call yesterday from an associate in Toulon. He was letting me know all was well and wished to pass along that Sophia is doing well too."

"This young man is he spending time with my Sophia?" Claire asked. "She never mentioned having a gentleman in her life before you mentioned it today. All she ever talked about was spending time with her girlfriend, Celine. Did you arrange for this to happen?"

Gregory saw the look in her eyes. "Yes, for her protection. Phillip is an honorable young man and I trust him to do as I ask. Both Sophia and Phillip are working at a business of an associate of mine. It's because of this work we need to talk, Claire."

"Is she in some sort of trouble?" Claire asked as the waiter brought over their coffee and food.

"Merci," Gregory said as he passed over money to pay the bill. "Keep the rest for yourself."

"Merci messier," the waiter replied, his eyes lighting up as he saw the 50-euro bill.

Returning to Claire's question, Gregory replied. "No, she's not in any trouble. However, Phillip heard of something which I need your help answering, though." He looked at the swirling foam his cream made in his coffee as he tried to formulate the question in his mind. "I'm scared to ask for your help again, you know," he finally got out, looking up at her.

"Gregory, you can rest assured I'm rather careful," she replied fondly. "You're not the only one who can manipulate people of importance, you know. Pasqual always said I'd make a good double-agent," mentioning her deceased husband.

"I'm still uncomfortable though," he said, sipping his coffee. "And I don't want to know how you handled Phillip's file either. But since you are willing to help, I need to find information on a person recently detained."

"And how soon do you need this?"

"Oh, I'm not in a hurry, so it need not be tomorrow. But sooner would be better," Gregory said.

"You said this person was detained? So, they've been released recently, I take it?" she asked, cutting a piece of her pastry. "It shouldn't be a problem at all."

"How do I say it... the person, he wasn't released," Gregory explained. "He was being escorted from a flight at the airport, and then 'poof', he's gone. No one has seen him since that day."

"If he wasn't released, he'll still be in the system," Claire said. "What is his name?"

"Talib. Hakim Talib. He's an Algerian," Gregory replied. "And you must know I'm not the only one wanting to find him, so you must be careful."

"Who else is looking for him?" she asked.

"There are at least two other men looking for him. I'm not sure of the Italian's name, but I'll find out tomorrow," he said. "The other man I know is an Algerian; his name is Omar Khalid. He leads a criminal component in Algiers and is very ruthless in how he deals with others. He might also have ties here in Marseille with the Maghrebi crime elements." Over the next few minutes, Gregory told Claire about his associate, François Laurent. Not only how they met but also how his murder took place at the hands of Omar's henchman.

"Not a pretty way to go, I'm sure," Claire said, visualizing the man's death. "Still, if this Algerian was detained and accounted for, I'll find his file," staring into her coffee.

"Is there anything you wish for me to give Sophia; I'm seeing her and Phillip the day after tomorrow."

Claire raised her head glanced at him, tears formed in the corners of her eyes. "No, just give her my love, and let her know I miss her."

***

Closing up her case file, Geneviève slid the series of folders into her desk before pushing the drawer closed and locking it. "Gentlemen, it's been a joy, but I must bid you adieu," She grabbed her bag and coat, ready to leave.

"Giving up so soon are we?" Nicolas asked, still working on the arrest report for Guillermo Ochoa.

"Yes, I'm meeting Monsieur Dupont for dinner," she said. "I promised him my company in cooperation for helping identify Louis Remesy."

"And where is he taking you?" It was Guy Masson's turn to ask, exercising his role as the big brother to the young woman.

"I'm not sure," she answered. "But if I don't get out of the office, I'll miss my bus." She offered a brief wave as she walked out.

Rushing through the lobby, she trotted down the stairs two at a time leading to the street. Just as she reached the Metro kiosk, her bus turned the corner and shrieked to a halt as the nearly full vehicle protested.

Geneviève stood next to the driver without many other options available, stretching above her head to hold on to the railing. Each stoplight on the route to her apartment brought the same worry that someone might grab her pistol from her hip and try to subdue her.

After a tedious twenty minutes, Geneviève stepped off of the bus and walked the last hundred meters to her apartment. She paused at the postal box to grab her mail, which comprised of two advertisement flyers and a credit card bill. Going up two flights of stairs, she came upon her flat and entered. "Oh, it's so good to be off duty," she sighed, slipping off her shoes, adding to the pile just inside the door.

She dropped the mail on the table in the front room on top of yesterday's newspaper. Entering the kitchen, she opened the refrigerator, only to find the week-ends contribution of leftovers crowding the shelves. Pushing aside a half-full bottle of Perrier, she grabbed a carton, sliding the lid aside, only to notice the slight tinge of mold beginning to form. So much for that, she told herself while tossing it in the trash bin.

Taking one last look, she shut the door before making her way towards the bathroom for a quick shower. Leaving behind a trail of discarded clothing while walking through her bedroom, Geneviève soon was standing in her shower, relaxing in its warm, gentle spray of water. The cascading water spilled over several faded and ragged scars on her back, visual reminders of past traumas.

She seized a towel and dried off before scampering into the bedroom to select the evening's attire. Never one to shy away from flaunting her feminine figure, Geneviève paused in front of her closet, unsure of which dress to wear. Moving her clothes left and right, she finally stopped, choosing a navy-blue dress for the night. Its plunging neckline was enough to expose a portion of her cleavage, yet the dress was still conservative enough to cover her back. She paired it with low-set heels she found on the floor of her closet, their color matching her dress.

Rummaging through cosmetics strewn across her dresser, she soon found her lipstick and twirled the tube to expose the dark crimson paste, sliding it across her lips. "And to finish the look, a few spritzes of Obsession," she murmured, squirting the perfume between her breasts. She definitely did not look like the police officer she had been earlier in the day. "I'm sure Hector will approve," she uttered as she grabbed her pistol and slid it inside a sequin clutch. Before she could grab her grey lace shawl, the intercom at the street entrance chimed.

"Hello?" she asked, scurrying to the door.

"Good evening, Miss Benoit," Hector's voice rang out. "I apologize if I'm too early."

"No, your timing is perfect. I'll be down in a moment." Snatching the clutch and her shawl, Geneviève stepped out, locking the door behind her before descending the stairs. Before leaving the building, she pulled the lace over her shoulders, tossing one side over the other.

"Good evening, Hector," she said as she met her date on the sidewalk.

The woman he saw exiting the apartment was not the same one he met in his office just weeks before. "You look wonderful," he said, placing a brief kiss on her cheek. "May I?" he asked, leading her to the open car door.

"Thank you," Geneviève said with a demure smile.

Slipping behind the wheel, Hector placed the Peugeot into motion, following the early evening traffic towards their destination. Neither occupant noticed the solitary figure standing at the curb watching their departure.

Benito Russo now had a very good idea who Geneviève's suitor was and how to spot him as he took down the vehicle type and license plate number. "Have a good evening, mademoiselle," he said to himself, walking towards the vacant apartment of the police officer.

Chapter Seven

A s soon as the sedan carrying Genevieve and Hector turned the corner, Benito Russo made his way to the front of the apartment building. Grasping the handle, he found it locked. "Damn," he muttered. Just as he pulled his lock picks from his wallet, he heard footsteps approaching from the other side of the door.

Stepping back from the ornate wood and glass entrance, he came face-to-face with an elderly woman exiting the building.

"Good evening," Benito said. "I was just ready to pull out my keys, but you've saved me the effort."

"Good evening," the old woman echoed. "And you're welcome," she replied as she shuffled past him pulling a rickety wire cart.

Holding the door while allowing the woman to pass, Benito slid inside behind her and peered at the mailboxes along the far wall. "G. Benoit, #301," he murmured. He quickly found the apartment, traipsing up the stairs two at a time, and used his lock picks to open the door. He was soon standing in Geneviève's front room, and he pulled out a penlight to surveyed the space. Rather ordinary furniture... no television, but a small stereo, he listed. Going to the window, he noticed an ordinary latch securing it and no signs of an alarm system. His flashlight landed on a small hutch where several framed pictures sat.

Benito could see the simple silver frames holding the photo's showed the onset of tarnish, a clear indication that the housework was not a priority to the young officer who occupied the apartment. Strewn to the right was a crystal ashtray, holding an odd collection of rings, bracelets and ear-rings.

Benito stepped to the bureau and picked up one showing a small girl between two older children, a boy and girl, and her parents on the steps of a church. "She was cute back then," he murmured. Setting it down, he held up another. This time it was Geneviève in her police uniform and her mother, alone. He placed it back, then turned to the kitchen.

Benito roamed through the kitchen, checking the back door, which led to the fire escape to the alley behind the apartment. He opened the refrigerator, and his eyes scanned over nothing out of the ordinary: a few staples and a couple of takeout boxes.

As soon as he stepped into the bedroom, he noticed what must be a common sight of single women everywhere: pants crumbled on the floor, a blouse, sports bra, and panties lying in a pile outside the bathroom, as she disrobed. A large, damp beach towel was hanging off the edge of the dresser. Peering into the bathroom, he recognized the remnants of the occupant's preparation for the evening, water droplets still clinging to the shower door.

Benito shifted his attention to the nightstand, and he gently pulled the drawer open. "Just as I thought," he said. Inside, he discovered two loaded magazines for a pistol and a collapsible nightstick along with a set of crystal rosary beads and a bible. Glancing over his shoulder, he caught the empty holster sticking out from under the coat which she had tossed on the bed.

He squinted at his watch, realizing he'd already spent over ten minutes looking around her apartment. After looking around the room behind him, he was satisfied anything he had touched was put back or still in its original spot. He hesitated at the front door, placing his ear near the crack and listening for anyone on the other side.

Stepping out of the apartment, Benito slid his hand inside, engaging the lock before closing it shut. He sauntered down the stairwell and walked out of the building, making his way to a local bar near his rental, already figuring out the next step of his plan.

***

A soft glow of orange painted the horizon outside the harbor while the city lights flickered sporadically on gentle waves from passing watercraft entering the marina. Sitting on the balcony overlooking the multi-million-dollar yachts, Hector Dupont was pleased to see his companion enjoying herself.

"I've never been to this restaurant before. You've made a wonderful selection, Hector. Thank you," Geneviève complimented between sips of her wine.

"I was hoping it wouldn't be too 'over the top' as they say," the security director said.

Feeling her face warming up as she became the center of attention, Geneviève spoke. "I've never spent a great deal of time eating out at restaurants to begin with, so this is a nice change."

"Well, I hope you allow me to entertain you again," Hector said, lifting his glass.

Over the course of the next hour, the pair exchanged pleasantries over dinner, oblivious to the others sitting nearby. When they were done, the server cleared away their plates and offered them each a dessert menu numbering over twenty delectable selections of pastries, some with photos, including several choices of coffee and teas.

"They all look so inviting," she said.

"I would recommend the strawberry gelato on shortbread," Hector said. "I've found it to be refreshing, but not as heavy as the other offerings."

"That sounds perfect. I need to watch how much I eat or I'll never hear the end of it from Claude."

Hector smiled at the answer, but his thoughts were focusing on her figure on a more personal level. Since meeting her at the airport last month, he thought of ways to be in her company without being intrusive. Her choice of unassuming perfume and clothing made her appear plain, but also mysterious and alluring.

"I would think you would be the one worrying about him more than he worries about you," he replied, finishing his wine.

"Well, since his wife Nadine passed away the year before last, he's found it hard to move on," Geneviève answered quietly.

"Were they together a long time?"

"Over twelve years," she said. "They met while Claude was on assignment in Nice. Nadine was a clerk working for Banque Palatine when someone tried robbing the bank. Claude, being a junior detective back then, was investigating and as they say, it was love at first sight."

"Sounds romantic, as if fairy tales can come true," Hector said. "Do you know how she died?"

Geneviève looked down at her tea, knowing how difficult it was to speak of Claude's wife in past tense. "She was assaulted by a drug addict while leaving the market near their home one evening," she said. "The assailant was high on PCP. She tried to fight back, but he ended up stabbing her six times before an officer shot him." Glancing back up at Hector, she continued. "Claude swore he'd rid the city of all the drug peddlers in her memory."

"I'm sorry for asking," Hector said, placing his hand over hers and giving it a gentle squeeze.

"It was during the recovery from her assault she was first diagnosed, just a small lump on her breast," she said. "But, after two more examinations, she was diagnosed with Stage IV metastatic breast cancer. It was horrific to look at such a vibrant soul taken by this disease." She wiped a tear from her eye with her napkin, careful not to mess up her makeup. "If you ever see a picture of her, you'll find her a beautiful woman," Geneviève said. "Look at me, I'm ruining the evening you had planned."

"Just having your company is enough to make this a wonderful night," Hector said. "Let's dispense with dessert and take a walk along the promenade, shall we?"

As they ambled out of the bistro, Geneviève pulled her shawl over her shoulders while sliding her free arm through Hectors' offered one. "Thank you for a wonderful evening," she said.

"It was my pleasure," the security director said. "It's been quite a while since I had the pleasure of entertaining such a beautiful woman."

Blushing at the compliment, Geneviève said, "You can't tell me you've trouble dating."

"In the past, most of the women I've been associated with have come to assume I can offer them perks with airlines or bend the rules at customs," Hector chuckled. "Because of this, I have… shall we say, limited my availability."

"I can honestly say I have no need for extraneous gratuities with any airline," she assured him. "And since I rarely travel outside France, I've no need for gifts from foreign lands which need taxes waived. But, I would enjoy the opportunity to make myself available for another date, if you'd like," She squeezed her arm against her date's.

As they strolled along the promenade, they stopped at a small bench along the seawall. Hector turned to her and pulled her close against his body. Dropping his face to hers, he gently kissed her.

The feeling of his body pressed against hers made her stiffen, caught between accepting his embrace and denying the feelings from her experience as a young girl in Cherbourg. Through the years, she had built her defense against intimacy, but found an odd sense of calmness in Hector's embrace. She didn't back away as he continued kissing her with increasing passion, persuading her mouth to open and gliding his tongue past her crimson lipstick.

Feeling Hector's lips against her, Geneviève pressed herself closer to his taller frame, feeling his arm around her waist, pulling her close. A dormant yearning for intimacy seemed to awaken in her, and she felt a pleasant ache, her nipples swelling against the silkiness of the dress.

Relaxing his embrace as he pulled his lips away from hers, Hector muttered, "I hope we can see each other again, and soon."

Geneviève caught her breath, peering upward into his emerald-colored eyes. "I'd like that very much. However, it's best if we each agree to move at a comfortable pace. I mean… I'm not in a rush, I just want to make sure if this is to last, we do it properly."

"I understand," Hector said. "For now, we can just enjoy tonight for what it is: a pleasant evening to become acquainted." Prompting her along, they soon came to his car. He held the door open and hoped she didn't notice his eyes focused on her well-toned legs as she slid into the car.

Hector was soon maneuvering the sedan amongst the other vehicles, navigating his way back to her apartment. As he changed gears, he recognized a gentle touch as Geneviève placed her hand on his. He caught a small upturn to her lips as she watched him drive. In minutes, they were in front of her apartment, where Hector got out and opened her door.

"Thank you again for a wonderful evening," she said, placing a kiss on his cheek.

"Please give me a call if you have time," Hector said. "I'd like to plan another evening with you as long as you're ok with seeing me again."

"I will," she said, sliding from his embrace and to her door.

Hector stood with his car door open, watching Geneviève enter the safety of her apartment building before getting into his car and driving away.

Making her way to her apartment, Geneviève entered, laying her shawl on the sofa and kicking the shoes from her feet before laying her purse on the bureau. As she glanced at the photos, she sensed something amiss, but couldn't put her finger on what it was. She headed into the kitchen, reaching to open the refrigerator, but recognized the hair she placed across the door seam was no longer in place. "Someone's been here," she whispered to herself.

Going back to the front room, she took the pistol from her purse while stepping toward her bedroom. She glanced at the open space as she nudged the door open before proceeding to the bathroom. Peering into the room, she noticed it was empty. Sitting on the bed next to her nightstand, opening the drawer to find everything in place there as well.

An uneasy feeling came over Geneviève, as she recalled the Italian they arrested for stalking her. Snatching the phone, she dialed the number for Claude. The groggy sound of her partner's voice greeted. "Hello?"

"Claude? It's Geneviève."

Peering at his watch, he noticed it was nearly ten o'clock. "Why are you calling me at this hour?"

"I was out with Hector Dupont," she explained. "But, when I came home… it seems someone's been in the apartment."

"How can you tell? Is something missing or damaged?"

"No, nothing has been taken or damaged," Geneviève said. "But I think several of the pictures on the bureau have been moved." She glanced over her shoulder just to make sure she saw correctly. "In addition, the safety 'tale' was disturbed in the kitchen. Other than those items, I can't find anything amiss."

"Contact the local office," Claude ordered. "I'll be there in twenty minutes."

"Thank you, Claude."

She telephoned the local police station near her apartment and several officers arrived minutes before Claude did. Making his way upstairs, he entered the apartment, still disheveled from waking up from his sleep. The officers allowed him inside after he showed his identification.

"Is everything all right?" he asked.

"Yes. I was just giving the last of my observations to Officer LeBlanc," Geneviève said.

The officer glanced at Claude's ID before speaking. "I've got all I need for my report, Captain Lemieux. This is the first instance we've had a break-in since I've reported for duty in the last three years."

"Things are cyclic in nature, officer," Claude replied. "It just might be time for them to begin again. Please see a copy of your report makes it to my office when you file it. And thank you and your partner for coming so promptly. I'll take care of things from here."

Nodding to his partner, the two local officers departed, leaving Claude and Geneviève alone in the apartment. Claude paced about the room, taking in the layout and trying to imagine the possible scenarios that would place his partner at risk.

"It turns out the Italians or even Khalid himself has upped the ante when it comes to you," he said, standing in the middle of the room. "We might have to move you for your own safety."

"I can take care of myself," Geneviève insisted, retrieving the open bottle of water from the kitchen.

"Then why did you call me in the middle of the night?"

"I did so only out of courtesy," she replied "After apprehending the voyeur, I thought it prudent to keep you informed."

"Like I said earlier, it's either another one of the Italian mafia families or the Algerian," Claude spoke. "Either way, you need to consider yourself a target from this point forward."

Sitting at the table, staring into the now almost empty water bottle, Geneviève considered what Claude was telling her. How do I explain this to Hector? she asked herself. The pleasant thoughts of her evening with her suitor swiftly faded, replaced with the uncertainty of what lay before her.

Chapter Eight

The judge and his clerks were busy shuffling the schedule to meet the growing number of cases the police were bringing in for sentencing. "It never fails, does it, Julia?" Sergeant Dubois asked her coworker. "Every summer season we seem to see the same foolish tourists."

"I was happier processing the football hooligans from England," Julia said. "It was much easier dealing with drunkards than today's drug users."

Getting out the next case folder, Claire handed it to her friend. "Here you go then, an Italian voyeur," she giggled. "This will give you something to talk about while you're playing cards on Saturday night."

As she leafed through the arrest report, Julia noticed the officer's name. "This is funny; Captain Lemieux was the officer on record for this arrest. Doesn't he work in the Drug Intervention office?"

"I believe he does," Claire said. "But it doesn't mean he can't make an arrest other than ones involving drug use, though."

The clerk's curiosity was getting the best of her, as she was soon thumbing through the notes, stopping on the third to last page. "It says here the suspect was conducting surveillance on a female detective," she said. "He had over a hundred images of her over a two-week period. He took some along the waterfront, in front of a market, even while she was exercising."

"Mind if I take a look?" Claire asked, holding her hand out.

"Sure, but remember... I get to deal with this one," Julia said as she handed the folder to the sergeant.

Flipping the cover open and scanning over the page, Claire began memorizing the details of the suspect, recalling what Gregory had told her the other day. "I've bumped into this officer," Claire said, recognizing Geneviève. "She's working with Captain Lemieux and Detectives Berger and Masson. They had the big drug arrest back in April, remember?"

"Claire, I'm lucky to remember fixing a cup of coffee, much less an arrest from three months ago," Julia chuckled.

"Still, I wonder why this man was watching her," Claire inquired, closing the file and passing it back.

"Turnabout is fair play," Julia said. "Here is the stack ready for the Judge Dionne's review; it's your turn to deliver them."

Shoving the pile on to the small office cart, Claire sighed. "I'll do my best not to let him talk my ear off. I shouldn't be too long," she called as she pushed the cart away from the table.

As soon as she left the file room, Claire stopped at her desk, grabbing a notebook and writing down details from the voyeur's file as fast as she could. Name, city, arresting officer and target would be important to Gregory. She wrote a reminder for herself on a sticky note to call him this evening and arrange a meeting. In moments after delivering the case files, she found herself politely nodding as Judge Dionne regaled her with his recent sailing adventure.

***

The streets of Lyon were still damp from the summer storm that passed through earlier in the morning as Superintendent Marcel Chevalier left the train station. Starting his way along the boulevard, he was soon walking towards the building entrance leading to the INTERPOL offices.

"May I help you?" the guard asked as Marcel approached the front desk.

"Yes, I have an appointment with Captain Bernard Fontaine this morning," he replied, holding out his identification.

"Oui, Monsieur Chevalier, just a moment," the officer said, picking up the intercom.

Moments later, a figure appeared from an elevator and approached the superintendent from Marseille. "Monsieur Chevalier, I am Captain Fontaine," he introduced himself, extending his hand.

Shaking hands, Marcel replied, "Thank you for seeing me, Captain."

"Please, if you'll just wear this badge and follow me, we'll get down to business." He took the visitors pin from the guard and handed it to Marcel.

He placed the emblem on his pocket and walked with the INTERPOL agent to the elevator which sped them to the ninth floor.

Getting off, he soon found himself assaulted by a din of conversation from all corners of the floor. Here, agents from different countries were in constant conversations with other law-enforcement agents in the world. Some spoke Spanish, others German, while most spoke French since it was the most common language between the gathered staff members.

"Sounds like I caught you at a bad time, Captain Fontaine," he said, following his host.

"This is benign compared to most days," Bernard Fontaine replied. "If the calls come through host nation services, many of the agents are shouting just to be heard by the others on the other line."

Holding open the door to his office, he showed Marcel to a seat across from his. "Please make yourself comfortable," he said. "Would you like coffee, tea, or perhaps water?"

"I'm fine, thank you," Marcel answered. "The services on the TGV are more than adequate."

Captain Fontaine took a seat behind his desk and pulled out a folder from his drawer. "Your call requesting access sent a few ripples across the office. I must caution you, Marcel. What you are about to hear is to be kept in strictest confidence," he warned, opening the folder on his desk.

"I understand," the senior police officer agreed.

"The man you have in custody is not from Paraguay," he said. "And he's not Spanish either."

Sitting forward in his chair, Marcel looked intently at the agent in front of him. "If he's not from Paraguay as his passport identity suggests, and you say he's not a Spanish citizen either, then what is his nationality?"

"He's an American."

This revelation from the INTERPOL agent nearly floored the superintendent. "And how did you come to find out about this?" he asked. "We've considered him part of a drug smuggling activity based on what the Guardia Civil and the German BKA have told us."

"You're not far off track with your suspicions, Marcel," the agent affirmed. Before he could continue speaking, there was knocking at his door. Closing the folder, he said, "Come in."

Ducking through the doorway from the noisy office space behind him was a formidable African-American, standing nearly seven feet tall. Bernard rose to greet his new visitor. "Charles, thank you for coming," he said, shaking hands. "Superintendent Chevalier, I'd like you to meet Senior Agent Charles Baldwin with the American Drug Enforcement Agency in Washington."

Standing, Marcel held out his hand. "A pleasure, Monsieur Baldwin," he greeted the agent.

"Please, call me Chuck, and the pleasure's mine," the DEA agent said while grabbing an empty chair. "Bernard here tells me you've come across one of my deep-cover agents."

"It would appear we have," Marcel said. "My question is what he is doing traveling with a passport from Paraguay if he's an American?"

Agent Baldwin looked at Captain Fontaine first, then back to Marcel before speaking. "He's been undercover for the last four years, tracking a lab rat with enough smarts to alter the chemical composition of PCP," he said. "I won't bore you with the science behind it. His last report to us, which came over eight months ago, mentioned the location of a facility, possibly here in France or somewhere in North Africa."

"But why has he been undercover for so long? And why here in Europe and not America?" the Frenchman asked.

"We first stumbled across a drug lab on a Louisiana sugar cane plantation," Chuck said. "It was more sophisticated than others we've found. From there, it led us to a larger one in the Dominican Republic. My agent, Guillermo was one of three officers we were able to have infiltrate the cartels operating the labs at the time."

Wringing his hands, he paused and took a deep breath before continuing. "You see, Guillermo Ochoa is the last of those three agents to survive. He's been following the trail of this scientist through the Caribbean, Africa, and now Europe."

"Gentlemen, it appears my department has stumbled, unwittingly, into the middle of your operation," Marcel said. "So, knowing this, how do you wish for me to proceed?"

Captain Fontaine and Agent Baldwin looked at each, with the INTERPOL agent speaking first. "Do nothing. Return to Marseille; release Mr. Ochoa with your apologies and let him continue doing his job."

"In the spirit of cooperation, can I ask if there's any information from his surveillance you could share with us?" Marcel asked. "We've stumbled across a shipping firm we believe is smuggling drugs from North Africa to France and just recently, to the United Kingdom."

Captain Fontaine looked at his American counterpart. "It wouldn't hurt to have someone at the grassroots level providing backup, would it?"

"No, I suppose not," the DEA agent said. "Marcel, you've got a deal. We'll give you with information pertinent to your investigation, while you channel information to Captain Fontaine on what you find. Do you agree with this arrangement?" holding out a bear's paw for a hand.

Accepting the offered hand and shaking it, Marcel replied. "You'll have our cooperation, Agent Baldwin." He turned to Captain Fontaine. "And I'll have our communication staff prepare the secure network so we can share information with INTERPOL. Provided you supply the access codes to send and receive the files, Captain?"

"I'll see they are prepared at once," Bernard said, glancing at his desk clock. "Do either of you have time for lunch?"

***

Standing curbside in front of the Central Courthouse, Claire Dubois paced back and forth. After informing Gregory of the information about the Italian 'voyeur' case, he agreed to meet with her at the end of her workday. She checked her watch again; it felt as if time had slowed to a snail's pace, and someone would question why she appeared so nervous.

As if answering her prayers, Gregory pulled up along the sidewalk, allowing her to get in. "I was getting a little worried," she said, fastening her seatbelt.

"Sorry, Louis and I needed to discuss some business. Shall we head to your apartment?" he asked.

"No, let's go to the Irish pub near the marina," she said. "It should be crowded enough that people won't bother us."

In a few minutes, Gregory was parking the car near the waterfront and the selected eatery. Aiding his sister-in-law from the car, they joined the early evening crowds walking along the promenade. "There it is," he announced, spying the Irish flag waving from the balcony.

They soon sat at a high table, drinks in hand before Claire began the conversation of her discovery earlier in the day. "It seems an Italian was arrested for conducting surveillance on a policewoman," she started, sipping her cocktail.

"Did the report show which police officer?" Gregory asked.

"It was Detective Benoit. She's part of the Drug Intervention Team," Claire said. "She's likewise the one involved in shooting your friend Louis," she pointed out. "And I heard she nearly stripped in front of your man Phillip while questioning him too."

"Oh, was this something you learned from her report?"

"No, it wasn't part of the report," Claire said. "One officer in interrogation was reprimanded for passing around a snippet of a video showing her pushing her tits up in his face during questioning."

Shaking his head at the gossip, Gregory took a slow swallow of his Guinness before responding. "So, it seems she's made herself an enemy of the Italian mafia. Was there anything else of importance?"

"The photos this man was taking, they covered different parts of the city she was visiting. Different activities and locations, essentially like he was trying to find a spot to abduct her," she said. "I recall her filing a report about a suspect for the British too. It was on a man named Remesy, the same one you asked about last month."

Hearing the alias of Nazim Aziz nearly caused Gregory to spit out his beer at her. "Are you sure of the name?" he asked, wiping the corners of his mouth. This would be an excellent bargaining chip if Nazim ever tried to double-cross Papillion, he thought.

"Yes, we had to place the report in our open files after she supplied it to Scotland Yard," she said finishing her drink. "Is this person someone you know?"

Glancing at the woman, Gregory though how he could tell her about his former business partner without endangering her. "He's a gentleman I've worked with in the past," he said. "We had a falling out over a transaction. I was hoping to avoid dealing with him if I could."

"Was this transaction legitimate?"

Gregory smiled at his sister-in-law. "Would you like to order some dinner? They serve a superb Atlantic cod filet in beer batter."

"Since you won't answer, I'll take your aversion to my question as a no then," Claire laughed. "I assume you consider this man a threat or you wouldn't be so quiet." Drawing the attention of the waiter, she held up her empty glass before turning to Gregory again. "Do you wish to know more if I come across information about him?"

"Yes, but only if you can get it without interacting with anyone," Gregory said. "Now, what's your answer about dinner?"

Chapter Nine

The early morning made for a quiet street to walk, as Geneviève scanned the windows and doorways of the various shops surrounding her apartment complex. *The prowler from the other night could still be watching or be close*, she thought as she approached the bus stop. Screeching metal surprised her as one of the local shop owners slid the security doors open. "Good morning," she said, passing the merchant.

"I didn't mean to startle you," the man apologized, rolling out a cart of fruit from inside the shop. "I've been meaning to have this old thing fixed. Some of our neighbors get cranky when I wake them up this early," he laughed, waving his hands at the surrounding buildings.

"Well, I'm not one of them complaining," Geneviève said, walking past the shopkeeper. In minutes, she was settling into the front seat on the bus making its way to the police station. The gentle swaying of the vehicle caused her to nod off, unnoticed by her fellow passengers.

"Mademoiselle, excuse me? I believe it's your stop," the driver said, shaking Geneviève's arm.

Sitting upright, she saw the other patrons looking at her. "I'm sorry, it's been a rough few days." She grabbed her bag and stepped off the bus, dashing up the steps of the police station. She passed by several officers exiting, one being Detective Masson.

"Whoa there, Benoit. You're going to hurt yourself," he said, stepping aside to avoid hitting her.

"Sorry, Guy," she replied, grabbing his arm. "I was just on the bus, but the driver had to wake me. I cannot believe I fell asleep. It was the first time I'd ever come close to missing my stop." Turning, she entered the building and made her way to her office, making a quick stop at the cafeteria for coffee.

In the office she shared with her three partners, she set her coffee down before placing her coat over her chair. Moving the papers in her basket, she came across a dispatch from the patrols near the shipping terminals. She skimmed over the report but realized something was missing. "Where's the information on the surveillance?" she asked aloud. Flipping through the pages, it didn't show anything on Papillion Transport and its office staff.

"You're in early," a voice came from behind as Captain Lemieux entered the office. "Did you remember to get me a cup too?" he asked, pointing to her coffee.

"Do you know the patrols have no information on Papillion from their surveillance observations," she said as she waved the report.

"No, I wasn't aware," Claude said. "And I take it you didn't buy me coffee either."

"It's been over a month since our inquiry. There's no evidence of someone entering the building? No sighting of anyone collecting the mail for the company?" she asked. "It seems they up and vanished, which is something I can't believe."

"I can't believe I have to buy my own coffee," the senior detective muttered, taking the report from her. It lacked any mention of members of the suspect shipping company in and around their office. "I'll contact the sergeant in charge of the detail and see why they're not reporting any activity. Now, my coffee?" he added sending her off. "And when you get back, we'll discuss the other night some more."

Making the short trip to the cafeteria, Geneviève was soon back in the office with Claude's coffee and was joined by her Nicolas Berger. "Here," she handed the cup to Claude, "large, black, and sweet."

"And I thank you," he said, nodding his head. He closed his eyes as he took a sip, savoring the caffeine. "Now, that's better. Where were we?"

"The surveillance on Papillion Transport has gotten us nowhere," she said. "How can we go from interviewing nearly a dozen employees to an abandoned office in a month's time?" she fumed.

"The surveillance team never noticed the lack of traffic?" Detective Berger asked as he nursed his energy drink.

"No. Four days after we interviewed the staff, it would seem they all disappeared," Geneviève said. "It's as if they had previously planned to move before we even served our warrants."

Claude sat back and listened, gathering his thoughts. "We never encountered the owners either, did we?"

"No, we didn't," she said. Foraging through her desk, she pulled out a notepad and flipped through a half-dozen pages of scribbling. "When I asked the receptionist, ah… Claudette Minot was her name," she read, looking over her notes. "She said the owner was in Venezuela on a business trip."

"I would bet you a home cooked meal we'll still find one of their vessels in the harbor though," Claude pointed out to her. "And if we do, they should be in contact with the office. Do you still have a list of their freighters?"

Moving more papers about, Geneviève pulled a sheet from the drawer. "Yes, the four registered here in France are on the top." She handed over the page. "And the ones registered elsewhere are identified below the freighters."

"What do you mean 'elsewhere'?" Detective Berger asked.

"The company has sub-leases on several oil rig tenders," she said. "Two of their vessels sail out of Scotland, with two more sailing out of Texas, in America."

"Seems like an odd arrangement," Berger said.

"It's how the inspectors from Scotland Yard determined they were moving the drugs ashore," Geneviève explained. "They suspect the freighters were transferring the drugs to the smaller boats so they could avoid inspections from customs officials."

"As soon as Guy returns," Claude started, pointing to Berger, "the two of you take a stroll along the waterfront again. See if you can find one of these freighters tied to the docks," He slid the list to the young detective.

"And what am I going to do?" Geneviève asked in protest.

"You and I have an appointment at 8 o'clock with the Captain to discuss your visitor from the other night," Claude said. "If your instincts are right, and someone was in your apartment, then we've got a bigger issue about your safety."

"What? Someone was in your apartment?" Nicolas asked.

"Yes, while I was out having dinner with Hector," she said. "I noticed something was amiss when I got home."

"And yet you still slept there knowing someone could break in? You're braver than me," Berger said, smashing the empty can in his hands.

"Or foolish," Claude chimed in. "While you still have a few minutes," he pointed to the clock, "you need to write up your suspicions about the intruder. We'll add it to the officers' report when they send me their copies later today."

Collapsing in her chair, Geneviève switched on her computer. "You know how I hate paperwork."

"Yes, you remind me every time we file reports," Claude said. "And every time, you chide me on how slow I am when you're done with yours. So, it's time to get busy." He waved his hands at her computer before getting up from his desk and heading towards the cafeteria for another cup of coffee.

Rounding the corner leading away from his office, he collided with the SWAT team leader, Captain Georges, before stumbling to his knees.

"Damn Pierre, make some noise when you get near these corners," Claude exclaimed, picking himself off the floor.

He helped Claude to his feet as he spoke. "Occupational habit Lemieux, it pays to keep in practice. How's Detective Benoit doing these days?"

"She's as well as ever," Claude said. "You're not thinking of recruiting her, are you? Working to gain some points with Chevalier by diversifying your teams, maybe?"

"She has the knack for it," Pierre said. "And she's a quick learner. Both team leaders were impressed with her ability to move with the men during the practice scenarios."

"Are you sure it's not the fact they liked to see her ass in those Nomex suits you wear?"

"I can't speak for them about their personal habits," Pierre said. "But, like I said, she's got a knack for it. I'm off to see the weapons tech; we've got a few new toys to play with,".

With a sigh, Claude stepped into the eatery. "I'd hate to lose her," he said to himself, pouring coffee into a large cup.

***

"Captain, we've got increasing waves between 3 to 5 meters coming from the southwest at two-minute intervals," the navigator reported. Peering at the computerized weather station, he added, "And the wind is picking up, steady at 20 knots with gusts to 35."

Dark and ominous storm clouds hung on the western horizon, signaling the approach of a weakening but dangerous cyclone in the Atlantic. As he watched various shades of swirling grey storm clouds approaching shore, Captain Adem Coetzee observed the navigator and second officer plotting a course from Tangiers towards Gibraltar and the Mediterranean.

"Hold your course and keep our stern to the waves," he commanded the helmsman.

"Aye, sir," the Malaysian sailor replied.

Striding up to the navigators' table, Captain Coetzee looked over the chart. Adem sensed the pending storm would have little effect on their path into the Mediterranean. "Once we passed the Straits, we'll be free of this weather." Turning to his 2nd officer, he said "Mr. VanSlyke, you've got the con. Have Mr. Walls join me in my cabin."

"Yes sir," the young officer said. Taking up the ship's phone, he relayed the request made by the captain.

In moments, First Officer Walls joined Captain Coetzee, sitting behind his cabin desk. "Take a seat, Kenneth. We need to discuss our new contract." He quickly motioned to the only empty chair in the room.

Grabbing his notebook from the side of his chair, Adem calculated his costs for the contract he had just negotiated. "We're being asked to pick up five containers in Algiers for delivery to Marseille," he said. "We then have scheduled deliveries between Barcelona and Nice, correct? Making port in Algiers before those stops would be simple, don't you think?"

"Are all five being dropped in Marseille?" the officer asked.

"Yes, from what I was told," Adem said.

"And how much did you charge them?"

"Two-hundred thousand euros for the five," the captain said. "Which means you and I will pocket 50 thousand each quarter, as long as we keep the contract."

"And what are we transporting?" the young officer asked, leery of being responsible for something dangerous.

"Knowing Youssef Raif like I do, I'd say we're moving drugs for him," Adem said. "Which is better than the villagers from Niger to Brazil, like the last time, huh? I'm not sure we can ever take a contract like that again. All those dead bodies put a foul stench across the decks."

"Not to mention the handful of crewmen we had to abandon because of their conscience," Ken said. "We're still running five men shy. Two in the engine room, a galley helper, and two deckhands. If word gets out about those natives, we'll be hard-pressed to get a loyal crew kept together."

Adem Coetzee leaned back in his chair, his eyes closed in thought, knowing his first officer was right. We'll need to be extra careful about this next trip, considering the consequences, he thought. "Are we still on schedule for Barcelona?"

"Yes, we'll off-load twenty-one containers and take on fifteen, which are bound for Genoa," Walls said. "Right now, we have no containers to drop off in Nice. Unless we get a communique while in port, we should make a quick transit this month."

"I like the sound of efficient sailing; very well then. I'm going to stretch my legs before having lunch," Adem said. "Make sure you pass through the bridge in the next hour and keep an eye on Mr. VanSlyke. I believe this will be his first time navigating the Straits, and I don't want him hitting anything."

"Aye, captain," the first officer affirmed, walking out of the cabin.

Captain Coetzee made his way out of his cabin, stepping onto the bridge wing and descending the stairs to the lower deck. Drawing out a cigarette, he lit it, but used his hand to protect the flame from the oncoming breeze. He made his way up the port side of the freighter, watching a flock of albatross gliding on the wind alongside. In the distance, he saw several other freighters making their own way towards the infamous narrows separating the Atlantic and Mediterranean.

Chapter Ten

The senior officer for the Drug Enforcement Unit let out a sigh as he finished reading the previous evening's account of the break-in to Detective Benoit's apartment. Captain Julien Duval closed the folder with a slap of his hands before looking up at his two officers sitting across from him. "Captain Lemieux, did you take into consideration your suspected voyeur might have had an accomplice?" He asked, tossing the paperwork onto his desk.

"No, I didn't," Claude responded, sitting a little straighter in the wooden chair. "When we conducted our search of his apartment, all we were able to find were maps of the city, photos of Detective Benoit, and a laptop computer. Forensics checked the hard-drive, and all they found was a host of folders with images from pornographic websites." "Even his clothing we found were plain by an Italian playboy's standards."

"So, you've already created a stereotype for him, Captain?" Julien asked.

"I think what Captain Lemieux is alluding to is how the suspect was conducting himself when we arrested him," Geneviève said. "It lent itself to a man needing to prove his sexual worth."

"Thank you for that observation, Detective," Captain Duval said, leaning towards the two officers and placing his elbows on the desk. "But it doesn't answer my question. You've reported someone has been in your apartment. And this came after arresting an Italian 'voyeur' who, by all accounts, had been following you for at least two weeks."

"You believe there's a connection?" Claude asked.

"I think it goes beyond a coincidence," Captain Duval said. "With the events from Detective Benoit's trip to Algiers, it's possible your suspicions about Omar Khalid being involved are correct."

"Well, we'll have our hands full here for the time being," Claude said. "Detective Benoit noticed the surveillance on our shipping company has failed to identify any activity over the last three weeks."

"What do you mean 'failed?'" Captain Duval asked.

"The latest report has no information about activity in or around the building used by Papillion Transport," Geneviève said. "It seems impossible that within days of questioning the staff, the company would cease to exist."

"No one has been seen entering or exiting the office spaces or building," Claude added. "I'm going to have Detectives Berger and Masson canvas the docks to look for the ships. If we can find one in port, we should be able to trace them to their offices."

"Have we heard anymore from Scotland Yard on the activities from their end?" Duval asked.

"No. They've just provided us with the lab results from the drugs they seized on the oil derricks," Geneviève said. "It appeared to be the same makeup as the drugs from the incident in Portsmouth back in May."

"Have we gotten any word on our mysterious guest from Paraguay?" Claude asked.

"I've not heard from Superintendent Chevalier yet," Captain Duval said. "He was supposed to return this morning."

"If we could question this gentleman, it might shed some light on how the drugs we're encountering are coming ashore," Claude figured. "Just based on the fact he's being tracked by us, the Spanish and Germans should justify questioning him."

"I don't disagree with you," Captain Duval said. "But we're a civilized police force and we must follow the rules or we'll be no better than the felons we arrest." He leaned onto his desk, tired of hearing and seeing his detectives chasing shadows. "Now, if we could get back to your dilemma, Detective Benoit. How would you suggest we move forward? You're now in charge, so give me my orders." He stared at the woman, waiting.

Geneviève blinked in disbelief. "I'm not sure what to say, Captain."

"This is where you get to make the hard decision," the senior officer said. "It's not so easy, is it?"

"No... no it's not," she said.

"It would be impractical moving you, and we can't dedicate a handful of officers to watch you and your apartment," Claude said, tossing his empty cup in the trash. "So where does that leave us?"

"Setting a trap for the prowler's return, I guess."

"You are close, Detective," Captain Duval said. "We go about doing what we do best: we canvas the neighborhood and begin to shrink the space your prowler feels comfortable working in. Now, who was the officer on scene?"

"It was Officer LeBlanc," Geneviève answered.

Scribbling down the name, Captain Duval said, "I'll contact his watch commander and we'll begin increasing patrols. Since this is their jurisdiction, I'll have them begin discreetly asking the locals about any new faces."

"Which still leaves me staying in my apartment," Geneviève sighed.

"I'm open to suggestions, Detective Benoit," the senior officer commented.

Peering at her partner, she had the feeling of being a pawn, used for baiting the king then discarded. On one hand, she was perfectly capable of defending herself. Showing the Algerians proved I could handle myself, she thought. On the other hand, not knowing when or where the prowler might make their move placed her at a disadvantage.

"Why don't I stay in one of the vacant villas at the police training grounds," she suggested decisively. "It's a controlled space and patrolled around the clock."

Both senior officers looked at each other before Claude spoke. "She makes a great point. We can leave your apartment as it is in the event the prowler returns. We'll just make it a point to stop by each day to make it look lived in and pick up your mail."

"If that's how you wish to proceed, I'll contact the barracks and make the arrangements for you," Captain Duval said. "And since we're focused on finding answers, why don't the two of you go and question this Italian voyeur. Let's try to find out if he has a friend still on the loose." He dismissed the two officers.

"And just how do you plan to commute between the training grounds and here?" Claude asked Geneviève, opening the door for his partner as they walked out of the office.

"I'll just borrow one of the cars in the motor pool," she said. "They must have a rotation schedule to move them between stations. I'll just become one of the drivers." She sat down at her desk. "Plus, it'll be a nice break from spending money on the bus."

Getting out a folder from his drawer, Claude slid it towards Geneviève. "Let's get back to find out about our mysterious shipping company, shall we? Here are my notes from the interviews; tell me what you make of them."

"Turnabout is fair play. Here, these are mine," she said as she passed her notes to Claude. "Our only problem is not having the notes from Inspectors McDermott and Fletcher and the people they talked to," she sighed, alluding to the Scotland Yard officers.

"You can always call them and have them fax their notes to us," Claude pointed out. Flipping the page, he let out a low whistle. "You mentioned the receptionist alluded to the owner being in Venezuela, right?"

"Yes, it's the story she gave me. Why?"

"Our latest guest," Claude said, "is supposedly from Paraguay. What are the chances he was here to negotiate the completion of a clandestine transaction? I mean, the shipping owner goes to South America, then we get a lead on this smuggler who's from the region from both Spanish and German police."

"It's too convenient," Geneviève said, shaking her head. "If we think along those lines, it would appear the officers from the Guardia Civil were passing their problems onto us. And who's saying the Germans didn't pass it to the Spanish for the same reason?"

Before Claude could answer, the phone rang, "Hello?" Geneviève answered. After a pause, she spoke again. "Yes, Detective Berger works in this office. What...? No, he's not here at the moment. Yes, I'll pass your message to him when he returns. Good day to you too... thank you." She hung up and turned to Claude.

"Who was that?" Claude asked.

"It was the communications clerk. Nicolas has a dispatch from the Spanish about our suspect," she said.

"And there might be the answer to all our problems," Claude said, getting up from his desk.

"And where are you going now?"

"I only have so much bladder space for the coffee, so I'm going to the men's room.".

***

"Do you ever think about settling down, Guy?" Nicolas asked his partner.

"You mean like get married, have kids, a home, and stuff like that?"

"Yeah, I mean, I come to work, I get off, and hit the gym or run. Then it's off to an empty apartment," Nicolas said, pulling the police car to the curb. "I have to fix my own meals, do my own laundry; it's becoming boring I guess."

"So, what sort of woman do you think could handle having you as a husband?" Guy asked, heading towards the waterfront. "She'd have to be athletic, right? A good dancer, pleasant on the eyes…"

"You're describing Benoit; you know?" He envisioned their female partner in the various scenarios Guy was depicting with his suggestions.

"She'd certainly be one I'd use as a benchmark for what you're looking for, though."

Leaning on the car's rooftop, he scanned the docks, then looked back to his partner. "Do you think it'd be better to date a woman in the department though?" Nicolas asked, stopping to stare at the ships. "We've got a few admin-types who are single. I mean, there's the one in accounting, ah, Bernadette. In addition, I've heard the lab was adding a few new girls. I mean, take the one now working in forensics, what's her name…?"

"You mean Francine LeBeau?"

"Yeah, she's fairly cute," Nicolas said. "I mean, sure she wears a lab coat all the time, but she's got a nice figure. She needs to ditch the librarian-style glasses and let her hair down occasionally."

Strolling past the second terminal, Guy stopped and pulled out his notebook with the list of freighters. "Ahoy, it looks like one of our ships pulled in." He pointed to the Motor Vessel (M/V) De Gaulle tied to the dock. A buzz of activity could be seen along the side of the freighter as several cranes removed containers of goods.

"I'll be damned. The old man was on to something, wasn't he?" Nicolas said, alluding to Captain Lemieux's theory. "So, do we go and see if anyone onboard can give us directions to their home office?"

"No, I'm thinking we sit it out and wait for someone to follow," Guy suggested. "We don't want to tip our hand too soon on what we know about them. Come on, let's get over to the harbormaster's office and see when it's scheduled to leave." The detectives turned back towards the car.

"So, getting back to my earlier question; should I date someone like Francine?"

"It might be easier that way," Guy said, sliding behind the wheel. "At least she'll know what you do for a job and won't ask a bunch of questions. Not to mention the ability to have an intelligent conversation, you know, with her being a science-type and all."

"You've got a point," Nicolas said. "But can she cook?" He carefully watched the ships pass by the window.

"You better hope she can tolerate your cooking," Guy teased, pulling into the parking lot for the harbormaster's office. Going into the building, the detectives approached the counter and receptionist.

"Good morning. Can I help you?" the young woman asked.

Each officer showed their police IDs, with Guy opening the conversation. "Yes, we were hoping to secure a list of arrivals and departures for the next month, if you don't mind?"

"And this is for official business?" the woman asked.

"Yes, it is," Nicolas answered ahead of his partner, letting his eyes roam over the young woman's figure.

"If you'll take a seat, I'll prepare the print-out for you," she said, directing them towards the corner and the empty chairs.

"You need to remember your manners," Guy said, noticing the stares of his younger partner.

"What? I was just making small talk with her," Nicolas defended.

After waiting for nearly five minutes, the young woman returned wheeling a wire basket cart with the manifests sitting on the top. "Here you are, gentlemen." She placing the box onto the counter with a thud.

The detectives both stole glances at each other as they noted the copier paper box on the counter. "Are you trying to say all this is a single month's listing of ship movements?" Guy asked.

"This is what you requested, isn't it?" the woman asked.

"Yes, it is," Guy responded.

"It'll take days to go through all these." Nicolas said, hefting the box into his arms.

"It's a good thing we're only looking to find four freighters then, isn't it?"

"Do you think Benoit and Lemieux had these many files looking for their drug smuggling cruise steward?" Nicolas asked, sighing with relief as he placed the box in the back seat.

"I wouldn't know. I was still working in Toulon at the time," Guy said backing the car out of the space and heading to the office.

"What restaurant would you recommend for a first date?"

Chapter Eleven

"You can't be serious, Marcel," Captain Duval exclaimed as he paced his supervisor's office. "We're given information about a possible link to drug trafficking and just because the American DEA says our suspect is working for them, we let him go?"

"Julien, everything INTERPOL showed me was legitimate," Superintendent Chevalier insisted. "All the information they've received so far shows this Monsieur Ochoa as legitimate according to Captain Fontaine." He continued, stirring a spoonful of honey into his tea. "Plus, we get the added bonus of being placed into the information loop for any future briefings. I'd think you would come to appreciate being included."

"My detectives will not be happy to see their efforts to bring in the suspect being discarded like the Sunday paper," the captain said. "Detectives Berger and Masson worked hard to track this man down."

Staring at his department chief, Marcel folded his hands on his desk. "I'm aware how hard your staff has been working. The judicial office has been seeking more clerks the last three months because of the number of arrests your group and the Gang Enforcement Task Force is making. However, we can't rely on just one person to bring down a potential drug empire."

"You're right," Julien agreed, sitting back down. "But if this man has been involved with the drug activities here, we should at least hear to what extent our troubles range."

"As it just so happens, I've gotten his last transcript from his supervisor." Marcel pulled two pages from a folder. "This was passed to his contact in Hamburg after a brief encounter on the docks and he was detained," he explained, passing them to Julien.

Scanning over the text, Julien let out a low whistle. "So this confirms he was on the freighter that docked in Portsmouth. I'm not sure the British will be happy to know several deaths were part of a clandestine transaction by the American's drug agency."

"I'll let INTERPOL and Captain Fontaine inform Scotland Yard, and they can decide if it's worthy of an inquiry," Marcel said. "As they say, better to leave sleeping dogs to lie. Now, what can you tell me about this Italian's fixation with Detective Benoit?"

Julien tilted his head back and chuckled.

"This is amusing to you?"

"No, sir. It's just Captain Lemieux deemed him a 'playboy' that's all," Julien said, suppressing his giddiness. "But in all seriousness, I'm having this man's background checked again." He spent the next five minutes explaining the break-in to Geneviève's apartment.

"Contemplating an accomplice is not a bad idea," Marcel said, finishing his tea. "Have we reached out to the Italian Embassy for confirmation of the suspect?"

"It was one of the first things we checked on," the captain said. "His passport came back nearly clean, with just a notation of entering Monaco without being stamped on arrival." He cleared his throat. "I'm further coordinating with the neighborhood patrols to look for any new faces milling about."

"It's summer time, Julien," the superintendent said. "The locals will point out every tourist renting a room as your suspect, you know. Are you ready to question each one? Moreover, what will Detective Benoit be doing for a place to stay? Is she remaining in her apartment or does she have someone she can stay with for a few days?"

"Since she's reported to us, I've not seen her spend any personal time with people outside of work. But in this case, we have been discussing her options," the captain said. "She mentioned staying in one of the VIP suites at the police academy for the time being.".

Superintendent Chevalier eyebrows rose, hearing the captain. "And what do we do if someone from Paris pays us a visit?"

"I'll handle it when the time comes sir."

"Of course, you will Captain. Now, if we can get back to our current dilemma with Monsieur Ochoa and INTERPOL. As soon as the communications department can set-up our equipment, we'll hopefully be a step closer to snaring the drug traffickers," Superintendent Chevalier said. "Until then, we'll have to continue doing police work the old fashion way, walking a beat. If there's nothing else, you're dismissed, Julien."

"Yes sir," the captain, said leaving the office.

***

"Do you have a color scanner available?" Benito Russo asked the FedEx clerk.

"Yes, it's in booth number 2," the young man, said pointing behind the Italian. "It's 5 euros for fifteen minutes."

Benito handed the money to the clerk who in return passed over the one-time passcode to use the device. Walking over to the cubicle, the Italian placed his messenger bag on the desk and sat, signing in the passcode to make the machine came to life, displaying various icons.

Sliding the map out of his bag, Benito placed it on the glass and selected the scanner function. "Now, to see if we can get this to save." He placed the flash drive stick into the empty port. Selecting 'scan' on the prompt, he saw the cursor change from an arrow to the spinning hourglass, showing the machine was at work, soon providing him with a computerized image of the city map.

Satisfied he was successful at saving the image, he placed the map back into his bag and shut the machine down. "Thank you," Benito said, waving to the clerk as he stepped out of the store.

Wandering down the avenue, he came upon the park his associate, Angelo Mazza, was arrested at two weeks earlier. "How could he be so foolish?" he asked himself. He took a seat on a vacant bench, pulling out his pad and making notes of the surroundings while keeping an eye on several patrons.

"Excuse us," a voice came from behind him.

"Yes?"

"Do you mind taking our picture?" the young man asked handing over the specially configured camera while his girlfriend stood behind him. "Just push this button," the man said, pointing to a spot on the camera.

"Certainly," Benito said, taking the instrument. "Don't forget to smile now." Holding it away from his face so he could see the image on the screen built into the back of the camera, he steadied his hands. He pointed the lens at the young couple and pushed the button several times, the digital camera recording the images. In doing so he unknowingly captured his own image as the camera was altered to record through the eye piece above the screen.

"Thank you," the couple said. The woman looked at his writing pad. "Are you a writer?" she asked, pointing at his notes.

"No, I'm an urban planner," Benito said, telling the lie with ease. "I work for a developer in Milan and we're looking at several cities and how they use parks and dwellings together." He waved his hand at the surroundings. "Several of our citizens have noted how much they enjoyed the availability and cleanliness of Marseille's parks, so my boss graciously allowed me to come here."

"Seems like a convenient way to add a little vacation to your work schedule," the young man said. "We'll let you go, and thanks again for the pictures." He walked off with his girlfriend on his arm.

"Such a sweet couple," Benito said to himself, picking up the pad.

"Do you think he suspected us?" the woman asked, leaning on her partner.

"No, I don't think so," the male officer said. "In any case, we'll have his picture for our files," slinging the camera strap across his shoulders.

Glancing at his surroundings, Benito noted several young women pushing strollers as they jogged around the dirt path. Likewise, in the distance, several young people were engaged in a heated game of volleyball on one of the sand courts. "It seems quite serene if you ask me," he noted, writing down possible areas where he could abduct his target.

***

"I'm sorry to be the bearer of bad news, Captain, but your suspect has to be released," Captain Duval said to his subordinate detective.

"I don't understand how the superintendent could agree to this," Claude said. "Doesn't he realize the epidemic these drugs are causing? My team has been making a dent in the street sales over the last two months but having someone connected to the trafficking is a prize worth exploiting. It's like getting handed a crystal ball and three wishes at the same time."

"I understand your frustration, Claude," Julien said to his friend. "But if this person offers information all police services can use, then we can make a major impact on the drug movement on a national level, not just locally."

Claude swirled his coffee around the cup. "But what if this man knows something about where the drugs originated? Shouldn't we get told about it?" He leaned against a dusty file cabinet. "You need a maid in here Julien," Claude brushed the dirt from his shirtsleeve.

"Superintendent Chevalier feels the sooner we release Monsieur Ochoa, the quicker we'll begin seeing tangible information," the senior officer said. "And your group of detectives has their hands full searching for this phantom shipping company, don't they?"

Dipping his head somewhat, Claude conceded the point to his friend. "Yes, we're still looking into them."

"On a more jovial note, the superintendent agreed to allow Detective Benoit temporary VIP status at the academy… so long as no visitors from Paris show up to spoil her accommodations."

"She'll be pleased to hear about the approval," Claude said.

"Have you heard back on the Italian's status?" Julien asked, alluding to the suspected stalker of Detective Benoit.

"Yes. It seems he traveled here from Naples via Paris," Claude said setting his cup down before pulling his notebook out of his jacket. Flipping it open a few pages, he continued. "He wasn't associated with any tour group, just someone traveling by himself. According to his credit card records, he stayed two nights in Paris before boarding the TGV and arriving here," he answered, picking up his cup and swallowing the last of his bitter coffee.

"Are the officers in Paris checking up on his activities?"

"We've asked them to look into the hotel and restaurants he frequented, but nothing out of the ordinary has turned up so far. Yet, here he is spying on one of my detectives," He wasn't afraid of letting his frustration show.

Captain Duval drummed his fingers on the desk's edge. "And where was he staying? I mean cost wise. The hotel in Paris?"

Shifting the page, Claude read off the notes. "It was a Marriott hotel, the one near the Champs Elysees, for both nights."

"It turns out your suspect likes to spend money," the captain said. "Which goes along with your 'playboy' theory, doesn't it? What about where he lives in Naples? Is it in an upper scale area befitting his persona?"

"We're still waiting for the Italian police to get us the information," Claude said.

"Let's not wait too long," Captain Duval said. "And let's make sure we're asking the right people our questions, shall we?"

"You don't think we'll get told what we need?"

"I'm saying their police agency is just as corrupt as the next," Julien said. "We need to exercise some caution, what with all the reports of the Mafioso bribing their way into the pockets of the police and politicians."

"So, you think this man is part of an attempt to abduct Detective Benoit?"

"Claude, you said so yourself; she made an enemy of the Algerian, right?" Captain Duval asked. "If the information Detective Benoit got from Inspector Haddad is correct, then this man could have the connections to make such an attempt. Or worse, offer enough money to have the Italians do it for him."

Sliding his glasses atop his head, Julien massaged the bridge of his nose. "I'm just saying, Claude, keep your eyes open and don't let your guard down, that's all," the captain said. "If we're wrong and there's more than one individual looking for her, we might not be as lucky as this last time, ok?"

"I understand, Julien," Claude said. "I'll keep a close eye on her. On another note, what can you tell me about Captain Georges' interest in Detective Benoit?"

Captain Duval tried his best not to laugh at the question but failed. "Yes, he's come and expressed his desire to include her in his team's next assignment. Only on an 'as needed' basis, mind you," the senior officer said. "He was really impressed with her ability to work within the team, and she picked up their tactics promptly too," He suppressed a chuckle as he continued. "Besides, he's losing one of his men to a special detail in Le Havre at the end of October, so there will be an opening."

"Well, I'm not going to give her up without a fight," Claude said of his partner. "She's been just as valuable to our department. I mean, she was responsible for the Algerians' ability to capture Hakim Talib." He explained, waving his glasses across the room. "And let's not forget she pursued the fugitive, Francois Laurent, as well."

"Are you done?"

"What?"

"I've already told Captain Georges he needs to coordinate a requirement for the replacement, and not go about stealing from other departments," Captain Duval said. "Which means if, and it's a big if, Detective Benoit wishes to apply, she can do so through the regular process."

"Well, since you put it in those terms, I'll table my concerns for now," Claude said.

"And with this discussion over, let's get back to catching criminals, shall we?" Captain Duval asked dismissing Detective Lemieux.

Chapter Twelve

Trundling into the office, Claude caught Geneviève dozing in her chair. "Are you not sleeping particularly well?" he said, giving her a nudge waking the young woman.

"What…? No, I'm sleeping fine," she said. "What time is it, anyway?"

"On your feet," he said. "We've got an unpleasant task to undertake." He guided her out of the office. "We'll take the stairs, just so you can keep moving," Claude said, pointing to the exit door.

"Where are we headed?"

"Captain Duval was directed by Superintendent Chevalier to release one of our suspects."

"Not the Italian, is it?" Geneviève asked, strolling down towards the basement.

Arriving at the bottom landing, he grasped the door handle and swung it open. "No, it's the gentleman from Paraguay," Claude said. "And when Berger and Masson return, we'll all sit down and discuss the 'why' behind the decision. Until then, I don't want to hear any questions out of you."

Strolling up to the watch-officers' window, Claude showed his ID. "We're here to release Monsieur Gomez," he said, pulling the logbook through the window.

"I'll get his personal effects ready," the officer behind the glass said.

"Your story better be good," Geneviève muttered into his ear as she leaned against the wall.

"If you'll follow me," the roving patrol officer said, heading down the hallway.

As they neared the cell holding Guillermo Ochoa, Detective Benoit stole a glance at the suspect in their voyeur case, Angelo Mazza. Peering out his cell door, he took in her features watching her stroll by, his gaze never wavering.

Feeling the eyes upon her, Geneviève felt her skin tighten as the felon followed her, walking along the hallway. A slight shiver coursed through her body, the subconscious feeling of the pallet scraping her back as she recalled the time when two assailants overcame her.

His attention drawn to Geneviève, the Italians failed to detect her partner. "I've got plans for you," Claude said, scaring the felon who recoiled from the cell door.

"You don't scare me, monsieur," Angelo said mocking the officer's French accent.

"Here you are, detectives," the officer said, opening the cell.

Standing back from the door, Claude waited for the officer to swing it open before speaking. "Monsieur Gomez, I am Detective Lemieux of the French DJSE," he said. Feigning a slight cough, he continued. "On behalf of the department, I'd like to apologize for the manner which you were treated. You see, there was a mix-up of information between yourself and another suspect." He ushered him out of the cell. "You'll find all your belongings accounted for at the front desk."

"But what about my missed voyage? The cruise ship has already sailed," Guillermo asked. "Are the French police going to see me to my next destination?" he inquired as he gathered his wallet and passport.

"Unfortunately, no we cannot," Geneviève said. "But I'm sure an arrangement can be made with the cruise lines; don't you think Captain?" She turned to her partner.

Nearly choking as he heard the comment, Claude replied. "Yes, I mean you paid for a ticket. I'm sure the cruise line can accommodate you on their next departure." Holding the door open to the stairwell, both detectives escorted Guillermo to the main lobby of the police station.

Entering the lobby, the noise, and chaos of officers and citizens conducting business confronted the trio as they made their way to the front of the building. "We'll be taking the white Citroen over there," Claude said, pointing to his car.

Pausing on the steps, Guillermo asked, "Ah, where are you taking me?"

"To the cruise terminal, of course," the officer said. "You mentioned wanting to continue your travels, and the only way to do so is back where they began." Claude opened the trunk. Grabbing one bag, he hefted it on top the spare tire.

"Monsieur, if you please," Geneviève said, motioning their guest into the back seat.

Pulling in next to Claude's vehicle, Detective Berger jumped out, shouting. "Where are you taking him?"

Claude walked up to his junior officer and spoke in a quiet, determined voice. "You and Detective Masson can meet us in the conference room in thirty minutes," he said. "At which point, I'll explain what I'm doing with this gentleman, do you understand?"

"Oui, Captain," Nicolas said as Guy stood holding their box from the harbormaster's office.

"What the hell's going on?"

"I don't know. But that's the Spaniard in the backseat," he noted, pointing at Claude's car. "And he doesn't look stressed like he's being taken to another holding area. We haven't finished our questioning," Nicolas said.

"Oh, and you've got a communique to pick up Detective Berger," Claude said before sliding behind the wheel.

"A lot of good it'll do now," the officer muttered to himself as he hurried after his partner. "Where do you think they're going, Guy?" Detective Berger asked, helping usher his partner through the lobby.

"Lemieux said he'd tell us when he gets back, so I guess we'll find out then."

"Yeah, but we haven't had the guy in custody for more than twenty-four hours," Nicolas said, pushing the door to the office open. Crumpling in his chair, the young detective grabbed the arrest report from his drawer. "Guess I can shred this, right?" he asked, holding it in front of his partner.

"If I were you, I'd hold off on doing that," Guy said. "Plus, he mentioned you had the response from the Spanish. Why don't you go see what they had written up on this guy? It might help decide if all this frustration is worth it."

"And if we find out this person was a serial killer instead of a drug smuggler, then what do we do?"

"We'll go find him again and see he gets what he deserves," Detective Masson said. "Hurry up, I don't want to review all these printouts by myself," he added, alluding to the ships' schedules from the harbormaster's office.

***

The pencil tip snapped for the third time that morning. Sweeping the broken lead from his paper, Pierre Segal spun his chair around, stuck the broken end into the sharpener, and counted to five. Coming back to his ledger, his hand, and pencil, shook somewhat as he glanced at the clock in anticipation for his meeting with Gregory Arsenault.

"Monsieur Segal," the young woman said, interrupting his work, "it's 9:30; you're late. They're waiting for you in the conference room," she continued, alluding to a scheduled gathering of senior bank staff. Grabbing the ledger and his notes, the banker scurried towards the waiting group.

"We're glad to see you making time to join us, Pierre," the bank president announced.

"My apologies," Pierre said, taking his seat in the middle of the room. Opening his notebook, he inhaled deeply, hoping to calm himself.

Over the next thirty minutes, each member of the bank provided the president with the status of his or her particular department. "And this concludes my report, sir," one of the women said, having spoken for the department handling credit card transactions. "Monsieur Segal, it's your turn," she finished, relinquishing the spotlight to Pierre.

"The commercial accounts for the quarter have…" he said, beginning his 15-minute monologue on his department's activities. Announcements of new accounts, the status of current ones, and the revelation of a long-standing client's decision to suspend their account contributed to his report. "I'll conclude my report by saying our association with Nordic Cruise Lines has likewise been suspended because of the police's investigation into their alleged drug trafficking operations. Because of this," Pierre said wiping his brow, "the bank will see a 250-thousand-euro loss each quarter for the next year or two."

The senior bank officer sat stoically in his chair before speaking. "It's not the first for this institution, and I'm sure it won't be the last. I trust you'll look to secure a suitable substitute for them, Pierre?" he asked, staring at his oldest staff member.

"Oui, I'll make every effort, Monsieur Reno."

"I'm sure you will, Pierre," the bank official said. "If there's no other business, we are adjourned."

Going back to his desk, Pierre saw a note sitting up on his desk blotter. Opening the paper, he took a moment to read its content. "Le Bistro de Asianic, 11:30 am, GA," was all the note had written on it. The initials at the end told Pierre all he needed as to who originated the note. With trembling hands, he crumbled it before shoving the paper into his pocket. Grabbing his hat and coat, he stepped out of his office. "Lily, I'll be taking an early lunch," he said, scurrying past one secretary.

After holding the door for several elderly patrons entering the bank, Pierre headed off towards the Asian-inspired eatery. Ambling along the sidewalk, he felt as if every person he passed was looking at him, each one knowing the illegal activity he was involved in for Papillion Transport.

As he neared a street corner, a conflagration of hair products assaulted his senses as they emanated from a local the beauty salon as several of the stylists tried to conjure the latest hairstyles for their clients. Passing the open door, he could hear the chatter as the women spoke of last night's television shows.

Flashing his timepiece, Pierre noted he would be a few minutes early, giving him time for a drink to help calm his nerves. Continuing along the sidewalk another fifty meters, he finally came upon the Asian restaurant. Greeting the hostess, he saw his guest sitting in the back. "I can see my party is already waiting for me," he said pointing to Gregory.

As the banker walked up to the table, Gregory Arsenault greeted his lunch guest. "Hello, Pierre."

"Bonjour, Adrien," Pierre replied, knowing Gregory only by his alias.

"I hope you don't mind meeting here," he said, "but I've had a craving for sushi, and this place has been voted best for three years running."

"I've never been shy about trying new things," Pierre said, picking up the menu.

Gregory sat quietly, observing the banker. Sipping his water, his brow furrowed as he considered how hard to push the older gentleman on the handling of his clandestine finances. As Pierre put down the menu, he took the opportunity to begin their negotiation.

"I understand the cost of living in our fair city is becoming a burden for you?"

"I'm not sure what you mean, Adrien. I'm rather comfortable," the banker said.

"Then why tell my associate your fee was increasing?"

Pierre sat, his scalp tingling as beads of sweat formed along his hairline. "The bank has a new president, and he's being more meticulous with the books," he stammered as the waitress came for their order. As the young woman left, he continued. "Several of the other accounts I've managed have pulled out and gone elsewhere. When this happens, he scours the ledgers looking to see why they left."

"Are you saying my account is at risk?"

"No, as long as we keep the transactions like we have in the past, yours will be fine Monsieur," Pierre said. "It's just, well, if Monsieur Reno digs deeper, he may find yours on accident," he continued. "If this happens, I'll want to make sure I can live comfortably since my banking days will be over," Pierre explained, gulping down his glass of water.

"Let's see if I understand what you're telling me," Gregory said. "You've mixed my account with others which are now at risk of being found out, am I correct?" he asked, giving the older man a cold and determined stare across the table.

"Yes, ah, it's possible," Pierre answered. "But I had to do the transactions like this because of how your funds were being accepted, Monsieur Richelieu. Several of the offshore entities are not welcome in our banking circles, so I had to mask them, for your benefit."

Gregory looked past his guest and out the window, contemplating whether it was time to end Papillion Transport's association with the bank. The question looming before him was how to leave the bank with their money intact without arousing suspicions by the new president. As the server brought their food to the table, Gregory was still considering his options.

"I'll need to discuss this position with the board of directors for the company, you understand," he said. As he poured some soy sauce into a dish, he continued. "If you don't have any objections, that is."

"Why would I object to you discussing things with your colleagues? I would expect nothing less," Pierre said. "But I hope you understand the position Monsieur Reno has put me in as well, though. If my current or past transactions are discovered, the assets for Papillion Transports will be seized and the police will come for both of us."

"Then I recommend we both exercise a greater degree of caution," Gregory said. "Would you like some wasabi for your spring rolls?"

Chapter Thirteen

S itting around the small table of the conference room, the three detectives looked at each other while waiting for their senior officer to arrive. Though Geneviève knew what they would soon learn, Berger and Masson were waiting to find out a practical excuse for their prisoner's release.

Claude stumbled through the door, spilling some of his coffee onto the floor. "Damn, I forgot a lid," he muttered, sidestepping the fresh puddle he made. "So, I've news about this Monsieur Gomez," he started, tossing a folder on the table and taking a seat. "He's an American."

"What do you mean he's an American?" Detective Berger asked.

"According to what Superintendent Chevallier told Captain Duval, yes; he's an agent for their Drug Enforcement Agency," Detective Lemieux said. "He's been working a special assignment for over three years. And we've been asked not to interfere with it."

"The Spanish provided us with some background about his activities," Berger said, waving the communique. "He was apprehended in Hamburg for inciting a melee on the docks before being arrested. When the BKB looked into his activities, they were told to turn him over to the Spanish," he explained, summarizing the message.

"So, he got drunk with the dock workers; what seaman hasn't when in port?" Masson asked.

"He wasn't drunk though," Berger said, reading more of the text. "It says when apprehended, they found several grams of hashish and nearly ten-thousand euros in his pocket. The odd part was when they ran his Spain-issued passport, it came back as invalid."

"So, we've been alerted to this guy because of several past instances of phony documents," Claude said. "And yet INTERPOL has asked us to look the other way? Something's not right," he said, looking at Geneviève sitting in her chair.

As the conversation between her fellow officers was taking place, she had fallen asleep, slouched in the oversized chair. It wasn't until Claude looked over did they see she was dozing, her breathing rhythmic and gentle.

"Should we wake her?" Berger whispered to his fellow officers.

"You can. I'm afraid of what she'll do to us when she wakes," Masson said.

"This break-in at her apartment has her pretty spooked," Claude said. "I'm surprised she's been able to go this long. Just yesterday, the young woman from the lab, oh, what's her name..."

"Francine," Berger replied.

"Yes, her," Claude confirmed. "She found Geneviève curled up on the sofa in the ladies' lounge." He stepped next to the young woman. "Excuse us, Miss Benoit," he said softly, shaking her. "Would you care to join our conversation?"

Drifting off like she did, the officer soon found herself clutching her school books, dodging puddles left from a passing shower. Roaming the back street near her home in Cherbourg, the young woman could sense the eyes of several sailors following her along the sidewalk. Feeling a hand touching her shoulder, Geneviève's first reaction was to assume a defensive posture, one of several her ju-jitsu instructor taught her many years ago.

"Whoa there, Geneviève," Masson said, catching her before she slid off the chair.

"I'm sorry," she said, shaking the cobwebs of sleep from her eyes. "I've not gotten much sleep the last few days. What did I miss?"

"Our former guest," Claude said, alluding to Guillermo Ochoa. "It seems Berger here might have some insight into his activities INTERPOL failed to tell Superintendent Chevalier. This, of course, wouldn't be the first time for them to withhold information."

"So, what can we do about it?" Geneviève asked, standing and straightening her blouse while pacing the room, trying to stay awake. "They're the authority on issues like this, aren't they? They've got the means of crossing jurisdictions to make sure the bad guys are caught."

"In normal circumstances, you're probably right," Masson said, weighing in on the speculation. "However, with something that's high profile or embarrassing to another country, they're most likely to keep things to themselves. Wouldn't you agree, Claude?"

Seeing his reflection in the window, the senior officer thought of the words to answer his colleague. "This involves something beyond our rank, I'm afraid," he answered. "Until we've been given more leeway to act with the information we have, we'll need to watch what actions we undertake."

"But we have the information right here. We know something isn't right," Berger said, holding the communique. "Unless someone created this to make us look foolish, I say we keep our options open to arrest Ochoa, or Gomez, or whatever name he's using now."

"If he was prone to selling drugs before, I'm sure he'll try again," Geneviève said, stretching her arms above her head. Transferring her weight, she tilted her body to the left, exposing one of the small scars on her back to her fellow officers.

"Captain Duval wants us to focus on the mystery of the shipping company," Claude said. "We know one, if not all, of their vessels was being used in drug smuggling. Moreover, since our first visit, the staff has vanished, but why can't we find them? It's time we go back to being detectives and try to decide what happened since our last visit."

"Nicolas and I still have nearly a hundred pages of vessel movements to review," Masson said, alluding to the harbormaster printouts. "So far, nothing except the De Gaulle coming in the day before yesterday from Naples."

"Then I suggest the two of you find who is the captain and first officer and keep an eye on them while they're in port," Claude said. "I can't imagine the master of a ship not wanting to boast to his employer about how well he and his crew are performing."

"And what are you and I going to do?" Geneviève asked, looking at the senior officer.

Claude walked up to her and placed his arm around her shoulders. "You and I are going to gather some of your things and move you to the police academy," he said. "Captain Duval has agreed to allow you to stay there for a few days while the foot patrols search for your prowler."

***

Yelling from the docks echoed off the warehouse and ships' side as workers continued to offload the freighter *M/V De Gaulle* as the sun began setting. "Don't you just love watching them sweat out a deadline?" Captain Sebastian Dubois asked of his first officer.

"Better they do it after sundown than high noon," Olivier Girard said. "Besides, this is probably the first time we've had a legitimate load for them to handle," he noted, referring to their illegal shipping practices from their history. "I still can't get past the expression on the harbormaster's face when he wanted his kick back, and you just shook his hand," the first officer said.

"If Gregory and Louis get their way, we could just become a legitimate business firm," Sebastian said. "It doesn't pay as well, but it's certainly less dangerous for everyone." He looked at a stranger with familiar features of his business partner approaching.

"Doesn't that person remind you of Clement?" Olivier asked, pointing to the man limping on the dock.

"The hair's longer and the beard seems out of place, but it could be," the captain said, studying the man approaching the vessel.

Dodging the trucks and other vehicles moving cargo along the docks, Louis Clement limped along the waterfront towards the gangway. Glancing towards the bridge, he saw the two officers in conversation, before one of them waved at him. He could see the man trying to yell, but he couldn't understand them over the noise.

Handling the ropes on the gangway, Louis pulled himself up the steep walkway until he could step over the edge and onto the deck. "Bonjour, mon ami," he said to the crew member. "I'm here to see your captain."

Before the sailor could call the bridge, a door swung open with a clank of metal on metal as the first officer came through it. "Louis, my friend," Olivier Girard shouted, hugging the man. "It's been too long. Why are you limping? What's with the cane?"

"A permanent gift, thanks to my tussle with Franco," Louis said. "I took a bullet from a policewoman the day he fled Marseille." He rubbed his thigh. "It's not too bad, but Gregory and I've been looking at office spaces we can move into, so I'm a bit tired at the moment."

Reaching them, Sebastian Dubois asked, "I practically didn't recognize you, did you forget to shave this morning?" he joked with his friend. "What brings you down to the docks? I thought we would be meeting tomorrow as scheduled."

Glancing about the deck, Louis sat on a vacant bollard along the ship's railing, glancing at the captain. "We've had to move our offices because of the police," he said. "Seems Papillion has gathered some interest after the last delivery to the Irishman," Louis continued, relating details about the *Bonaparte* delivery in the North Sea to the men.

"So, the entire enterprise is in jeopardy?" Sebastian asked.

"I would be willing to say we're in a more tenuous position," Louis said. "However, I'm confident as a group, we've got the means of overcoming this obstacle just as we have in the past. Since we've cut ties with Aziz and his Algiers connection, we don't have to scour the vessels to remove the stench of the drugs." He glanced at the seaman for his reaction.

Sebastian looked at Louis, surprised to find out his disdain for their former drug operations. "So, how will we earn our living then? Am I supposed to be an honest sailor now?" he asked, chuckling at the thought.

Meanwhile, as the two men talked about the future, first officer Olivier peered over the side, observing the activity of several dockworkers near the warehouse entrance. The lead worker, wearing the cleanest work clothes, was arguing with a man standing in the shadows. Two of the dockworkers were stepping closer to their supervisor as he became more animated in his discussion. "Captain, we might have an issue on the docks," he said, turning to Sebastian and Louis.

Both men moved to the rail and glanced over, watching the event unfold. The supervisor, now flanked by four of his workers, had surrounded the one man, who was still obscured in the growing shadows. "I haven't seen the workers get this agitated since the dock strikes two years ago," the captain said. "Jules, go see if you can find out what this is all about," he ordered.

"Oui, Captain," the young man said, scurrying down the gangway.

"How soon can you prepare a defense?" Louis asked, sensing something wasn't right.

Glancing at his friend, Sebastian said, "A few minutes, no more than five. Why?"

"I'm getting an odd feeling about this," Louis said, watching the work come to a halt while the workers gathered at the end of the warehouse. "How much cargo do you still have to off-load? And how soon can you get underway?"

"Olivier, get a count of what's left to discharge and get Max up here," Sebastian said, more as an order than a request.

"Oui, Captain," the first officer replied, climbing the stairs to the bridge.

In minutes, Olivier's voice could be heard over the ship's intercom requesting the engineer topside, and soon he was seen traipsing down the ladder back to his captain's side. "We've twenty-two containers left to off-load according to the logs," he said, catching his breath.

"Are any of them perishables?"

"No. Ten are dry-goods, eight are machinery parts, and four are empties being returned," the first officer said, citing the list he'd committed to memory.

Meanwhile, the engineer of the ship, a hearty and stout-figured German from Munich wearing a pair of white coveralls emerged on deck. "What's the problem, Captain?" he asked. It was uncommon for him to called on deck, so he was naturally curious for this instance.

"How much time do you need to get us underway?" Sebastian asked with Louis looking on.

"We just got into port last night. Why the rush to leave?" the engineer asked.

Gesturing to the rail, the captain pointed out the gathering crowd. "Seems the natives are restless," he said. "I don't want us caught up in a strike or worse, a melee amongst the dockworkers and vehicle operators. I'm not in the mood to have anything endangering us."

The engineer began to understand their plight. "We've enough fuel to make it to Toulon if need be. The power plants are still warm, so getting them ready wouldn't take long, maybe an hour at the most," he said, calculating the time to bring his engines online. "But I've just the three snipes onboard. Vysaily and Alec are off the ship," he added, alluding to his first and second engineers.

"When do you expect their return?" the captain asked.

"You gave them until tomorrow evening," the engineer said, reminding his captain it was his decision to release several of the crew members. "I'm not sure if they have their phones, but I can try calling them back if you wish?"

Sebastian looked at Louis. "What is your gut telling you?"

Louis peered over his shoulder. "It's not getting any worse, but...." he started, knowing things involving the docks could turn in an instance. "I would keep a watch at the ready and consider calling your men back at first light."

Meanwhile, the seaman Sebastian sent to the docks had returned and stood off to the side. Motioning the seaman towards them, he asked, "What did you find out Jules?"

"The harbormaster was advised tomorrow morning, the police will be sealing off all the commercial docks," the young man said. "They plan on searching every vessel for contraband. The supervisor was being told he and his workers will be escorted off the docks and all work will end."

"That explains why he and his men are so pissed off," Olivier said. "No work, no pay."

Walking away, Louis took a few steps from the group, motioning for Sebastian to follow. "How much spare cash do you have onboard?" he asked.

"The usual sum we agreed to keep for bribes and such, why?"

"I recommend you prepare to get underway," Louis said. "I'll go and see how much it will cost us to help you leave the docks. Between the dockworkers and a sympathetic tug-boat captain, we might need to start a collection." He chuckled at the thought of passing a hat.

Chapter Fourteen

The sound of a paperback book falling to the floor startled Geneviève, causing her to bring her pistol to bear on the noise. Dammit. Grabbing her wristwatch, she saw it was practically six in the morning, as the faint glow of sunrise outlined the curtains. Getting up from the chair, she plodded into the kitchen to fix coffee. Searching through the cupboard, she found a cup to hold the mahogany liquid.

Tugging open the refrigerator, she noticed how bare the shelves were. "I'm going to need a few things," she said as she grabbed the creamer. "I'm sure Claude won't mind stopping after work." Stirring her coffee, she brought the cup towards her lips for that first sip. "Near perfect," she uttered with a sigh.

Before she sat, a knock at her door stopped her. "Just a minute," she shouted, trotting into the bedroom to grab her slacks and a t-shirt. Sliding on her shirt, she walked back to the front room, clutching her pistol as she approached the door.

"Detective Benoit, we're going to be late," her partner said through the door.

Opening it, she saw the haggard look which was becoming all too familiar from her partner. "How many bottles was it last night?" she teased, knowing his after-hours routine.

"Good morning to you, too," he said, stepping into the villa. "You've got fifteen minutes to get yourself ready or I'll report you as an absentee." Wandering into the kitchen, he grabbed a cup and poured his own coffee and glanced over the counter. "Don't you have any sugar?"

"No," she said as she entered the bedroom. "And you didn't answer my question."

"You're right, I didn't and I won't," Claude said. "Now, get going or I'll leave you to walking yourself to the office."

After twenty minutes of showering and dressing, Geneviève emerged from the bedroom, only to catch Claude asleep in the easy chair. Sliding her holster onto her hip, she secured her weapon before shaking him gently on the shoulder. "Claude, I'm ready," she said.

"Good, I've waited long enough," he said, easing himself upright.

"You really need to slow down," she said, locking the door behind them. "Have you considered discussing things with Captain Duval? I'm sure he'll understand if you need to take a few weeks off."

"I'm fine," the senior officer said. You handle your pain in your own fashion, he thought. "And what makes you think Julien... I mean Captain Duval, would understand what my social life is like?"

"I'm just saying you need to consider your long-term health," she said, observing the police cadets exercising as they left the grounds. "You won't find a replacement for Nadine in the bottom of a wine bottle."

She's right, he thought. But my life with Nadine was much more than just companionship, recalling their moments together. We laughed, held hands, and talked. Oh, how I miss talking with her, her cute laughs... A tear rolled down his cheek. "God's punishing me by taking her, but I don't expect you to understand," he muttered under his breath.

Recognizing the emotion of talking about his former wife, Geneviève tried to soften the pain. "Claude, I'm sorry, I didn't mean to say anything to hurt you. It's just that I'm worried about you," she said. "You realize I'm here to help when you need it, and I'm sure everyone else would be there for you as well."

"I know mon Cheri, I know." Maneuvering his car into the station parking lot, he took a deep breath, collecting himself before he got out.

Meanwhile, as Claude and Geneviève were approaching the police station, Francine LeBeau was just stepping off the cross-town bus in front of the district office. Clutching her handbag, she strolled up the steps towards the entrance when she spied Detective Berger striding towards the entrance to her left. Gathering her courage, she maneuvered closer to him. "Good morning, detective," she said.

Caught off-guard by the woman, Nicolas stammered, "Oh... hi. It's Francine, isn't it?"

Blushing at the encounter, she replied, "Yes, Francine LeBeau." Feeling empowered by the meeting, she continued. "I'm working down in the forensics laboratory. I understand you work with Detective Benoit?" she asked, making her way through the entrance.

"Yes, Geneviève and I are partners, so to speak," he said, holding the door for her. "She didn't mention the two of you were friends, though," he said with a smile. "Maybe if you're free later this week, we can get a cup of coffee?"

Her pulse quickened at the thought of seeing the detective again. "I'd like that," she said. "I'll give you call and let you know when I'm free, ok?" she said, turning towards the stairwell.

"Sure, I'll be waiting," Nicolas said, walking away towards the elevators.

"Someone special, Nicolas?" the voice asked from behind his back.

"Damn, Geneviève, you nearly gave me a heart attack," the detective said, turning to see the woman holding two coffees in her hands. "And no, she's not someone special. I mean, yes, she's... it's just Francine, from the lab," he babbled like a school boy.

"I know who she is. Francine's a nice girl. Just be gentle with her, Nic," Geneviève said, entering the elevator ahead of him. "I get the impression she's not as graceful in social circles as you might think, ok?"

Feeling the conversation was becoming more personal than he'd like, Detective Berger posed a question to his partner. "How's life as a VIP?" he asked, alluding to her stay at the police academy.

"I forgot about the cadet's morning and evening routines," she said. "Between the calisthenics and weapons training, it's not as quiet as I'd like. But, I'm not having to worry about someone breaking through my door either."

Stepping in, they found Guy pouring over the last of the vessel movements provided by the harbor master, while Claude's chair was vacant. "Where's Claude?" she asked.

"He came in, dropped his coat, and left," Guy said.

"His coffee's going to get cold again," she said, placing the cup in the middle of his desk.

Grabbing his stack of notes, Detective Berger leafed through the last few pages. "Any luck with the lists?" he asked, glancing at Guy.

"The M/V De Gaulle just pulled into port yesterday, and they'll be tied up for the next three days," Detective Masson said. "Because of this, we'll have three days to check out the officers' movements in hopes they lead us to their home office," he continued, alluding to Papillion Transport and its workplace.

"No time like the present is there?" Detective Berger said, getting up. "Shall we go and act the part of bloodhounds?"

Tossing keys across the desk, Guy said, "You're driving, then."

As the pair of officers left the Geneviève alone in the office, she sat and wondered what to do about her partner, Claude, and his struggle to handle his wife's death. I hope he's talking with the captain, she thought. How is his turmoil any worse than yours? The fear she'd carried since adolescence quickly rekindled.

***

Having cleaned up the small kitchen, Benito Russo was out of his apartment heading toward the bus stop. Having spent the last few days preparing his plan, he needed to put the steps together now to make it happen.

Walking along the street, he passed the market where he had last seen the police officer as she made her way to catch her ride. "Good morning, sir," he said, doffing his cap at the store owner.

"Bonjour, monsieur," the older man replied.

"I was wondering if you could help me," Benito asked. "The other day I was talking with a very charming young woman and I was hoping to meet her again and ask her to join me for coffee, but I haven't run into her since then."

"Oh, you mean Miss Benoit," the merchant said. "I can see why you wish to meet her again. She and her partner came by the other day and collected a few things, like they were going on a trip."

"Was it the tall gentleman driving the red Peugeot?" Things just got harder, Benito thought.

"No, Monsieur Lemieux drives a white Citroen C4," the older man said, sweeping the front step of his market.

"Did they mentioned where they were going or for how long?" he asked. "I'm only in town for a few weeks and don't want to miss an opportunity to see her again." Forming a mental note of the name and vehicle description, he added them to his list for the target.

As the two men spoke of Geneviève and Claude, Benito didn't recognize the two police officers pulling up to the market. Getting out, the officer approached the two, while his partner stood behind next to the car.

"Bonjour, Jules," the officer said. "Bonjour, Monsieur...?" he started, turning to the Italian.

"Russo, Benito Russo," the mafia member said.

"You're new to the city?" the officer asked.

"I'm originally from Milan."

"You're here on holiday then, Monsieur Russo?"

"Work actually, as well as a holiday," Benito replied. "My employer sent me here to gather ideas for a community project back in Milan." He pulled out a business card for the police man.

Peering at the card, the officer noted the company name before handing it back.

"This young man and I were just discussing a beautiful woman who lives nearby," the shop owner said. "Seems he's taking a liking to one of our fair citizens."

"And what is this woman's name?" the officer asked, looking at Benito.

"That's my problem - we only had a brief encounter, and I didn't have a chance to ask," the Italian said. "I was hoping this gentleman might help me find her." He motioned to Jules. "I can assure you, officer, I'm just interested in having coffee with her."

The officer felt uneasy with Benito and his answers. "Can I see some identification please?" he asked while extending his hand.

"Of course," Benito said, reaching into his bag.

"Slowly, Monsieur," the officer said, placing his hand on his sidearm. This caused his partner to take a more defensive stance next to the car, his hand going to his weapon.

Getting his passport from the bag, Benito handed the document to the officer who flipped it open, studying the photograph against the man standing before him. All the features listed appeared correct, including the information about his country of origin and residence.

"Monsieur Russo, I would caution you on contacting our citizens," the officer said. "What you consider as innocent conversations could be suspicious by others." He handed back the document. "Are you staying in one of our hotels?"

"No, I've rented an apartment off Avenue Clot Bey," he replied. "The young woman I met was at the bus stop, but she was stepping in as I was exiting. As I mentioned, it was a brief experience."

Before Officer LeBlanc could ask another question, the radio crackled with a request from dispatch, requiring their response to a disturbance near the waterfront. "If you'll excuse us," the officer said, climbing back into the car as his partner gunned into motion.

"Why did they sound so suspicious?" the shop owner asked.

"I'd be concerned if they hadn't, Monsieur Jules," Benito said. "If they were too complacent, then who would catch the criminals? I look forward to seeing you again sir, good day." He doffed his cap before strolling down the street, beads of sweat dripping down the back of his neck.

Meanwhile, an interested spectator observed the Italian as he walked away from the shop, noting the direction he took and his attire. It wasn't long before Giuseppe Ricci had made his way behind Benito

Russo as he entered the local bistro. "I've got information from Mister Scuderi for you," he said just loud enough to be heard.

Bristling at the name, Benito fought the urge to turn and face the voice, knowing he had just avoided the police earlier in the morning. Walking to the counter, he ordered his drink and a small sandwich, and after receiving his change, took a seat along the wall. Here he took stock of the man who had stood behind him earlier.

Giuseppe did the same, buying a bottle of water before walking out to a bench in the park across the street from the eatery. Sipping from the bottle, he kept a watchful eye on the other Italian, noting when he got up to retrieve his food and exited the bistro.

"May I join you?" Benito asked.

"Please," Giuseppe said, offering a space on the bench. "It's a very pleasant day, isn't it?"

"Yes, it is," Benito answered. Turning somewhat, he looked at the other man. "Do I know you?"

"We have a mutual acquaintance in Alberto Scuderi, my friend," Giuseppe said. "He asked me to come see how you are faring since your friend Angelo became careless," he explained, mentioning the previous mafia member now in custody.

"Angelo was a fool," Benito said. "He can't keep from pretending to be something he's not."

"Let's not dwell on someone else's failure shall we," Giuseppe said. "Alberto would like to know when you plan on acting against the police officer. The client is growing impatient and if we can't deliver the woman, we are all going to lose a share in the bounty."

Staring straight ahead, Benito took a bite of his sandwich, washing it down with his coffee before speaking. "My plan was to abduct her by the end of the week, but there's a new problem."

"And what problem is that?"

Benito turned and looked at Giuseppe. "She has disappeared."

Chapter Fifteen

An early morning fog bank obscured the ships resting at anchor in the bay and moistened the streets around the docks. Drips of condensation fell from his beard as Louis made his way towards one of several commercial tug boats tied to the dock.

A lone figure stood on the fantail, the glow from a cigarette outlining the face at each drag on it. "Can I help you?" the seaman asked, tossing the stub towards the water.

"I'd like to talk with the boat's master if I could?" Louis asked, standing at the foot of the gangway. "I've got a business proposition for him, but I need an answer now." He moved to steady himself between the cane and his good leg.

"I'm the captain," the seaman said, striding down the gangway, his face becoming clearer as he approached. "Bonjour, my name is Tiago Cartier," introducing himself while extending his hand.

"Arnaud Guerini," Louis replied, using his alias as co-owner of Papillion Transport.

"What is it you need moved? A yacht going to Monaco, maybe?"

"I need you to aid a freighter from the docks and into open water," the Legionnaire said. "She's the *M/V De Gaulle* tied up on the southern berth at the Transport La Portuaire facility. She's manned and ready when you arrive, and I trust her captain explicitly."

"A motor vessel you say. How big is she?" Captain Cartier asked.

"She's 134 meters and 12,000 metric tons," Louis said. "However, she's carrying a partial load. They are carrying 22 containers, and her fuel bunkers are at 28 percent."

"A vessel that large usually takes three tugs to maneuver. Why is it so important to have her moved?"

"I've heard rumors of a wildcat strike amongst the dockworkers, and I don't want my vessel stuck here for an extended period," Louis lied. "I've made arrangements in Toulon to off-load the remaining containers and take on fuel, so you see, I need to get her underway."

"Carrying out something like this normally requires the harbormaster's agreement," the seaman said. "But I'm getting a sense they won't be advised of this movement. Work such as this could come with a heavy fine for me if I choose to do it," he noted, lighting another cigarette.

Finally, we're getting to the money part, Louis thought. "How much would it take for your help?" he asked as several crewmen emerged from the vessels interior, the lights from inside the ship silhouetting the captain from behind.

"Something like this might cost ten, maybe fifteen thousand per hour," Captain Cartier said. "But with the fog, the risk of collision increases. Not to mention, there's filing your departure with the harbormaster, and..." his voice trailing off as he heard the rumble of another tug getting underway.

"Will thirty thousand in cash be enough?" Louis asked, knowing he had his hand on fifty thousand euros from the ship's safe in his jacket. "Time is precious, Captain; I'd like an answer."

"You can have my services for thirty-five," Captain Cartier replied, holding out his hand, "and my personal guarantee of my crew's silence."

"Done."

Turning to the two members of the crew smoking at the fantail, Captain Cartier shouted an order to them. Hearing their captain, the men tossed their cigarettes into the water and hurried back inside the vessel. In minutes, they reappeared and handled the lines preparing the tugboat for departure.

"Here's the radio frequency for talking with the freighter. She's captained by Sebastian Dubois," Louis said, handing over a slip of paper to Captain Cartier.

"And the payment?"

Louis reached back into his jacket and pulled out an envelope containing the money. Tolling out the hundred-euro bills, he handed the thirty-five thousand to the tugboat master, sliding the rest back into his jacket.

"Bonne chance, Monsieur," he said, turning away from Louis. Meanwhile, as the captain climbed the ladder to the bridge, Louis pulled his cell phone out, dialing the number for Sebastian who was waiting for his call. The call was answered practically at once.

"Louis, tell me something good will happen soon," the freighter captain said.

"You'll be getting an assist from Captain Cartier on Tug No. 458 in a few minutes," Louis said. "Make sure everything is ready for his arrival. I need to contact Gregory and let him know about your departure. Bonne chance and safe sailing my friend."

Turning to the green and white vessel, Louis was surprised to see it already slipping away from the dock without belching acrid smoke from its stacks. What he noticed was the high-pitched whine of an electrical motor just before the marine diesel roared to life.

***

Driving his car through traffic, Detective Lemieux pulled to the curb near the small police station in the Bonneveine district of the city. Peering at his partner, he sat waiting. "You're being too quiet; why don't you ask me whatever's on your mind?"

Geneviève shifted herself in the passenger seat. "What did Captain Duval say?"

"About what?"

"Whatever you went upstairs to talk about," she said. "You were in his office for roughly an hour. You both had to be discussing something," she continued, brushing her hair aside. "Did you talk to him about Nadine?"

Taking a deep breath, Claude answered. "Yes, I talked to him about Nadine. I likewise talked to him about other issues, like what I'm going through," he said, dropping his head. "Between her death, Claudia returning home, and the promotion, it's all getting to be a burden." His hands twitched on the steering wheel.

"Claude," Geneviève said, her voice soft and comforting. "You're not alone in all this. Nicolas, Guy, myself, we're here for you. I'm sure Captain Duval said the same thing, didn't he?"

"Yes, yes, he did," Claude replied, taking a deep breath to calm himself. "He mentioned if I need a few days to take them, but where am I to go?" He looked at the young woman. "The apartment is a prison nowadays..."

"I don't know," she said. "Maybe book a room on a cruise ship, take a few days away from the city just to relax and not worry about things." Putting her hand on his, she continued, "Claude, the work, the criminals, it'll still be here when you get back. I promise not to catch all the bad guys while you're gone," she teased, smiling back at him.

"I'll think about it," the detective said. "Now, let's find out what the officer's working with Sergeant LeBlanc have for us, shall we?" He grabbed his coffee cup before climbing out of the car.

Since the break-in at Geneviève's apartment, the officers patrolling the neighborhood had been trying to find any person of interest who they deemed suspicious. Ambling into the small police office's, Claude and

Geneviève were escorted to the small conference room where Sergeant LeBlanc was waiting.

"Bonjour, Captain, Detective," he said, motioning to the two empty seats at the table. "I'm happy to say we might have a possible lead on your suspect," he said, nodding to Geneviève. Dimming the lights, he keyed the projector to the first image. "This gentleman has been seen in the vicinity over the last two weeks," he explained, displaying the image of Benito Russo.

"Who is he?" Claude asked, slurping his bitter coffee.

"An Italian by the name of Russo," the sergeant said. "He's here working for a firm based in Milan on an urban development plan. We've contacted the consulate and they've confirmed the passport as genuine." He clicked the next image to the screen. "Here we have him meeting with a local merchant. He admitted to looking for a young woman he'd met earlier the week before." LeBlanc advanced the image to show the Italian talking with the shopkeeper.

"That's Monsieur Jules," Geneviève pointed out, seeing the image.

"Yes," the sergeant said. "He confirmed later in the day Monsieur Russo asked about you by name, Detective Benoit. He even went as far as asking about a gentleman you were seen with, someone who owns a red Peugeot."

"Hector?" she muttered, looking at Claude.

"Is this person someone we need to know about, Detective?"

"What, uh... no. I mean, he's an acquaintance. Monsieur Hector Dupont is his name; he's head of security for the airport," she said. "We've seen each other socially on one or two occasions," she explained, blushing at her admittance of the affair.

"You might wish to discuss the case with him," Claude said, glancing at his partner. Turning to the sergeant, he continued. "Have you brought this man in for questioning yet?"

"No, we haven't done so yet," the officer said. "We encountered him at Monsieur Jules's market, but before we could detain him, we were called to the waterfront to help in a quarrel amongst some Hungarian soccer fans."

"Do you have an address on this man?" Geneviève asked.

"No, just that he was renting an apartment off Avenue Clot Bey," LeBlanc said. "We haven't followed up on it yet. But it's on our docket for each patrol to review." He held up their daily status sheet each officer received before starting a patrol.

Holding one sheet, Claude noticed the sergeant had followed proper protocol by listing specifics about the person of interest without revealing their name. "I'll take this for my records sergeant. If given an opportunity, sergeant, the next chance you get, detain the individual," the detective said. "It's easier to apologize for a mix-up to a potential tourist than to the next of kin of the victim." Tossing his empty cup in the wastebasket, he motioned to Geneviève. "Let's go. Thank you for the briefing, sergeant," he said, nodding to the officer as he walked out.

Finally, outside the station, Claude leaned against his car, his hand stroking his chin.

"Don't you think you were a scant rude to the sergeant?" Geneviève asked.

"Why? Because he didn't realize our suspect was standing in front of him and did nothing," the senior officer said, stepping away from the car. "He'll be a better officer for the rebuke, trust me." Spinning around, he turned to Geneviève challenging her, "And why did you just sit there and let him go like that? We're talking about a person who was in your apartment, aren't we?"

Several of the uniformed officers from the station had stopped outside the building and took in the exchange between the detectives. Each of them was surprised at the manner which the female spoke to her partner being the greatest concern.

"You need another cup of coffee," she said, sliding into the passenger seat.

Yanking the driver's door open, Claude settled behind the wheel. "That's it, I need more coffee?"

"For the moment, yes," she said, staring ahead and avoiding his gaze. "There's a bakery near the school. we can stop there," she suggested, directing him to their destination.

"I expected you to show more emotion," Claude said, driving through the traffic circle. "The sergeant is giving us the person who violated your privacy. Doesn't learning this inspire you to want this man in custody?"

"What if Captain Duval is right?" Genevieve asked. "What if this man is just one of several out to abduct me, like the first one? So, we detain him, but if he's the second, who's saying he's the last one? There could be more, and I'm interested in getting them all."

Pulling the car to the curb, Claude placed it in park and shut the engine off. "Ok, say you're right and there are one or two others; what would you do?"

Geneviève turned to face her partner. "The man's a foreigner, so he most likely is getting help from someone locally," she said. "We need to find out who the person or persons are, then we apprehend them all. Until then, we're just plucking petals off a flower."

Snickering at the metaphor, Claude replied, "At least we'd get to the one in charge."

"We know who's in charge of this; it's Khalid - he's behind it," Geneviève answered, her voice growing louder. "His ego can't take being bested by a woman. It's part of his nature, part of his culture," she said.

"I agree," Claude said. "But who's the Italian helping him? What part do they play in all this, heh? Are they repaying a favor, or is it a debt the Algerian is calling them in on? Let's not forget this all started with the drug smuggling we uncovered with the inspectors from Scotland Yard."

Slouching back in her seat, Geneviève sighed. "Which one takes priority though?" she asked, the frustration in her showing. "If we apprehend the Italian, does he give us Khalid? Or another Italian? And what of the shipping company and the drug smuggling? If we catch them, do we get enough information linking their activities back to Khalid? It all goes back to him."

Cracking his door open, Claude glanced back the young woman. "First thing is a fresh cup of coffee, then we can make our plans, ok?"

Stepping out onto the sidewalk, she looked back at him, "Just as long as you're paying this time. I can't afford to keep you caffeinated every day, you know."

Chapter Sixteen

Weaving the police car amongst the containers and the slow-moving cargo vehicles, Detective Berger felt like a rally car driver on his trek to Dakar. Passing a container trailer, he approached the dock where the freighter belonging to Papillion Transport was secured. Parking behind the warehouse, Berger and his partner Detective Masson walked towards the corner of the building.

"It's gone," Guy exclaimed.

A wide expanse of blackish green water greeted Detective's Masson and Berger as they returned to the berth where the freighter De Gaulle once sat. The fog, hanging low on the horizon, obscured the view of the harbor and the lone tug guiding the freighter towards open water.

"The report said it wouldn't leave for another two days," Berger said, reading his notes.

"Come on, we're going to find out what the hell is up," Guy said, trotting towards their car.

Making the short drive to the harbormaster's office, a solitary watchman met them at the door.

"Where is Monsieur Clerc?" Detective Masson asked showing his police credentials.

"He's on his way to Terminal A for a meeting with the union leaders," the watchman said. "The longshoremen are threatening a strike. It's my understanding they want a five-euro-an-hour pay increase for the junior laborers. They make up 65 percent of the workforce on the docks. If they can't get an agreement signed by tomorrow, the harbor comes to a standstill."

Hearing the clerk mention this provided Guy and Nicolas with the reason for the M/V De Gaulle's sudden departure. "Who's responsible for dispatching the tugboats?" Guy asked.

"We are. All the vessel movements are coordinated from this office. There's fee's which needs to be paid, signing of documents," the man said. "It's not like your pleasure craft for fishing or water-skiing. Much of the taxes and fees are used to pay salaries for everyone," he explained, folding his hands on the counter.

"What's the penalty for moving a vessel without permission?" Nicolas asked.

"For a merchant vessel? It's ten-thousand euros for the first offense," the clerk said. "And a letter of reprimand is filed with the Maritime Commission. If a vessel owner receives enough reprimands, they'll lose their berthing rights and be kept out of French waters."

"What are you thinking?"

"This company, Papillion Transport might have enough influence to overcome a fee of 10,000 euros," Nicolas said, explaining his theory. "Not to mention they could have a plant inside the Maritime offices to miss route certain paperwork, even destroy records."

Turning to the clerk, Guy Masson asked, "How would you deliver a letter to a company at fault of missing payment?"

"We send it by courier," he said, walking around the counter to unlock the door for his co-worker. "Morning Claudia," he said, greeting the woman. "We've all the respective addresses for the companies sailing from Marseille."

"What address do you have for Papillion Transport?"

"Give me a moment, I'll look it up for you." She walked to a desk and powered up the computer.

Finally, after five minutes of pacing the small office, the clerk produced the address for the detectives. "They filed a request to change their address from here to one in Toulon," he explained, pointing out the note for them. "A copy of the letter was likewise sent to the principal owners of the company as well. One copy went to Monsieur Emilio Carbone in Brest while the other was dispatched to Claude Guerini in Lyon."

"Do you recall the date Benoit and Lemieux questioned the staff?" Masson asked his partner.

"No, I didn't think I needed to keep track of their investigation."

"Come on, then," Guy said. "We need to learn if this date aligns with their session with the company staff," He walked towards the door and turned to the clerk. "Merci, monsieur."

***

Detective Benoit sat in quiet thought while sipping her coffee, watching a solitary figure walking through the park. "Can you see that man, Claude?" he asked nodding toward the park.

Setting his coffee down, Claude shifted his chair until he identified the person she was alluding to. "What about him? He's taking a stroll through the park," he said, turning back to her. "Is he doing something illegal? Maybe spying on someone we can't see?"

"He has the same rough features as the photo from Sergeant LeBlanc," she said.

"And you can tell that from a hundred meters, can you?"

"I've got younger eyes than you do," she teased, ribbing her partner. "He's taking a seat and pulling something from his bag," she said, describing his actions to Claude. "What if he's making notes on the best place to abduct someone, or his escape routes, or...?"

"You're being paranoid now," Claude said. "But, if you promise to sit still, I'll take a stroll past him to decide if it's worth facing a harassment suit," he said, getting up from the table.

"Don't forget your coffee.".

Starting his way across the boulevard, Detective Lemieux entered the park, walking in the opposite direction so he could approach the man, moving towards Geneviève. Several children occupied themselves on the swings under the dutiful eyes of their mother. The closer he came, the more defined were the man's features, which were nothing like those from the police photo. Claude continued strolling past the gentleman who had sat and began sketching the city skyline on an artist's pad.

Giuseppe Ricci looked up from his sketches and nodded politely at the officer strolling past him. Benito was right. The police are getting more active, he thought, brushing dust from the paper.

Rejoining his partner, he tossed his cup in the trash. "He's sketching the city," Claude said. "And unless he's an expert at theatrical makeup, I don't think he could've grown a beard in 24 hours." Looking at his partner, Claude could detect the worried expression on her face. "We need to give Sergeant LeBlanc and the rest of the officers a chance to find this Italian again. We can't go chasing ghosts at every turn."

"Just an hour ago you argued about him arresting this man, now you're saying to give them a leeway," Geneviève said. "Which one is it supposed to be, Claude? Point out their failure or give them a break?"

"I was wrong..." he said as his cell phone rang. "Hello? Yes, Nicolas, we'll be there in a few minutes," he replied, ending the call. "Come along, Masson and Berger have some new information on Papillon Transport they wish to share. While I get the car, grab me a fresh coffee please?" he asked, tossing the empty cup in the trash.

Watching her partner turn the corner, Geneviève went into the bistro and bought Claude another cup. "Merci," she said, paying for the drink as Claude tapped the horn as a sign for her to hurry. "Impatient old man," she muttered, walking away from the counter.

Finally, after a twenty-minute course in driving patience through traffic, the detectives arrived back at the main police office. Taking the elevator, they were soon back in their office where Guy and Nicolas were discussing the disappearance of the M/V De Gaulle from earlier.

"What do you have for us?" Claude asked, setting his coffee on his desk.

"Last night, we located one of the freighters from Papillion sitting at the docks," Detective Masson said. "Going back this morning to begin our surveillance, the ship was gone. Poof. Vanished into thin air."

"But the harbormaster's record shows it should still be in the harbor," Nicolas added. "And according to the clerk, no vessel enters or departs without documents and fees."

"Of course," Geneviève said. "Money makes everything so much easier."

"When I pressed the clerk about a vessel being fined, he said they send a letter to the owners by courier," Masson said. "So, being the good detectives, we asked for the address for Papillion they have on file," he started, holding a slip of paper in his hands. "And low and behold, Papillion requested a change of address to Toulon," he stated, passing the notice to Claude.

"Pull the file, Geneviève," Claude said. Taking a large gulp of his coffee, he pulled his pad from the desk drawer.

Sliding the file from the cabinet drawer, Geneviève opened it before handing to the senior detective. "We did our initial questioning on the 20th of June," she said, pointing out the date.

Studying the notes, Claude noticed the same thing. "They submitted the change of address on the 22nd according to this. Which goes along with your notion of possible inside information on our investigation and where it was leading."

"And we can't forget the secretary's statement," Geneviève said. "She said the owner was out of the country, but who's saying he wasn't in Toulon negotiating a new lease for office spaces?"

"The tax office in Toulon would have records of the new business," Detective Berger said. "It wouldn't take much to get our hands on those. Not to mention something simple as electrical and phone services being in their company name."

"He's right," Guy said. "We keep looking for a single instance when we should be thinking about it from a business viewpoint."

Leaning back in his chair, cup in hand, Claude followed the logic in Guy's statement. "Nicolas, you mentioned it first, so you take the utilities angle in Toulon," he said. "And Guy, you begin looking at merchant business leasing prospect. You walked the streets there, use some of your old connections," he instructed, taking another gulp of coffee. "Geneviève, you look for a money trail. Let's see how they pay their fees at the harbor master's office and find the bankers."

"And what are you going to do?" she asked.

"I'm going to have a talk with Captain Duval about Sergeant LeBlanc's report," he explained, getting up from his desk. "I'll be back." Claude left the room, closing the door behind him.

"What's with LeBlanc's report?" Nicolas asked.

"It turns out the sergeant came across the prowler the other day," Geneviève said. "During a chance encounter, he and another officer met an Italian at a local market. While talking with the shop owner, they found out he was questioning the merchant about me. The problem is the sergeant didn't realize it until after he returned to the station and read up on the previous report," she said, sipping her coffee.

"Didn't they get any information on this man?" Guy asked.

"Oh, they did," she said, pulling a copy of their daily incident report from her pocket.

Taking the copy, the detective scanned it before speaking. "His name is Benito Russo. Lives in Milan working for an urban development company," Nicolas read aloud. "Did they do a background check on him?"

"Yes, and so far, he's legitimate," Geneviève said. "The sergeant found out a general vicinity of his apartment, and the patrols will concentrate their efforts to try to locate him," she said, brushing her hair from her eyes.

Staring at the woman, both men sensed there was something more she wanted to add to the story. "What else Geneviève?" Guy asked.

Licking the coffee from her top lip, she paused before answering. "It's possible this Italian also has information on Hector," she muttered, glancing at the empty cup. "According to Monsieur Jules, he gave a general description of his car, which means he was close by when Hector and I met for lunch or dinner one day."

"Have you said anything to him?" Nicolas asked.

"No, not yet."

"What are you waiting for, an invitation? His well-being is at risk the longer you wait," Guy said. "He's got a right to know someone out there has placed a target on you and he's potential collateral damage in the making."

"I'm... I'm not sure how to broach the subject," she said. "I don't want to scare him off because I'm a police woman, or there are risks to being seen with me."

"Geneviève, he needs to know," Nicolas said. "Tell you what - let Guy and I have a word with him. We'll let him know about the case so you don't jeopardize your relationship with him."

"I appreciate the offer, but I think it's something I need to do," she said. "Besides, all this fuss could be for nothing in a day or two if Sergeant LeBlanc locates the Italian again," she said, forcing a smile to her face.

Meanwhile, as the three detectives were discussing the situation with Geneviève's prowler, Detective Lemieux was discussing the same matter with his senior officer, Captain Duval.

"So, the sergeant had the suspect, but let him go?" Duval asked.

"I don't think it went down like that, Julien," Claude said. "My take on how the sergeant described the situation was more along the innocent discussion with a shop owner trying to derive information without arousing suspicion."

"But he was still able to get something on this man, wasn't he?"

"Yes. He recalled much of what was said," Claude replied. "And when Sergeant LeBlanc returned to question the shop owner, that's when other pieces fell into place. I'd say the sergeant and his staff will come across him sooner than later."

"Let's hope it falls into the 'sooner' category, shall we, Claude?" the captain said. "Now, how are you holding up?" He asked, noticing Claude's bloodshot eyes and the constant need to hold something in his hands.

"I'm doing ok," Claude said, sitting back.

"I don't want to push you to doing something if it's not needed, Claude," Julien said. "But, for your own good, I will if necessary, you understand?"

"I appreciate your concern, Julien," he said. "And I know I can turn to you and Annette if it comes to it," he started, standing. "But I'll be ok, mon ami. I promise."

Chapter Seventeen

Gregory sat across the table from his friend, listening to his story about the *De Gaulle* and the dockworkers. Finishing his drink, he glanced at Louis before saying anything. "So, you decided spending 35,000 euros was the right choice?"

"Don't you?"

"I wasn't there, so I can't say what my decision would have been," Gregory said. "But I'd like to think I would have done the same thing," he said, sipping his coffee. "Losing a single day sailing by any of our freighters would be hard for us to recover from, seeing how our income has been slashed in half. Or worse, having the vessel confiscated by the authorities."

"Have you received anything from our contacts?" Louis asked. "We should have gotten something from the Greeks or Turks by now. They've been the steadiest and most loyal customers the last three years."

"I'm optimistic we'll learn from them by the end of the month," Gregory said. "I would not be surprised if they found out of our split from Nazim and are waiting to see what our next step will be. Which brings me to our newest issue," he started, pulling out a folder from his desk and sliding it in front of Louis before he continued.

"Seems Giuseppe has been in town meeting with another member from Italy," he said, pointing to the grainy photo of the two men sitting in the park. "Based on what I've learned from Claire, the Italians are not only looking for Nazim's cousin but also planning on abducting a police officer."

"I don't see it being an issue," Louis said. "One less patrolman on the streets won't matter much to us."

"What if the officer being abducted was the one who gave you the limp?"

"The female detective? She's the target for the Italians?" he asked. "Where can I be of help then?" He grinned like a fool. "If they can snatch her off the street, I'm definitely in favor of it."

"She's also the one involved in making Nazim's cousin disappear," Gregory said. "Which has me concerned that the Algerian, Khalid, is the one asking the Italians to do the dirty work." He got up for more coffee. "If it turns out Giuseppe or someone he knows is helping Khalid or

Nazim, I'm considering we might do one last operation," he continued, gazing out the office window.

A ship's horn echoed across the water before Louis could respond. Studying his friend, he knew once Gregory decided, especially one involving the use of force against an adversary, he would be committed.

"And who do we strike first? The Italians or the Algerians?"

"If we plan it properly, we can make it appear like they went after each other; what do you think?"

"Set them both against the other?" Louis said, stretching his leg. "It's been a while since we planned something like this, you know. You're not afraid of being rusty, are you?"

"I'll admit we've been out of the game for a few years, but have you forgotten what the sergeant major taught us on the Farm?" Gregory asked. "The reason we spent four months training was to have the skills ingrained into our psyche, our ability to react," He leaned on his desk as he spoke. "We'll have Julien prepare a limited obstacle course. And I'll contact Romain to see if he can offer us with some materials."

"Make sure you tell Romain to keep his dogs at home, though," Louis said. "The last one kept trying to hump my leg." Chuckling at the thought and rising, he stepped next to Gregory. "I suggest we move against the Italians first. They're closer, and I would assume Giuseppe has fewer people to call upon in Toulon," he said as he walked out of the office.

***

Fixing the map onto the wall, Benito Russo took the photos his fellow mafia member took of Geneviève, placing them around the perimeter. Running string, he linked the photo to the maps location, identifying the pattern Angelo Mazza created during his two weeks of observing the officer.

"What was your plan?" he asked himself. Manipulating the string, he linked each spot on the map, making a crude circle. He saw two random photos set aside. One was showing Geneviève at the police academy entrance while the other was her and her gentleman friend at the airport. "There was no mention of you traveling, was there, detective?" he said aloud. "Why are you at the airport?" he asked, knocking his knuckle against the image.

The buzzing of his cell phone interrupted his thoughts. "Hello?"

"Benito, it's Signore Scuderi calling. How are you?"

A slight shudder coursed through his body hearing the voice of the mafia don. "I'm well, sir."

"I'm not going to waste your time, Benito," Alberto said. "Tell me, how is your plan coming along to abduct the woman?"

"The police have increased their presence around the woman's apartment. Because of their activities, it's causing me to make other arrangements," he lied to the mafia member. "But I've determined a means of apprehending her without risking injury. To do so, I'll need the assistance of another person, though," he explained, formulating the abduction.

"My associate, Signore Ricci, will be in contact with you later today," Alberto said. "Your task needs to be accomplished by the end of the month. The officer will be handed off to a merchantman for delivery to our client then, you understand?"

Benito was looking at the calendar on his laptop. Eight days from now, he saw after counting the spaces. "I understand, Alberto; the plans will be completed by then. How much help will Signore Ricci make available? And will he have the information on this merchantman as well?"

"He's capable of undertaking much of what you will need, I'm sure," Alberto said. "And he's able to contact me if there are other issues outside his control. After he contacts you, I'll give the information to him about the hand-off with the merchantman," He was careful to keep the identity of the ship and captain secret. "But, keep in mind, Benito, the more help you are given, the less you're paid."

"Understood, Signore Scuderi," he replied. "If you'll excuse me, I've work to do."

"Of course. Addio," the older Italian said, ending the call.

Setting the phone on the table, Benito looked at the photo of the officer and her friend at the airport. "How formidable are you?" he asked himself. The image of Hector Dupont didn't answer him, nor did it offer any sign as to the difficulties he was soon to be engaged in.

Staring at the photos of Geneviève, he grabbed a copy of the police report from her encounter in Algiers. "Subdued three assailants, placing two in the hospital," he read aloud. "That's why you're exercising so much, isn't it? You're busy trying to prove you belong and hide any of your weaknesses aren't you," thumbing through the photos on his counter.

Once again, his cell phone rang, but he didn't recognize the number. He let the caller leave a message which he retrieved, listening to what they had to say. "Signore Russo, my name is Ricci. Please contact me at..." The man left a local phone number. Scrolling through his call log, he selected the number and hit the talk button.

"Hello?"

"Yes, is this Signore Ricci?" Benito asked.

"Yes, it is. May I ask who's calling?" Giuseppe asked.

"My name is Signore Russo. I'm an associate of Signore Scuderi," he said. "I understand you are to offer me with some help here in Marseille. Am I correct?"

"Yes, Signore Scuderi asked that I make myself available if needed," Giuseppe said. "But I'm not in Marseille, at least not this moment, so any meeting would have to take place tomorrow at the earliest." He was able to tell the lie with ease.

Benito frowned, hearing the man being sent to help was a day away. "What is the soonest time we can meet, and where do you recommend?" he asked, looking at the map.

"Parc Balneaire du Prado. I'll be wearing an away jersey for your home club," Giuseppe said. "I'll be sitting along the walking path, so you don't have to go traipsing the sand searching for me amongst the sunbathers."

Searching the waterfront on the map, Benito came across the location with his pencil, drawing a circle around the name. "What time would you like to meet?"

"Let's make it 10:30, shall we?"

"Fair enough. If you don't mind, I've several errands to make before then, so if there's nothing else, I'll bid you addio," Benito said.

"Ciao," Giuseppe replied, ending the call.

Benito took one last look at the map before grabbing his satchel and leaving the small apartment. Departing the building, he turned right and strolled towards the waterfront and the location of the next day's meeting.

Sitting in his car, Giuseppe observed Russo leave, noting his attire and the bag. In a few minutes, he got out of his car and followed Benito from the opposite side of the boulevard. He kept pace, making sure he didn't lose sight of the other mafia member.

After fifteen minutes, both men stood facing the waterfront promenade. Giuseppe noticed the number of pedestrians growing by the minute as locals and visitors alike took in the summer sun. "All these people will make surveillance by the police a nightmare," he said to himself as he crossed the street.

Walking from his apartment, Benito thought through his plan. "It's simple," he told himself. "I grab the boyfriend, and in exchange for his life, the woman agrees to take his place." He couldn't help but laugh at the simplicity. "And as busy as the airport is, it'll be the best place to execute." He knew the influx of travelers would add to the chaos of the getaway. Glancing out at the harbor, he spied several freighters plying the waters as they entered open waters.

"Which one of you am I contacting?" he said aloud, watching the diminishing images fade at the horizon.

Giuseppe noticed Benito stop and look out to sea. "Guessing which ship the woman is being taken to, aren't you?" He knew Alberto would tell him when the freighter would arrive, but only when it was certain they had Officer Benoit in their hands. "I'm not one to second guess, but I'll say it's not here yet," he muttered to himself.

The concentration of both men was soon interrupted by sirens of emergency vehicles making their way along the boulevard. Peering right, Giuseppe saw smoke billowing from one of the international hotels as fire equipment converged in front and police cars stopped at intersections to control traffic.

Now there's a diversion, Benito thought as he observed the scene unfold before him. "But we can't get too crazy, can we?" he uttered. Walking along the promenade, he soon came upon the park Giuseppe mentioned for their meeting. The image of smoke curling along the front of the hotel had captured the attention of many walking along the path. Getting to the sign announcing the park space, he saw several benches and tables, some occupied while others were not.

"It's about the time we'll meet," he noted, glancing at his wristwatch. "So, I just need to look for a lone figure wearing an Inter Milan jersey."

Meanwhile, Giuseppe had made his way close to where Benito stood, and began making his own mental notes. "Benches are all facing the water, and not all the tables are being used," he told himself. "It shouldn't be a problem finding an empty seat and seeing the world pass me by."

Walking up to a small vendor selling refreshments, he bought a soda and a bag of chips before sitting at a table. What can I do with 75 thousand euros? He thought of the bounty placed on the woman. "A new oven would be nice, maybe some new tables and chairs," he chuckled, conjuring up a list of items for his restaurant back in Toulon.

Just 100 meters to his right, Benito Russo leaned against the wall separating the roadway and the promenade. "What can you do with fifty-thousand euros?" he asked, contemplating the fee he would receive for handing over the police woman. "Maybe one of the new Alfa Romeo convertibles," he said, smiling. "Red with leather interior would suit me fine."

Shouting from down the boulevard broke through his thoughts as he turned to towards the noise. Looking at several of the crowd pointing skyward, he noticed why the screaming took place as a lone figure was poised on a balcony of the burning hotel.

Commands from the fire brigade could be picked up, but the person stood frozen against the wall. As smoke continued pouring out, it changed color, from sickening black to hopeful grey, signs the firemen were making progress fighting the fire inside the building.

Just as the figure moved towards the edge, attempting to escape the flames, an arm reached through the curtains, grasping an arm of the person and pulling them away from the rail. A cheer arose from the crowd gathered along the promenade as the rescue was completed.

Chapter Eighteen

With Detective Lemieux sending each detective on their respective tasks, Geneviève was dropped off at Banque Palatine to question the staff about the account for Papillion Transport.

"Excuse me, is your senior executive on site?" she asked the receptionist.

"And who may I say is calling?"

"Detective Benoit of DJSE," she said, showing the woman her police credentials.

Soon, Geneviève was being escorted past a row of desks to an office between the teller stations and the vault. As the receptionist opened the door, she said, "Monsieur Reno, Detective Benoit to see you."

"Thank you, Giselle," the executive said. "Detective, please have a seat," he said, motioning to the couch. As he got up to sit next to her, he asked, "What can I do for the police today?"

"Monsieur Reno," Geneviève started, "we are investigating a local company and we are hoping you can offer us with some background information."

"I'll do my best," he said. "But you understand, we have a clause in all our corporate accounts covering confidentiality related issues. If your questions don't cross those lines, we should be able to help you," he started, leaning towards her. "And if not, maybe we can come to a mutual understanding for cooperating."

Perceiving the executive's advances, Geneviève looked the man in the eyes before answering. "We're looking to question those involved in dealings with Papillion Transport, it's a shipping firm here in Marseille."

"That would be my commercial accounts director, Pierre Segal."

"Is he in the office today?" she asked.

"Yes, if you'll follow me," Monsieur Reno said, getting up from the couch.

Walking behind the executive, Geneviève noticed many of the staff lowering their gaze as he walked past them. Interesting, she thought, almost like they consider him a deity or if he had something he held against them.

Reaching the desk for Monsieur Segal, the executive passed the secretary. "Where is Pierre?" he asked, seeing the empty seat behind her.

"I'm sorry, Monsieur Reno," Lily said. "Monsieur Segal called earlier to say he was feeling ill and wouldn't be in," the petite woman said, a quiver in her voice as she relayed the message.

Turning to the officer, Monsieur Reno apologized. "I'm sorry for this, Detective Benoit, but as you can see, my staff member is absent today. Maybe if you furnish me with your questions, I can look into the matter and contact you when I find something."

"I appreciate the offer, Monsieur Reno," Geneviève said, "but I'd like to discuss this with as few people as possible. Several questions I have to ask are sensitive in nature, you understand?"

"Certainly," he said. "Please feel to contact me for any need you have," he told her, handing over his business card.

Taking the card, Geneviève replied, "Either myself or one of my fellow officers will follow up later this week." As she strolled out of the building and stepped onto the busy street, her luck improved as the city trolley designated for the harbor pulled up. Stepping onboard, she soon found a seat near the driver.

***

While Geneviève was discussing matters at the bank, Detectives Berger and Masson returned to the harbormaster's office to question the staff about their missing freighter, the *De Gaulle*.

"Monsieur Clerc," Guy continued with his discussion, "don't you have the means of tracking the vessel movements?"

"Of course," the master seaman said. "We have the latest radar operation associated with the harbor activities. We can see over 100 kilometers out to sea and track the coming and going of each vessel bound for Marseille."

"Then how come you can't tell us where the *De Gaulle* is right now?" Guy asked.

"Much like an airplane, each vessel has a device to help us recognize which ship is transiting the water outside the harbor," the harbor master said. "If it's not transmitting, we can't see them. All they become is a dot on the screen," he explained, pointing to the radar image behind him.

"So, any of those dots could be the freighter?" Detective Berger asked.

"Unfortunately, the answer is yes," Monsieur Clerc said. "And as you can see, we've nearly twenty or more sailing without the aid of their transmitter conveying a signal."

"Let's get back to our other situation then," Masson said.

"The freighter's owner," Clerc answered.

"Yes. When was the last time you had an encounter with them?" the detective asked.

"It was about two years ago," the harbor master said. "Monsieur Richelieu and his associate came to us to negotiate berthing rights for his vessels. It's billed and paid via wire transfer from Banque Palatine by Monsieur Segal," he said, alluding to the banker.

"What was the name of Richelieu's associate?" Berger asked, taking down notes.

"It's here on file," he answered, pulling out a folder from the file cabinet and passing it to the detective. "Monsieur Giles Dumont from Toulon."

"Is this the only document on file?" Berger asked, writing their names into his notebook.

"Yes. It's not up for the renewal until the year after next."

"Does the name Dumont ring a bell for you?" Berger asked, looking at Guy.

"Not this minute, no. But then again, I wasn't investigating corporate issues when I was assigned there either," Guy said. Turning back to the harbormaster, he continued. "What disciplinary actions do you take against the tugboat operators? Say, finding one moving a freighter without your blessing," he asked, trying to piece together a theory.

"They'd be reprimanded and could lose their license," the harbormaster replied.

Before another question could be asked, Detective Benoit came through the door, joining her colleagues. "Gentlemen, sorry for the intrusion," she said, folding her blazer over her arm.

"How did you get here?" Guy asked.

"I jumped on the trolley," she said. "Then took a stroll along the docks. It's a what, oh... five-, ten-minute walk at most from the end of the trolley service to here." She wiped her forehead of perspiration. "I knew you two would still be here anyway."

"Monsieur Clerc," Guy said. "May I introduce Detective Benoit," he said, gesturing towards the woman.

"Bonjour, Detective Benoit," the harbor master said. "We were just discussing the complexities of tracking ocean-going vessels."

"And did you learn anything?" she asked, ribbing her fellow detectives.

"Yes," Nicolas said. "It turns out we don't know enough about freighters and their movements," he said, admitting to their naïve and rudimentary knowledge.

"Monsieur Clerc was just explaining how they use a transponder to track vessel movements," Guy said. "But the crew has the means of turning it off, so they can't be tracked on radar." A sense of defeat was apparent in his statement.

"But, on the bright side," Nicolas added, "we have the names of the freighter's owners," he bragged, flapping his notebook in front of her.

"Claude and I already have the names," Geneviève said. "We got those during our previous investigation. It's old news, I'm afraid."

Glancing at the clock on the wall behind the detectives, Monsieur Clerc realized he was needed for an incoming cruise ship within the hour. "If you'll please excuse me," he said. "It's my turn as the harbor pilot. I must leave now."

"We understand," Guy said. "Thank you for the information. We'll contact you if we have any further questions. Shall we?" he asked, motioning to Nicolas and Geneviève towards the exit.

Walking outside, they noted Monsieur Clerc hustling towards one of the bright orange speedboats idling at the docks. No sooner had he pulled his foot off the dock, the motor roared as the boat was propelled out into open waters.

"He didn't even have time to sit," Nicolas said, watching the spray of water soar upward as the boat sped up. "But damn, that looks like it would be fun."

"You better hope Francine can swim before dragging her out onto one of those," Guy said.

"Are you seeing Francine?" Geneviève asked.

"What? No, I haven't asked her to do anything yet," Nicolas stammered, surprised by the question. "I'd be afraid to take her on a speedboat. For all I know she gets seasick in a bathtub."

"Where should he take her on a first date, Benoit?" Guy asked unlocking the police car.

"Good question," she said. "It should be somewhere neutral, a place where she can feel comfortable and not pressured into something too soon," she continued, climbing into the passenger seat. "I know she's very much into eating healthy though, so keep that in mind."

"Wonderful, a woman who prefers eating sprouts instead of scallops," Berger said.

"I didn't say that," Geneviève said. "I just said she eats healthy, not what she eats. Oh Guy, can you swing me by the airport? I need to see Monsieur Dupont."

"Finally going to let him in on your trespassing prowler?" the detective asked, pulling the car into traffic. "I'm betting he'll understand if you just be honest with him."

"Sure, any guy would totally get being associated with a person being stalked by the mafia," Berger added from the back.

"I'm going to use you for jiu-jitsu practice for thinking such things," she remarked. "Hector spent time in the Air Force; he can handle himself."

"He'll take it just fine," Guy said, glancing at Geneviève. "And you need to zip it, Berger." Just remind him that we're all covering your back on this."

Finally, after a quiet ten minutes of driving, Detective Masson pulled the police car to the front of the terminal. "I'll give you ten minutes, ok?"

"We'll be waiting right here," Nicolas said from the back seat as he opened his notebook.

Getting out, Geneviève hurried into the building, making her way to Hector's office. Catching a clerk as they unlocked the security door, Geneviève said, "Hold it open, please."

The clerk turned, hearing her voice. "I'm sorry, miss. I can't let you through this door."

Pulling her police ID out, Geneviève said, "I'm here to see Monsieur Dupont."

Ushering the officer to her director, the clerk knocked on Hector's door.

"Excuse me, Monsieur Dupont, this officer said she needs to speak with you," she called, motioning to Geneviève who stood outside the doorway.

"It's fine," Hector said with a smile. "I'll see her now."

"I'm sorry for showing up unannounced, Hector," Geneviève said, "but I need to tell you something, and you need to keep it to yourself." She sat down across from him.

"All right. What's so important it couldn't wait until Friday evening?" he asked.

"Last week, while we were at dinner, someone broke into my apartment," she said. "Nothing was stolen. But during the investigation, we've learned there might be a criminal element planning an abduction," Geneviève said, lowering her eyes. "And I'm the target."

Hector sat back in his chair, his steel-grey eyes focused on his companion. "And?" he asked knowing there was more for her to say. "What else is there Geneviève? I can see it in your expression. There's something you're not wanting to tell me."

"The officers learned the suspect knows of you," she said. "I mean, he's gotten a description of you, your car..." She turned away to avoid revealing her tears to him. "Hector, I don't want anything to happen to you because of my actions, or an association with me."

"I grew up in an era where chivalry had not ended," he said with a smile. "First, I'm capable of defending myself. Second, if you and I are continuing this relationship, I won't allow anything to happen to you," Hector said, leaning onto his desk. "And my impression of Detective Lemieux is that he won't stand by while you try to handle this alone, will he?"

"No," she said with a sniffle. "Claude wouldn't, and neither would Guy nor Nicolas for that matter."

"Who are they? Your brothers, cousins...?"

"Sorry, no, they're the other detectives I work with," she said. "They're here, well, I mean they're parked in front of the terminal to be exact. They gave me ten minutes to let you know what I was dealing with," she continued, looking at her watch. "And my time is about up."

Getting up from his desk, Hector walked around and leaned over Geneviève, kissing her on the cheek. "We will be fine, you and I," he said. "Come, let me meet these two protectors before one of my sergeants tries to cite them for double parking in front of the terminal."

Walking out of the office, they made their way towards the entrance. "Oh, I should tell you," Geneviève said. "I'm staying at the police academy until we catch this person," she explained, walking through the sliding doors.

Coming to the police car, Guy and Nicolas were standing on the curb, waiting for their partner's return. Seeing Geneviève walking out with Hector, Guy spoke first. "Monsieur Dupont, I'm Detective Masson and this is Detective Berger," he said, motioning to Nicolas.

"Gentlemen, it's a pleasure to meet both of you." Hector briefly shook hands with the detectives. "I can see Miss Benoit is being looked after by accomplished individuals."

"So, she told you what's going on?" Nicolas asked.

"Not in detail, but enough to convey the importance," Hector replied.

"What type of weapon are you carrying?" Guy asked, motioning to the slight bulge under Hector's jacket.

"You're rather observant. Very good, detective," the director answered. "It's a Sig-Sauer, 9-millimeter. A hold-over from my days in the Air Force. I have the right to wear it as director of security, if that's your concern."

"I never noticed," Geneviève muttered under her breath.

"You were distracted," Nicolas whispered in her ear.

"I hate cutting our conversation short, but I have an airport to manage," Hector said, shaking hands with the two men. "I'll call you later." He gave Geneviève a kiss.

"Use my cell number," she said, getting into the passenger seat.

As Hector turned away, entering the terminal, he disappeared from their view, as Guy pulled the car from the curb and joined the traffic leaving the airport.

"Detective Benoit," Guy said, maneuvering through traffic, "we approve of your gentleman friend. Don't we Nicolas?"

"Of course," the younger detective answered, his thoughts drifting off, wondering where he could take Francine LeBeau on their first date.

Chapter Nineteen

Detective Lemieux walked through the lobby, making his way towards the cafeteria for more coffee. As he reached for the door, he heard an unfamiliar voice. "Detective Lemieux, can I see you for a moment?" the woman asked.

"Do I know you, Mademoiselle?" he asked, seeing the visitor badge hanging from her blouse.

"I'm sorry, detective. My name is Doctor Louise Beringer," she said, holding out her hand. "I was told by Captain Duval you were leading an investigation on a new strain of hashish being peddled throughout the city."

"Yes. Please, call me Claude. Do you mind if we get some coffee?" he asked, motioning to the cafeteria. "Then we can sit and discuss this in my office."

"I take mine black with sugar, if you please," the woman said.

Claude ordered the two coffees and nodded to the cashier who placed them on his police department tab. Passing the cup to the doctor, he directed her towards the elevator. Moments later, they stood in front of his office. "If you'll follow me," he started, holding the door open.

Entering, Louise noticed the stack of empty coffee cups in the detective's trash can as she took a seat. "Your other officers look to be busy," she teased, pointing to the trash can. "Putting in a lot of hours chasing leads on the case I take it."

"Most of those are mine," Claude replied, embarrassed. "Now, you said you sought me out so we can discuss the drug issue. Is there something you wish to add to the investigation, maybe new evidence, or something left off the autopsy report for Miss Bakker?" he asked, recalling the young Danish woman.

"Yes, detective. We came across something new," Louise said. "My colleagues were treating a victim from yesterday's hotel fire; when the bloodwork results, they noted the use of an illicit drug," she explained, taking another sip of her coffee. Opening her purse, she displayed a print-out. "Our lab was also used to run beta tests on your samples from several months ago, so the technicians ran a comparison."

"I wasn't aware the hospital staff were given any samples of the evidence," Claude said, making a note to discuss it with Julien.

"It's a practice we've had in place for years, Claude."

"So, your staff confirmed this victim was exposed to the same drugs we're finding on the street," the detective said. "It shouldn't be much of a surprise since the drug dealers outnumber the police five-to-one in most areas of the city."

"But what we found was the same markers for hashish, but a mere trace of an unknown," the doctor said, finishing her coffee. "The lab noted the earlier sample had a greater concentration of your unknown chemical."

Claude leaned back in his chair, laying his tablet on his stomach. Scrawling a few ideas down, he looked up. "It seems your lab has stumbled across an important issue, Doctor."

"Please, it's Louise," she said with a smile.

"I'm sorry, Louise," Claude said. "What I'm seeing between your tests, both earlier and more recent, is the unknown chemical is breaking down over time. Am I correct with this theory?"

"Whatever this unknown is seems to have a short lifespan once exposed," the woman said. "Most drugs, legal or illegal, can only keep their potency for a finite period. It's like a fine wine. Once you open it, you must finish it before it becomes stale."

"I wholeheartedly agree with your analogy, Louise," Claude chuckled. "However, if what your staff has identified is true, the drug is becoming less lethal, doesn't it?"

"The hashish is still a dangerous drug by itself," Louise said, "including the unknown drug I believe made it worse. But as it circulates, it seems to lose its desired effect. There is still a need for the person to achieve their high. The drugs are still an addiction."

"Thankfully my only vice is wine," Claude said, finishing his coffee. "Not to mention this." He lifted the empty cup in his hand before adding it to the pile.

"Alcohol is an addictive product just like drugs, Claude," Louise said. "The distinction is wine being legal and hashish, in this case, is not. It all comes down to the extent consumed when we're talking alcohol, or even caffeine." She tossed her empty on top of his.

Claude was sensing his friend Captain Duval set this meeting up more to have the woman discuss his emerging signs of alcohol abuse rather than the drug case. If he did, he chose an attractive woman to deliver the message.

"So, where does this leave us, Louise?" he asked.

"Catching the drug dealers is your business, Detective," the doctor said. "But what you might see is that individuals getting the hashish laced with the more potent unknown will continue to seek it out. The ones with the weaker version, they'll most likely be happy with hashish or marijuana."

"And the ones abusing other drugs?"

"They'll continue to do so," Louise said, looking into Claude's eyes. "Either until they get the help they need, or when it becomes too much, they die."

He sat there, torn between wanting to learn more about her as a woman and questioning her motive behind their chance meeting. Seeing the time, he knew he couldn't do either, lest he showed up late for his department meeting. "I'd enjoy continuing our conversation," he said, "but you'll have to excuse me. I have a meeting in a few minutes."

Sliding her card across the desk, she said, "I understand. Call me when you wish to continue our discussion."

"I'll see you to the lobby," Claude said, getting the door for her.

Just as Claude finished escorting Louise to the reception desk, Detectives Berger and Benoit entered through the side entrance, watching the woman walk away.

"Who was that?" Geneviève asked, walking up on Claude.

"What…? Oh... that was Doctor Beringer," Claude said, caught by surprise. "She was discussing some new findings related to our case."

"She's quite attractive," noted Nicolas, watching her skirt sway as she stepped towards the street.

"I hadn't noticed," Claude said, lying to the younger officer. "Where's Guy?"

"Parking the car as always," Nicolas said.

"I'm going to be late for my meeting," the senior officer said, hearing the clock chime throughout the lobby. "When I get back, we'll talk about your meetings."

"What do you make of the doctor's visit?" Nicolas asked.

"I'm not sure," Geneviève said. "I don't think Claude will admit to anything, either."

***

The public-address announcement was repeated every five minutes, reminding drivers that the zone in front of terminals was meant for letting passengers out and not for loitering. Benito knew the timing since he'd been sitting in his rental car for the past two hours, watching for his target to leave the building.

Misleading the clerk at the vehicle registration office, he got information on Hector Dupont, including a special access pass he was afforded as a director at the airport. Learning this, Benito proceeded to the parking complex where he soon spotted the red Peugeot he spied Detective Benoit entering on their date.

"Your plan seems simple," Giuseppe said, sitting in the passenger seat. "But it depends on the woman being willing to sacrifice herself. What if she decides he's not worth it? What is your backup plan?"

"From what I saw," Benito said, "she'll accept the exchange. You've seen the photos Angelo took; the woman is young and naïve."

"And a police officer," Giuseppe said. "I'm sure she's received some training on how to handle being abducted, if nothing more than hand-to-hand combat. Are you ready to subdue her if she becomes difficult?"

"Of course," Benito said, grabbing his backpack and showing off the Taser. "I'm sure this will be enough." Turning back to the terminal, he spotted their target leaving the building, making his way towards them and his vehicle.

In minutes, the Italians were entering the expressway behind Hector Dupont, following him towards the city. "Which part of the city do you think he lives in?" Giuseppe asked as road signs identifying the Verduron district appeared.

"We're close," Benito said, speeding up and changing lanes to keep the car in sight. "The registration is for an address in Saint Antoine." Slowing down, he saw Hector preparing to exit, causing him to cut off the truck he just drove past.

Sitting at a traffic light, Hector Dupont was oblivious to the Italians who were following him. With the change in the signal, he proceeded to his apartment complex. Moments later, he pulled into the driveway and next to the security kiosk, punching in his code to enter.

Seeing the Peugeot turn into the building entrance, Benito slowed down long enough for Giuseppe to see Hector entering his pass code to open the gates. "The building has security gates and cameras," he said as Benito pulled to the curb. "Taking him at his apartment will not be easy if this was part of your plan."

"Have faith my friend," Benito said. "I'll gain access for both of us." He noted the property management listed on the front of the building. "You forget I have a legitimate job which I can parlay into almost anything. One call to the manager and we'll have freedom to execute the plan, trust me."

Taking out his laptop, Benito was soon searching an online map, looking for the location of the property management office. "Seems we're only a few kilometers from their business," he noted, pointing to the red dot on the screen. "Give me twenty minutes at the most, and we'll be a step closer."

"This better work. The merchantman will only be available for a short period and we can't be late," Giuseppe said, alluding to the passing freighter Southern Warrior sailing toward Genoa.

Thinking of the general vicinity of the office complex, Benito was soon parking the car outside the building. Grabbing the satchel and two cardboard tubes from behind his seat, he headed towards the central lobby.

As Benito disappeared behind the glass doors, Giuseppe pulled out his cell phone and called Alberto Scuderi.

"Hello, Giuseppe?" the voice asked.

"Yes, Alberto, it's Giuseppe. It turns out Signore Russo will be able to complete his contract on time," he said, describing their current situation for abducting the police woman. "He has a simple plan which will work, just as long as the police woman concedes to protecting her lover."

"We mustn't fail, Giuseppe," the older Italian said, groaning as the young woman massaging him pressed down on his spine. "We only have one opportunity to use the passing freighter. If we miss it, we'll have a much harder time seeing the woman into Italy."

"I understand," the young man said. "I've already arranged for a boat to take us out to sea. It's just a manner of timing as you know. I'm confident all will work out," Giuseppe said just as Benito emerged from the lobby. "I'll contact you later."

Opening the door, Benito tossed the tubes into the back, then placed his satchel behind the seat before getting in. "And we are in business my friend," he said, holding a business card with a series of numbers.

"And those will allow us access?"

"Not just access," Benito said. "But complete access. Gates, laundry, sauna, the whole complex is ours to roam," he bragged, starting the engine.

"I'm not sure I want to hear how you pulled this off," Giuseppe said, somewhat in awe of his companion. "So, we can walk about with immunity? What is the next move? We know they have cameras recording all the movement taking place outside the vehicles and the utility buildings."

"We just need to conduct a short survey of the occupants," Benito said, pulling in front of a local café. "After ten or twelve patrons see us, they won't notice anything strange when we enter Monsieur Dupont's apartment and subdue him."

"Why are we stopping?"

"I'm a bit hungry," Benito said. "A need a little something for the drive back to town."

Getting back to the issue of meeting the renters," Giuseppe began, "after meeting all those people living in the complex, the police will have plenty of witness and descriptions of us. Do you have a plan to handle that?"

"Do you trust me?" Benito asked.

"I'm not sure I have a choice in the matter," Giuseppe said.

"After you buy me dinner tonight, I'll explain and show you how we get around the issue you just mentioned," Benito said, grabbing his order from the counter.

"And what makes you so sure I'm willing to buy dinner?" Giuseppe asked.

"You have the means, don't you?" Benito asked. "I mean, you own your own pizzeria in Toulon, manage certain affairs for others... you must be paid well for all those things."

"You're well informed, Benito," Giuseppe said. Maybe too well informed, he thought, taking a drink of his coffee. "Let's get back to the city and make our plans, shall we?"

Chapter Twenty

The hourglass spun in circles as the computer searched for clues to the inquiry. Raising her glasses, Sergeant Dubois ran her fingers over the bridge of her nose, the indentations ever present. "God, I hate these damn things," she sighed.

"I think you look good in them," Julia said. "They're rather fashionable."

"As if anything we wear in uniform could ever be considered a fashion statement," Claire said, joining in her friends' laughter. "Come on computer, get a move on." She tapped the screen with her pen.

"It's not a race horse, Claire; you can't whip it to the finish line," the woman said.

"I know, but it would sure be nice if we could," the officer spoke as the file was opening on her screen. "Finally." Typing in some new commands, the file flashed several times before settling on a new page.

"I'm done for the day. Are you joining us for drinks?" Julia asked.

"What, um... no, I've got a few original files I'm trying to clean up. I'll see you tomorrow," Claire said, dismissing her co-worker.

"Ok, then," the other woman said walking out of the office.

Shifting her attention to the file labeled as a summary report, Claire read, "Hakim Talib, male, age 28, a citizen of Algiers, Algeria." She scanned down to the next paragraph, "...was remanded into custody on 2 July. Suspect was cleared by medical staff and housed in the detention cell D-5." Jotting down the details, she read on. "On 4 July, the suspect was transferred to the interrogation center at Ile d'If until further notice." Looking through the remaining pages over the next five minutes, all she found was typical patrol officer jargon.

"What do they mean by Ile d'If center, I wonder?" she asked herself.

Moving back to the first page, she noticed a link to another file. Peering over her shoulder, she hesitated, hovering the cursor over the blue lettering before clicking on it. In moments, another report appeared, this one from the police medical officer.

This report included text and a recording of a conversation between the doctor and his patient, Hakim Talib, according to the headings. Grabbing a disc from her drawer, she copied the recording.

Printing out the reports, she placed the paperwork and the computer disc in the lining of her jacket before shutting her computer off. "This is something Greg will want to see and hear," she muttered to herself, shutting off the lights while closing the office door.

Walking out of the police headquarters, she headed away from the crowd waiting for the evening trolley and pulled her phone from her purse. Dialing her brother-in-law's number from memory, she was soon greeted by his voice.

"Good evening, Claire. What a pleasant surprise," he said.

"I was wondering if you're free for dinner?"

Glancing at his watch, he noticed it was almost six in the evening. "Sure, where are you?"

"I've just left the office," she said. "Can we meet at La Cantine near Rue Sainte, say... eight o'clock? It's important, Greg," Claire said, emphasizing the term.

"Fine, I'll call them and set a table aside for us," he replied.

Stepping onto the trolley, Claire ended the call. "Thank you, see you then."

"Who was that? Louis asked.

"Claire. She wants to meet for dinner," Gregory said.

"Did she say what it was about?"

"No, she didn't. Just that it was important," he said, sitting behind his desk. Putting the restaurant name into his computer, he soon found the number and dialed. In a few minutes, he had secured a table for Claire and himself. "I guess I better get cleaned up,"

***

"Who is dropping you off tonight?" Detective Masson asked, glancing at his partner past his feet resting on the desk.

Dropping the folder on her desk, the woman looked at the soles of size twelve Chukka boots. "I usually catch a ride with Claude," Geneviève said, leaning to one side. "But he's not back from his meeting. Which one of you are heading my way? Nicolas, how about you?" She tossed a wad of paper at the younger detective.

Losing his focus from the computer screen, Nicolas Berger glared at the culprit of the intrusion. "I'm making plans, so it'll have to be Guy or someone else," he said, turning back to the listing of four-star restaurants for the city.

"Come along," Guy said, grabbing his coat and motioning for the woman to follow him. "I'll drop you off at the front gate. It's just a brisk 1000-meter walk to the villa from there."

Grabbing her blazer and purse, Geneviève followed Guy Masson out of the office as Nicolas picked up the phone, dialing a number from the computer. "Yes, good evening," he said. "La Cantine? Can I get a table for two for this evening? Yes, eight o'clock will do fine. The name, um... Berger. Thank you, see you then." He replaced the phone, a tremble to his hand.

Grabbing his coat, he left the office, racing to his car. Pulling out, he fought the urge to cut across the other lanes to the exit, lest he incur the wrath of a senior officer heading home. Darting around, he noticed Guy and Geneviève several cars ahead, pulling onto the boulevard.

Finally, after thirty minutes of wrestling with the other commuters, Nicolas pulled into his apartment complex and parked. Making his way to the third floor, he was soon in his studio, stripping out of his work suit and cleaning himself up for the evening.

After making their way from the city center, Guy pulled his car to the curb in front of the gates leading to the police academy grounds. "You going to be ok?" he asked, glancing at Geneviève.

"Yes, I'm sure," she said. "And thanks for dropping me off. Hopefully this won't be a recurring event." She slid out of the passenger seat. "Bonne chance, Guy."

Showing her ID to the security officer, she strolled the sidewalk towards the residences. Each step gave her a moment to think through her relationship with Hector, and how their investigation into the Italian prowler was impacting it. He doesn't deserve having to look over his shoulder all the time, she told herself.

Nearing the Administration offices, a shadow appeared from behind, causing her to flinch. Twirling around, Geneviève nearly caught the cadet from Senegal with a back-handed punch. "I'm so sorry," she said, catching herself before impacting the man's face.

"You've got good reflexes, officer," the cadet said, gathering himself. "If you'll excuse me." He continued his march towards the office building. At the top of the stairs, a senior instructor stood, applauding softly at Geneviève. "You've still got it, Detective Benoit."

Blushing at the complement, she waved to the instructor. "You taught me too well, Margot," she called as she continued to the villas.

But, Hidecki-san instructed me in ways you never could, she thought, recalling her sensei from the dojo in Cherbourg.

Finally, she reached the small residence assigned to her. Entering, she tossed her blazer across the chair and pulled her pistol from its holster while releasing the magazine, rendering the weapon safe. Kicking her shoes off, she padded barefoot into the small kitchen and began preparing something to eat.

As Geneviève was settling down for the evening, her partner Nicolas was leaving his studio to pick up his date for the evening. Taking the slip with the woman's address in his hands, he placed it into his car's navigation console and selected 'go' while starting the engine. Soon, he was following the blue line and a red dot showing him the way to Francine LeBeau's apartment.

***

Reaching the restaurant, Gregory caught sight of his guest stepping out of a taxi. Walking up to the driver's window, he pulled his billfold out, "How much?" he asked, surprising Claire.

"Eight euros," the driver said.

Passing over the money, Gregory stood back as the car drove away. "You should have told me you needed a ride," he said, giving her a brief kiss on the cheek.

"I didn't want you driving across town just to drive back again," she said. "Plus, you never know who might be watching. I hope you don't mind the sudden call, but I've got some interesting news for you," Claire said, waiting behind a couple conversing with the hostess.

"Let's hope it's good news, then," he said, stepping alongside the hostess. "We've a reservation; the name is Richelieu," he told her, using his alias. "Like you said, you never know." Taking Claire's elbow, he trailed behind the hostess as they were shown to their table.

Taking their seats, they scanned the menu as the waiter took their drink orders. In minutes, they soon placed their dinner order before Gregory began their conversation. "So, what is new and exciting?" he asked, sipping his wine.

"Have you heard of Ile d'If?"

"Of course. It's the ugly rock out past the harbor where the old fort stands, why?"

"It seems your friend from Algiers is spending his time there," she said. "And he's been there for more than just a day or two. Seems an

128

agency has arranged for him to occupy one of the cells," she explained, taking a gulp of her Pinot grigio.

"I wonder if it's possible to pay him a visit," Gregory asked as their salads were brought to the table. "Can you be certain of this?"

"I read the reports," she said. "There are even several audio files between your friend and his physicians. If I had to guess, he wasn't a willing partner in what was being discussed." Nibbling at some of her salad, she continued. "At one point, he mentioned working at appliance repair facility north of the city."

The expression on Gregory's face changed as he heard about the warehouse. "No specifics?" he asked.

"No names, but he provided enough to find a location," she said. "Friends of mine toured the facility but found nothing worth mentioning. Just a few old suits and a carton of wine bottles."

Gregory's mind reeled from hearing about the items left at the warehouse. We took every precaution; we should be fine, he told himself. Turning his attention back at Claire, he continued asking his questions. "So, my North African friend is doing well?"

"From what I gather, yes, he is," Claire said. "However, I'm only looking at a small part of information. Everything was contained in one file, you understand."

"Does the facility have many members, caretakers, attendants, those sorts of people?" he asked, formulating a plan to double-cross Nazim.

"It's well-staffed," she said. "A compliment of a dozen is on-site at all times, not to mention those caring for the guests, why? What are you wanting to do?"

"I need a reason to discredit a former business associate," he said, sipping his wine. "This person's ego might be his undoing if he had the right information. Is there a need for special identifications at the facility?"

"I can ask a few innocent questions, I'm sure," the woman said.

"Was there anything on his female companion?" Gregory asked, changing the focus of their conversation.

"Yes, she seems to be well-liked," Claire said. "She's being lavished with VIP treatment while the paparazzi are being kept at bay. Seems she went into seclusion somewhere near Plan-de-Cuques." That was the district where the police training area was located. "It seems an Italian consortium bidding for her services has sent a second suitor to negotiate."

As Claire provided Gregory with the information on Hakim Talib's location and the Italians' effort to abduct Detective Benoit, his mind was racing through the possible actions. If the police found out about the warehouse, what else did they learn? he asked himself. And what of the woman, how can I use her against Nazim or his mentor, Omar Khalid. So many options, and so little reward.

"Gregory, did you understand me?"

"I'm sorry, Claire. What did you say?" he asked, embarrassed for ignoring her.

"I was asking how Sophia was. Have you heard from her or the young man since the last time?" the young woman's mother asked.

"Both her and Phillip are doing well," Gregory said. "She's keeping busy at a local restaurant. And Phillip is close by making sure she stays safe. I can arrange for you to see her if you'd like." As he waited for Claire to respond, Gregory caught a glimpse of a man waiting to be seated near the hostess' podium.

Walking up to the entrance ahead of Benito Russo, Giuseppe Ricci looked in on the patrons enjoying their evening. As he scanned the men and women, including several children, he froze as he recognized one. Spinning away as casually as he could, he pushed Benito toward the street.

"What are you doing?"

"We need to leave now," Giuseppe replied, reaching the curb. "I saw someone I didn't expect to see," he explained, striding down the sidewalk and hailing a passing taxi. "We'll find somewhere else to eat."

Peering back at the entrance, Giuseppe was hoping the former Legionnaire didn't recognize him and his companion. If he was found out, he wasn't sure he could explain being in Marseille and the business he was doing for Alberto Scuderi.

Chapter Twenty-One

The sound came from behind, footsteps splashing through puddles on the sidewalk as the rain intensified. Eerie shadows cascaded across the street alternating between their source of lights. As she passed the shop entrance shrouded in darkness, Geneviève felt a hand grasp her arm, pulling her down as she screamed at the intruder.

The weight of her assailant pressed her down onto the shipping pallet as calloused hands tore at her blouse. The rough-hewn material scraped her flesh as she attempted to free herself, her legs refusing to move under the shadowy figure.

As her heart pounded heavy in her chest, the screams continued until she realized they weren't hers. Opening her eyes, Geneviève found herself in bed, covered in sweat. Another scream came, this time subdued from outside the villa. Clambering out of bed, she grabbed her pistol and bolted out of the building.

A glint of light shone to her right from a small stand of trees, showing movement when she heard the muffled scream again. Rushing towards the noise, she soon came upon a man dressed in dark clothing trying to subdue a female cadet.

The sound of approaching footsteps caused the assailant to let go of the woman and take off in the opposite direction. Turning to see if he was still being followed, he didn't realize Geneviève had cut across his path and was now upon him.

"Freeze!" she yelled, leveling the pistol at his head.

Staring down the length of the weapon, the man stood still, his chest heaving as he tried catching his breath.

Standing near the man, Geneviève noticed he looked like the cadet she encountered earlier in the evening. "On your knees, hands on your head," she yelled as her breathing slowed down from sprinting after her prey.

Finally, two patrol vehicles came towards her, their spotlights illuminating the scene. "Identify yourself," an officer ordered as he came close to the detective, his own weapon drawn and poised.

"Detective Geneviève Benoit," she said.

"Where are your credentials?" he asked, glancing at the woman's lack of attire.

"Back in my villa, number 4," Geneviève replied, keeping her weapon on the suspect.

Soon, two of the other officers approached, handcuffing the assailant and allowing her to lower her pistol. "Did you come across a young woman back there?" she asked.

"Yes, she's being taken to the infirmary," the officer, a sergeant as his uniform suggested, said. "She's shaken up, a few scratches, some bruises," he said, "and very grateful for your quick response."

Watching the other officers place the suspect into one of the patrol cars, Geneviève realized how cold the early morning air had become. "Can you give me a lift back to the villas please?" she asked, folding her arms across her chest.

"Of course," the sergeant said, showing her to his vehicle.

Showing up at the villa, she rushed in, coming out five minutes later clothed and cleaned, knowing she need to assist the officer while he filed his report. "I've seen the suspect before," she said, sliding into the passenger seat. "Earlier in the evening. He's a cadet."

"Really?"

Over the next few minutes, she related the events from earlier where the cadet had caught her off guard while she was walking to the villa. "Officer Cote saw everything," Geneviève said. "She was standing in the front of the Admin office."

"And how do you know Officer Cote?"

"She was instructing the courses on victim psychology and negotiation techniques," Geneviève said. "They were very interesting. I was surprised at the length of time a hostage can succumb to 'Stockholm syndrome' while in captivity as well."

"She seems to relish her role here," the officer said, sliding the report in front of her. "If you can just sign at block 16a, I'll see you're escorted back to the villa."

Geneviève took the pen the officer held out for her and turned the paper to one side. With a flourish, she signed as witness to the assault, recalling how her signature had evolved from the first police report she signed twelve years ago.

***

A cup of coffee sat steaming on the table in front of Giuseppe Ricci as his guest prepared a small breakfast for them. Seeing the former Legionnaire in the restaurant was a surprise, but hardly unexpected.

"So, this acquaintance of yours, he's the one helping you against the Corsican mafia?" Benito asked. "If what you say is true, I can understand why you wish to avoid being seen as an 'agent provocateur' to them."

"The worst part is after they helped me, I was asked to check on a possible partner for them," Giuseppe said. "Turns out the man they were looking to associate themselves was part of the 'Maghrebi' organization. His name is Nazim Aziz, and he's fronted out of Algiers by a ruthless sheik who is partnered with the Corsicans," he explained, sipping his coffee. "It's a vicious circle."

"I don't understand," Benito said. "What makes this such a bad situation?" he asked, cooking several eggs to go along with the bacon.

"Their partnership soured after a shipment of hashish was stolen from a freighter bound for the United Kingdom," Giuseppe said. "Nazim blamed Gregory of collusion with an Irishman to steal the drugs and keep the money he was paid to alter the shipment. As it turns out, Alberto learned from contacts in London, an Irishman was trying to work a deal against South Americans who were muscling themselves into his region."

"So why doesn't Scuderi turn everything over to the Corsicans and let them handle things?" Benito asked, serving up the food. "Why should we be placed in the middle of a turf war? We have our own issues in Milan."

Taking a bite of the eggs and bacon, Giuseppe washed it down with some coffee before answering. "There's something between Scuderi and this Algerian," he said. "I haven't been able to figure it out though."

"Why would you?"

"It's never a bad thing to have an idea who is working for whom," Giuseppe said. "Plus, if I ever come across something for the don which could cause conflict, I want to make sure I'm on the right side."

Benito sat across from his guest, pondering how he could put the information he'd heard to good use, either for Scuderi or the Algerian Giuseppe was describing. Dipping his toast into the egg yolk, he considered his options.

"Now, back to our situation," Giuseppe said. "What is your grand plan to avoid being detected when we abduct the policewoman's suitor?"

Getting up from the table, Benito retrieved a case from the bedroom and opened it to display the contents.

"What the hell?" Giuseppe whispered. Inside he was looking at the makings of an artist's makeup stand. "A theatre kit, am I right?"

"Very good," Benito said. "My sister was part of a local troupe and she taught me a few things so I could help her get ready," he explained, pulling out several wigs. "I've gotten good at doing my own disguises: wigs, false teeth, small scars and a few nose corrections," he said with pride. "We can walk through Monsieur Dupont's complex wearing these and when we're done, no one will be the wiser."

"I'm impressed, Benito," Giuseppe said. Taking up one of the wigs, he considered what he might look like wearing it. "I always fancied the blonde look," he said, glancing in the mirror. "What about clothes?"

"Our normal clothing should be fine," he said. "Remember, we're part of a consulting firm taking a survey on how well the patrons like their complex." Pulling out his satchel, he retrieved the generic forms they would use. "See, we just need to fill in their names, apartment number, and check a few boxes off. Once we get to Dupont's door, we'll strong-arm our way in, subdue him, and then leave later in the evening."

"You make it sound so simple," Giuseppe said. "There must be fifty units to approach. How do you plan to time it when he's there?"

"It's simple. But more important, it works every time," Benito said. "I've done eight such abductions over the last four years for Alberto like the one I just described," he explained as he closed the case. "It works."

"How much time do you need to prepare both of us?"

"An hour for each of us, maybe 90 minutes," Russo replied. "Not much more since it's just wigs and makeup."

"We've got to make this happen by Friday," Giuseppe said. "The transport for the woman will not linger; we'll be delivering her on the move."

"Are we tossing her from car to car?"

"No. We'll be meeting several members of mine from Toulon at the marina. She's being taken by speedboat to a passing merchantman," Giuseppe said. "And the ship won't be stopping. It has a scheduled arrival in Genoa on Saturday morning which can't be missed."

"So, we literally can't miss the boat," Russo chuckled, shaking his head.

"Not if you wish to see your chunk of the bounty, we can't."

"Then I suggest we go over the routine we'll use," Russo said. "Because tomorrow, we'll begin our charade, say about 10 o'clock. We can take a few samples and then meet near Dupont's unit before hitting a few more. This way, the patrons will get used to us being near the unit without being suspicious."

"If this is the plan, I'll inform my man to be ready after sundown on Thursday evening," Giuseppe said. "Now, what do you have for weapons beside the Taser?"

***

Stepping out of the bedroom, Geneviève slid her feet into her shoes before grabbing her blazer from the foot of the bed. She'd contacted the desk sergeant after returning to the villa, securing a ride to the police station, and looking at her wristwatch, she noticed she was cutting things close.

Walking into the small kitchen, she poured the last of her coffee into a paper cup as a knock came at the door. "Coming!" she shouted, putting a splash of milk in the cup.

Rushing to the door, she nearly forgot her sidearm, forcing her to go back to the bedroom to retrieve it. Getting to the door, she was surprised to see her partner standing on the porch. "Claude, I didn't expect you," she said, pulling the door closed.

"I'm getting used to phone calls in the early morning about your escapades," he said.

"The patrol sergeant called you?"

"Yes, after you took up residence, I instructed them to let me know if you ever cause a problem," Claude said, sliding behind the wheel. "Seems running around the grounds half-naked with your gun is out of the ordinary, don't you agree?"

"I woke up hearing screams, what would you want me to do?"

Pulling out of the training facility, Claude swerved to miss a passing trolley. "How about getting dressed for one thing," the older officer said. "And then call for backup before you go chasing down people in the early morning darkness."

"I was more concerned about stopping the crime than being in uniform," Geneviève said. Watching the buildings pass them by, she realized they weren't heading to their office. "Where are we going?"

"It seems your assailant's family has a checkered past," Claude said. "We've learned his uncle has been associated with one of the African black gangs here in the city. It would be interesting to see if he's part of the drug smuggling."

"I wasn't aware of their involvement in drugs," she said. "All the reports I recall seeing associated the black gangs with racketeering efforts along with the Corsicans. The last big raid was against Les Caids des Cites here in the city."

"They're spreading out and flexing their muscles," Claude said. "One of the undercover operations also identified their possible involvement with the groups associated with Maghrebi crime families in Lyon, Lille and here in Marseille."

"If they are, we should see more movement, but we're not," she said.

"A lot of the gangs' action would be in the less desirable areas of the city," Claude said, pulling into a neighborhood known for Maghrebi gang activity, "such as this part of town." He waved his hand at the graffiti riddled buildings. "We've always been assigned to the more glamorous areas, like the waterfront, for our investigations."

Glancing at the boarded-up storefronts and spray-painted symbols across the building facades, the outlook for the area was bleak. "This looks like a war zone," she said, dismayed at the scenery.

"It is in a large part," Claude said. "As local gangs gain strength in their members, they move the weaker elements out." He stopped, pulling in behind a marked police car. "Keep your eyes open to everything," he warned her.

Getting out of the car, Claude approached the uniformed officers standing behind their car. "Good morning, Andre," he said, shaking the officer's hand.

"Bonjour, Captain Lemieux," the officer replied.

"I appreciate you taking time for my partner and I this morning," Claude said. "This is Detective Geneviève Benoit," he introduced, motioning to the woman beside him.

"Bonjour, Detective," the officer said, acknowledging Geneviève. "Your call was a surprise this morning, Claude," the officer said. "Monsieur Bolaji was never considered a contributor to the crimes here in the neighborhood."

"His nephew is being investigated into an assault," Claude said, following the officer down the sidewalk. "There was a flag on his file about possible connections with one of the Corsicans' families."

Turning into a small grass area, the officer lead Claude and Geneviève to a flat piece of granite inscribed with a name and two sets of dates. "Here lie the remains of one Monsieur Bolaji," the officer said. "Unless there's someone else posing as him, the report you have has been tampered with by someone."

The detectives each shared a glance between themselves before Geneviève spoke. "Now what do we do?"

Chapter Twenty-Two

Gregory Arsenault sat at his desk, reviewing the communiques from his contacts in Istanbul and Naples. Each one relayed similar information: the groups stood committed to Papillion Transport activities and vowed to continue having the freighters move their cargo.

Steadying two cups of coffee in his hands, Louis Clement entered the office, his limp becoming less noticeable. "Can you grab one of these?" he asked, extending the cup towards Gregory. Taking a seat across from his friend, he noticed the papers on the desk. "Are they good news or bad?"

"Oh... these; they're good news for us," Gregory said, holding the telex. "Reading these, our customers in Turkey and the Italians in Naples have confirmed their continued support. Now, it's a matter of scheduling the freighters," looking at the board behind his desk identifying each of the ships that comprised Papillion Transport.

"We just moved Sebastian and the *De Gaulle*," Louis said. "Once he off-loads in Toulon, we can have him make a pickup in Naples, can't we?"

"Not until we get a bill of lading for goods," Gregory said. "I'm not going to commit to anything until I know we'll see money coming in to account for the action. It's time we think more like a regular business, remember?"

"I remember," Louis said. "So how did dinner go with Claire last night?"

"Enlightening to say the least. She found information on Hakim," he said. "It turns out the police have him holed up on Ile d'If, but the only structure is the chateau. Which makes little sense since it's a tourist attraction now days," he continued, sipping his coffee.

"Maybe he's chained up in the dungeon. Can you imagine it, just like Laurence of Arabia," Louis laughed, alluding to an old silent movie? "But why there?"

Glancing at his partner, Gregory considered the question too. "You ask a very good question: why hide Hakim there, and for what reason?" He swirled the remaining coffee in his cup.

"Do you think he talked?"

"I don't know," Louis said. "But I learned Hakim said enough for the police to learn about the warehouse," he explained, alluding to the building where they transferred the drugs. "It would explain the rumors Julien heard from members of a black gang in the northern part of the city. He was told the police raided an abandoned warehouse; it could have been the one we used."

Gregory shrugged his shoulders. "Who cares? We're no longer in that business. But if Hakim talked and the police used the information to raid the warehouse, we can turn it against Nazim."

"Do you hate him that much?"

"I wouldn't call it hate," Gregory said. "It's more like a need to demonstrate one's importance. He put his own greed above the partnership, so he needs to learn a lesson." He stretched his arms over his head. "If he gets arrested, so much the better. Now, let's get things ready for a first order, shall we?" he began, removing his ledger from the desk drawer.

***

The ringing of a cell phone interrupted the silence of the police car as Claude and Geneviève made their way back downtown and to the police station. "Hello? This is Detective Benoit. Yes, he's with me. Yes, we'll be there in ten minutes," she spoke, ending the call.

"And where do we need to be now?" Claude asked, stopping for a traffic light.

"Gare Maritime office," she said. "A foot patrolman came across another dealer passing hashish to tourists. And he had a torn picture of our arrest from two months ago."

"We're becoming popular, aren't we?"

"Is it possible we've been looking in the wrong direction?" Geneviève asked her partner.

"What do you mean?"

"We've focused on the shipping company, but there are still drug dealers," she said. "We're still missing the middleman, so to speak. It's either the ones on the street or the smugglers. We keep missing the ones collecting the money."

"If we keep picking off the pushers, we'll ultimately get to them," Claude said. "We've a city of over 850 thousand living here. We can't expect the bad ones going around wearing sandwich boards advertising their wares now," he explained, pulling the car to the curb.

Seeing the patrol officers and the suspect along the seawall, Detective Benoit made her way towards them, pulling out her ID. "Good morning, officer."

"Seems you're becoming popular, Detective Benoit," the officer said. "This young man has taken a liking to you and your partner." He handed over the remains of a CCTV printout.

"Can I see that?" Claude asked, extending his hand. "This looks like the arrest from the promenade near the flea market," he guessed, noting the background. "How did you come across this?"

"It was in the bag. I didn't ask for it," the young man said.

"So, your supplier just happened to include this with your stash for no apparent reason?"

"Yeah, I guess so."

A police van was soon pulling up to the curb to transport the suspect. Glancing around the waterfront, Claude couldn't decide if the picture was meant as a clue to something bigger or a cruel joke to confuse them. After transporting the suspect and booking him for possession and selling drugs, the detectives made sure he was placed into an interrogation room.

"While we wait for your public defender to arrive, why don't you and I discuss your dealer," Claude said. "Right now, you're looking at 30 months' time, but if you wish to have it reduced…"

"You're joking," the suspect said. "I'd just assume do the two and half years then turn against the…" he paused, stopping himself from implicating his supplier.

"You were going to say something?"

"Not another word until the lawyer arrives," the suspect said, pushing his chair against the wall.

After ten awkward minutes of silence where Claude and Geneviève stood staring at the suspect, a harried and disheveled attorney stumbled into the interrogation room. "I'm sorry for keeping you waiting," the young man said to the detectives.

"What about me?" the suspect asked. "Don't I get the same courtesy? You are representing me remember?"

"Yes, I'm sorry," he said to the suspect. "May I see the arrest report?" he asked, holding out his hand.

"Detective Benoit, could you see to getting a copy for Monsieur…"

"I'm sorry, my name is Monsieur Moreau. And you are?"

"Detective Lemieux," Claude responded. "While my partner is getting a copy of the report for you, shall we discuss the terms of his arrest?"

"It seems the arrest was premature, detective," Moreau said. "He's not guilty of possession or selling. All I see here," he started, holding the report up, "is his possession of someone else's bag."

"And you've determined this in what manner?" Claude asked as Geneviève re-entered the room. "The bag in question contained drugs, did it not?"

"There's not even enough for personal consumption," the lawyer said, reading the report.

"The bag was used to carry much more," Claude said. "When it was tested, there were traces of hashish and marijuana inside the pouches. And need I point out your client was also carrying almost two thousand euros in small bills." His temper was beginning to show.

"So, my client likes to carry cash with him. Who doesn't?" Moreau replied, pointing to Geneviève. "How much cash do you carry, miss?"

"You'll address me as Detective Benoit first and foremost, Monsieur Moreau," she said sharply. "Second, it's none of your business on how much money I carry since it's not pertinent to your client's activity."

Taken aback by Geneviève's rebuke, the lawyer was prepared to unleash a torrid lecture on protocol but was cut short by Detective Lemieux.

"The other issue we have with your client is why he's in possession of city property," he continued, holding the evidence bag containing the partial photo.

"He was apprehended with a torn page from a magazine, so what?"

"This is not a page from a magazine," Claude said. "It's a printed image from a city CCTV camera. Moreover, it happens to be one capturing police activity during an arrest. So, we'd like to hear his version of why he has it"

"I told you, it was in the bag," the suspect stammered.

"There, he's told you the truth," the lawyer said. "As I see it, he's looking at a minor offence, which carries a thirty-day sentence at most," Moreau said, trying to get Claude to admit to a lesser charge.

"I'm sure the judge will have other ideas on his sentence," Claude said. "Unless your client wishes to offer us with some useful information. Then I'd be willing to add a statement of cooperation for the judge to consider. I'll give you time to think about it," he finished, getting up from the table.

Stepping outside the room, he turned to Geneviève. "We need to find out how he got his hands on a picture of you and Guy arresting the woman from this drug bust. The only way he could have gotten his hands on it was either a city worker or someone in the department."

"The easiest answer is a city worker," she said.

"Yes, but, if it's someone in the police department, who could it be?"

"I'm not sure."

Before they could speculate further, the door opened and Monsieur Moreau motioned them inside. "My client wishes to make a statement. However, he wants to know what his sentence will be before he speaks," the lawyer added, sitting down.

"I have no control over the judge," Claude said. "But, as I mentioned earlier, I'm willing to annotate your cooperation; it's all we can do." He looked back at the attorney. "And you know this."

Putting his hand on the shoulder of his client, Moreau whispered something to him while the suspect nodding in agreement.

"This is all I'm able to tell you," the suspect began. "The picture was a copy of one got by a city worker. There're copies being handed out to all the street dealers, basically a warning to look out for her," he explained, pointing to Geneviève. "Word's gotten out to everyone on the street not to confront her for a sale of any kind."

"What's the name of the city worker?"

"I don't know. All I know is the picture was passed to me by another dealer."

"Where did you and the dealer make contact?" Claude pressed the suspect.

"I'd say we're done," the lawyer said, sensing Claude's approach.

"Was the other dealer French or another nationality?" Geneviève asked.

The suspect looked at her. "How'd you know he wasn't French?"

"He was Italian, wasn't he?"

Glancing at the lawyer, the suspect continued the dialogue with the detective. "Yeah. The guy, he said he was from Milan and was looking for you. Now, how about the recommendation?" he asked looking at Claude.

"What you just said makes you part of a larger issue, I'm afraid," Claude said. "Monsieur Moreau, I'd like to discuss something with you in private."

"What's he talking about?" the young suspect asked.

"It's better for your health if you didn't find out," Geneviève said. "As a dealer, you should be well-versed in all the potential trouble walking the streets these days" She leaned against the wall. "Sometimes it's better to turn and walk away when someone offers you a deal that's too good to be true."

"I'm on the street. I can't turn my back on a thousand euros just for pointing a person out," the suspect said. "Having that much money in my hand gives me a week in the hostel. A clean bed to sleep in, a shower, some food…"

Claude and the lawyer looked on through the glass. "For the record, your client just confirmed the solicitation for information regarding a police officer."

"This can't be used in court, you know, detective," the lawyer said.

"He wasn't coerced into making a statement, was he?"

"It's not admissible in a trial, though," Moreau stated. "The judge will throw it out."

"You're right," Claude said. "But if the prosecutor never mentions it, it won't matter, will it? The department is investigating a kidnapping plot, and your client just confirmed a possible suspect's nationality," he continued. "I'd say it's worth a six-month reduction in his sentence."

"You'd agree to recommend it?"

"Sure. Once the parties your client is involved with find out what was discussed," Claude said, forcing a smile in the direction of the lawyer. "Six months off his sentence won't matter much, will it?"

"You can't let prisoners know what he said or didn't say. It's like committing him to a death sentence," Moreau said. "You have to protect him."

"He's a pusher. He's lucky to survive on his own," Claude said. "If he's as smart as he seems, he'll come out of his time in prison with just a few scratches and a maybe new look on life. Now, if you'll excuse me, I've an arrest report to file," he said, leaving the lawyer with the patrolman and technician who recorded everything.

Chapter Twenty-Three

With the sun shining down the undercover agent basked in its warmth. Luck was still on his side being able to catch the cruise ship before sailing. *Thank god for mechanical malfunctions*, he thought. Sitting on the sundeck of the *M/V Concerto*, he noticed that the cocktail tasted sweeter than usual. Relaxing in the warmth of the sunshine, Guillermo Ochoa reflected on his latest excursion with the police. *Damn Germans*, he thought. *They should have listened in the first place when I told them I was DEA.*

Trying to flee the French freighter in Hamburg when one of the engine crew suspected him of being a police officer, he had grabbed the wrong passport from his cabin. Devoting the last three years chasing the chemist from Venezuela was taking its toll on his psyche.

"Senor Gomez, would you like another drink?" the attendant asked.

"Si, uno mas, por favor," he replied, holding up his empty glass.

Watching the couples stroll the deck, he wondered if he'd ever get to living a normal life again. As soon as I can hand over all my files and reports, I'm done, he told himself. Shielding his eyes from the sun, he glanced to his left making sure his target was still in sight. He's enjoying himself, noting the bikini-clad Dane lounging against him with her oily skin. Once I can confirm his association in North Africa, I'll contact Chuck and he can send in the cavalry.

"Señor, your drink," the attendant said, holding his Mai Tai.

"Muchas gracias, señorita."

***

Detectives Berger and Masson sat and listened to their captain explain the situation he and Geneviève encountered with the drug dealer from earlier in the day. "So there seems to be someone offering cash to people on the street for information on our activities."

"And this guy said it was the Italian we've got locked up for being a voyeur?" Nicolas asked.

"He pointed straight to him during the line up," Geneviève said.

"But what has the Italian said since being fingered?" Guy asked. "I can't believe he'd willingly agree to what a street dealer says."

"It doesn't matter," Claude said. "We already have the Italian for stalking a police officer. Now we can add attempted bribery to the charges. The best-case scenario is to arrest another dealer with the same photo, then we've got the collaboration to make our case airtight against him."

"So, we can keep the one Italian locked up. What about the one who's still on the street?" Nicolas asked. "He's still out there somewhere, and we don't know if he's got any help."

Claude glanced at his three detectives before speaking. "I know, and it's why we need to stay sharp. And why Geneviève will continue to live at the training facility until we catch this person." He left the room with his empty coffee cup.

"There's a rumor you subdued a cadet last night?" Guy asked as the door closed.

"It's not a rumor. It's true," Geneviève said with pride. "I heard a woman screaming and found him accosting a fellow cadet in the bushes near the villa."

"And you subdued him in your sports bra and gym shorts," Nicolas pointed out.

"I was more concerned about the victim's safety than my own comfort. But yes, I should have put something else on," she said, turning red at the statement. "I'm sure you would run after someone in your briefs if you had to, Nic."

"I don't wear briefs," he said, laughing.

"Enough, this isn't a locker room," Claude said, returning with a fresh cup. "Your fellow officers' choice of loungewear is not up for discussion. What is up for discussion is our current effort to track down Papillion Transport and its location. Where are we?"

Guy grabbed his notepad from his jacket. "I reached out to a former partner in Toulon who said he's never heard of the company. He's looked into the utilities being set up near the waterfront but came up dry."

"I've scoured the business license bureau, and they have no listing," Nicolas chimed in. "Unless this business has several means of being identified, we've hit a wall," he sighed, folding his notebook closed.

"What about the banks?"

"Well, the commercial account manager wasn't in the other day, so I'll need to go back today," Geneviève said. "But it was strange walking with the executive, besides the fact he was trying to hit on me," she said. "All his staff seemed submissive around him. Almost like they were afraid to make a mistake or they'd get fired on the spot."

"And this has a bearing on our investigation?" Claude asked, slurping at his coffee.

"No, it just gave me the creeps," Geneviève said.

Before she could continue, the phone rang. Picking it up, Claude answered, "Yes, this is Captain Lemieux." The three detectives looked as Claude's face twisted as he listened to the caller on the other end. "Thank you," he said. hanging up the phone.

"Time to earn our pay," he said, standing up. "Grab you stuff; we've another lead to follow on the Italian."

"Where was he seen at?" Geneviève asked.

"A citizen in the Sainte-Antoine district reported seeing someone matching the description," Claude said. "The suspect was spotted stopping at a local bistro with another man," he continued, striding down the steps toward the parking lot.

"So, it seems he does have someone helping him then."

"Possibly, but we'll know more when we get there," Claude said, putting his coffee into the cup holder.

Meanwhile, Detectives Berger and Masson were following their partners in another car.

"How'd your date with Francine go last night?" Guy asked.

"Ok, I guess," Nicolas answered

"Just ok?"

"Yeah, I mean, we had a nice dinner down at the waterfront. We chatted, nothing much more to say," Nicolas said. "I can attest though: she does clean up well. She was wearing a nice skirt and blouse. Nothing fancy, but it was fashionable."

"And the librarian glasses?"

"Oh, no, she was wearing contacts," Nicolas said. "She said she wears the glasses so she doesn't have to adjust the microscopes. Turns out she has hazel eyes, bordering on grey-green."

"What restaurant did you end up going to?" Guy asked, pulling in behind the other patrol car on the expressway.

"It was the seafood restaurant off of Quai du Port," Nicolas said. "You know, the one they always mention on the radio with the Sunday evening jazz sessions."

"I'll take your word for it since I'm not one to listen to the radio much unless it's for a soccer match."

As Guy and Nicolas discussed the previous evening's events, Claude and Geneviève sat in awkward silence as they drove to interview the shop owner who spied the Italian.

"Are you upset with me?"

"What...? No... what gave you that impression?" Claude asked.

"Because you're driving, but not talking," she said. "Usually you have something to say. Is it about this morning?"

Claude glanced at the young woman. "Ok, yes. I'm concerned about this morning. The doctor who examined the victim wrote in his report the young woman didn't mention screaming or crying out when the assault took place. But you said you heard screams."

Geneviève looked away for a moment before answering. "I heard screaming, Claude."

"I believe you did," Claude said in a softer tone. "But was it more in your mind, rather than from outside, maybe? Is it just possible the thought of this Italian has you slightly spooked or something like that?"

"I know what I heard," she said.

Pulling the car in front of the bistro, Claude turned to Geneviève, but she was already stepping out of the car and walking towards the shop. Pulling her ID from her purse, she greeted the owner who stood at the front door.

"Bonjour officer. How can I help you?" he asked.

"We understand you reported seeing a possible suspect. Is that true?" she asked.

"Oui, several officers were passing a flyer around," the shop owner said. "When I noticed the picture, I recalled seeing the man stopping just the other day. He bought a coffee and a sandwich."

As the three stood on the sidewalk, Guy pulled the other patrol car in behind Claude's and got out with Nicolas.

"He looked very much like him," the shop owner said, pointing to Nicolas. "Except he had straighter hair, and it was a lighter shade of brown."

"Are you sure?" Claude asked.

"I can show you; my CCTV camera is brand new," the owner said, waving them into his shop. Walking into the small back room, he turned the surveillance camera on. Both Geneviève and Claude could see Guy and Nicolas standing outside, their images showing up on the screen.

"Here is the man I saw," the owner said, pushing play to let the video from the other day run. In moments, the detectives had a clear view of Benito Russo buying his coffee and the sandwich, even glancing at the camera for a mere instance.

"We'll need the file, if you don't mind," Claude asked.

Passing over the computer disc to Claude, the shop owner asked, "Is there a reward for helping you?"

"Not officially, no. But I'm sure my partners and I can make your assistance worthwhile," Claude said. "We'll discuss it when I return your disc, is it a deal?"

"Oui, you have a deal," the owner said, holding out his hand which Claude shook.

Coming back to the front of the shop, Claude and Geneviève walked up on Guy still questioning Nicolas about his date with Francine LeBeau.

"You went out with the young girl from the lab?" Claude asked.

"You mean Francine?" Geneviève replied correcting him.

"Yes, we had a nice evening," Nicolas said, blushing in front of Geneviève.

"Did she wear those glasses of hers?"

"No, come to find out, she wears contacts when she's not at work," Nicolas said.

"Tell them about her eyes," Guy ribbed his partner.

"What about them?" Claude asked. "Don't tell me she's cross-eyed or something like that."

"No. Her eyes are fine," Nicolas said. "A very nice shade of grey-green hazel. And before you ask, yes, I was a gentleman. We had a nice dinner, then I drove her home to her apartment," he told them, leaning against the patrol car.

"And your next date is when?" Geneviève asked.

"We didn't discuss another date," Nicolas said. "At least not last night. If you don't mind, can we get back to being police officers?"

"He's right," Claude said. "What do you recommend we do with this?" he asked, holding the computer disc in his hands.

"What's on it?" Guy asked.

"A very clear image of the Italian we're looking for in Geneviève's prowler case."

"I say we get as many copies to the foot patrols as possible," Nicolas chimed in.

"I've a better idea," Geneviève said.

"Do tell, please," Claude replied, noting her mischievous grin.

"We use the population to help," she said. "Just as he's doing with the drug dealers, I say we turn the tables against him. Let's get the image on an 'All Points Bulletin' order and supply it to the television stations, plaster his face all over the airwaves," she suggested, spreading her arms skyward.

Guy and Nicolas both exchanged grins while Claude frowned outwardly at her exuberant behavior.

"Do you know what trouble you're asking for… do you?" Claude asked. "Every citizen will point out every suspicious tourist in the city; is that what you want? We cautioned Sergeant LeBlanc about this very thing."

"But if it puts more pressure on the Italian, then he'll do something foolish," she said.

"Where's my coffee?" Claude asked, running his hand through his hair.

"You finished it," Geneviève said.

"Someone get me a coffee; I need to think this through before I present it to Captain Duval," he sighed, holding out a ten-euro bill.

Grabbing the money, Nicolas went back into the shop to get Claude's coffee. "And don't forget, black and sweet," he heard over his shoulder as he walked through the doors.

Staring at Guy and Geneviève, he let out a sigh. "This could backfire in our face you, know?"

"Or it could flush him out and we'll be rid of the problem altogether," the woman said to both men as she slid into the passenger seat.

"Or it'll invite more trouble," Guy said, turning to his captain.

"I'm afraid it will be the latter," Claude replied.

Chapter Twenty-Four

"**B**onjour, Madame," Benito said, greeting the tenant. "My name is Claudio Silvia, and I'm conducting a survey of your complex for my company," he explained as he handed over his business card. "We're looking at how best to incorporate various comforts of inner-city lifestyles with those in the suburbs."

"And how long will this take?" the woman asked, glancing back at her television show.

"Not long, maybe five minutes," Benito said, pulling out the generic form.

This scenario played out for he and Giuseppe over the next two hours, each going door to door, announcing their business while asking questions from their bogus forms.

As Giuseppe walked to the car, he caught sight of the apartment used by Hector Dupont. Nothing distinguished it from the other units except a small decal of a Fleur d'li at the bottom edge of the window. "Are we done for the day?" he asked Benito, walking up to the car.

"For the morning, we are," the other Italian said. "We should get something to eat and come back, say in ninety minutes. It'll give us with an opportunity to show consistent activity during normal hours," he explained, unlocking the rental car.

"And what have we learned from this?" Giuseppe asked.

"Some of these tenants have some odd habits," Benito said, maneuvering the car out of the parking lot. "But the ones I talked to were all women. Some had children, but most were older women with no jobs," he noted, sliding behind the wheel. "And you?"

"The same, but I came across one tenant," Giuseppe said. "He's disabled from the shipyard, but he seemed awfully fit for being injured," He pulled out the man's form. "He's been here for eight years and commented on the lack of a tavern nearby."

"Doesn't sound like a problem," Benito said, pulling the car out of the complex.

"I got the sense he could be if provoked," Giuseppe replied. "I also noticed our target's unit has a decal on the window; it'll help keep it in sight as we move about the units. Are you sure this will work? We've only three days to get our hands on the woman, you know."

"Relax. I've told you, this is not the first time I've done this," Benito said. "All we need to do is get our hands on this man and then trade his life for hers." If my observation is correct, she won't think twice about trading his well-being for hers."

"Which means we need to get our hands on him today, or tomorrow at the latest if we're to meet our deadline," Giuseppe added.

"And we will," Benito replied, pulling the car into a vacant parking spot outside a local restaurant. "We'll eat, go back and do a few more surveys, and by then, our target will arrive home."

"How can you be so sure?" Giuseppe asked.

"Have faith my friend; it'll work," Benito said. "Now let's see what this establishment can offer us for lunch, shall we?"

***

The short, one-hour drive to Toulon gave Gregory time to consider what to do with the information provided by Claire. How best to use it against Nazim? he asked himself. Certainly, just leaking the location of his cousin would entice the former partner to act. And how should I act on the Italians looking for the police woman?

Maneuvering his Peugeot sedan into the space near Sophia's apartment, a slight smile came to his face as memories of his past exploits in the city emerged. "Maybe I'll go see if the small market is still open," he muttered, recalling the neighborhood he and Louis frequented. Locking his door, he proceeded towards his niece's apartment when he spied Phillip exit the building.

"Good morning, Phillip," he said to the young man.

Caught by surprise, Phillip Gaston turned at the greeting to see his boss. "Ah, bonjour Gregory," he replied. "I didn't know you were coming to town."

"I'm sorry for not calling, but I have some information I wish to discuss with Monsieur Ricci," Gregory said. "And I promised Sophia's mother I would check up on her while I was here as well. Is she home?"

"Um... yes, she's in, but still in bed, I believe," the young man stammered. "Oh... and Monsieur Ricci has been out of town the last few days."

"Really? Do you know where he might have gone?"

"I'm sorry, Gregory, I wasn't told. But I believe Tony, his manager, could tell you," Phillip said, looking at his watch. "And he should be opening the kitchen by now."

Gregory stood on the sidewalk, trying to decide what to do. "Since I'm arriving unannounced, I'll let Sophia have a few more minutes' rest while I go have a talk with Geno's manager."

"Do you wish for me to go with you?"

"No, I think it's best the people working for Geno don't associate you and I together," Gregory said. "At least for the time being, that is. Your time to step up will come, I'm sure."

Phillip looked down, somewhat dismayed he couldn't prove his worth to his boss. "As you wish, Monsieur," he said. "And how is Louis doing? And the rest of the men?"

"They're doing well. And they do ask how you are doing," Gregory said. "In time, we'll have you back in Marseille with the rest of us, don't worry," he assured him, patting the young man's shoulder. "By the way, there's a ship, the De Gaulle, pulling into harbor later today. I need you to deliver this to the captain. And only the captain. No one else, you understand?"

"Oui, Gregory. I'll see it's delivered," Phillip said, taking the envelope.

"Now, you go run your errand. I'll go visit Tony," Gregory said, walking away towards Giuseppe Ricci's restaurant, Pizzeria La Italia.

Walking along the sidewalk, Gregory took his time. His thoughts flittered between the present and his past, just after his release from the Foreign Legion. He and Louis chose to set up their shipping firm, Papillion Transport, which they "inherited" for murdering the two gay members of their unit, out of the city.

"Do you have a light, Monsieur?" The voice came from the shop entrance.

"Excuse me?" Gregory asked, his thoughts interrupted by the stranger.

"A light. Do you have one?"

"No, I don't smoke," Gregory replied.

"Then I'll take your wallet," the thief said, stepping in front of him, knife by his side. At the same time, a second man stepped out of shadows and behind Gregory.

"Of course," the former Legionnaire said, reaching his hand behind his back when he noticed the second criminal move closer. As he pulled his wallet out of the pocket, Gregory stepped back, kicking the second man on the left knee, causing him to crumple to the ground.

The first assailant saw the move and lunged at Gregory with the knife.

Gregory sidestepped the assailant while swatting the hand aside that held the knife. Swinging around, both men were facing him. While the one with the injured knee stayed down, the other switched the knife back and forth in his hands. Gregory undid his belt, wrapping one end around his hand, waiting for the next assault.

The robber made another lunge for the Frenchman, which Gregory defended with his belt, swinging the buckle across the assailants' face and opening a deep cut across his cheek.

Moving his hand to his cheek, the would-be robber pulled it away finding it covered in his own blood. By this time, his partner was struggling to his feet and limping away from the melee, leaving the first assailant alone.

"You wish to continue?" Gregory asked, belt swaying at his side.

With little fanfare, the assailant turned, making his way toward his friend, who was now over a block away from where they made their attempt to rob the Legionnaire.

Watching the two men walk into a building's entrance and disappear, Gregory replaced his belt onto his pants. "This proves I need Romain to get me back into shape," he told himself while turning to finish his walk to Giuseppe's restaurant.

In minutes, he came across the small eatery, its entrance closed, but he could see several men standing in the alley smoking cigarettes and joking while one struggled with bags of trash. Wandering through the narrow space towards the men, Gregory noted a delivery van pulling up behind them.

"Excuse me," he said. "Is Monsieur Ricci around? I'd like to speak with him."

"One moment, I'll get someone," one man said, stamping out his smoldering cigarette.

Gregory noticed the delivery van driver was making his way into the alley carrying loaves of fresh bread. The man who struggled to carry out the trash stepped aside, letting the driver by and into the restaurant.

As soon as the driver entered, a squat, pudgy man walked out, making his way towards Gregory. "Bonjour, Monsieur," he said. "I understand you wish to speak with Monsieur Ricci, yes?"

"Yes. I'm a friend of his and I came into town on business and thought I would stop by," Gregory said, sizing the man up.

"I'm sorry, but he's not available," the Italian said. "But maybe I can be of assistance. My name is Antonio Moscone, but you can call me Tony." He extended his hand.

"Thank you, Tony," Gregory replied. "Is it possible to get a message to Geno? It's rather important I speak with him in person," he explained, formulating his idea to conspire against Nazim and the Italians looking for the police woman.

"I can see he gets your information," Tony said.

"Please let him know I'll be in Marseille tomorrow," Gregory said. "And if he could, call me about 10 am at the following number."

Tony pulled out a notepad, scrawling the number down as Gregory dictated. "I'll see he gets this right away. Is that all?"

"Yes, thank you," the Frenchman said, shaking the Italian's hand before leaving the alley. In less than ten minutes, Gregory found himself outside the apartment of his niece, Sophia. Walking up the stairs, he could hear the soft cries of a small child under the voice of its mother trying to console it. Coming to the door, he gently knocked and waited.

As the door swung open, Gregory was greeted by the sight of his niece, her hair a tousled mess. "Good morning, Sophia," he said, seeing the surprised look in her eyes growing wider. Her mouth was agape as her face froze in disbelief.

"What are you doing here?" the young woman asked.

"I needed to speak with Giuseppe, but he's not around," Gregory said, stepping into the apartment, noticing for the first time that the floors creaked under each step. "I was just at the restaurant speaking with Tony."

"And what did the doughboy of Pompeii have to say?" she asked, her description failing to hide her disdain for the Italian.

"I just left my number for Geno to call me," he said, sitting on the small sofa. "And, so you know, I ran into Phillip, too. He's going to run an errand for me later today, so don't panic if you don't see him at the restaurant."

"Something important?"

"Yes. He's going to hand over a package to a ship captain," he said. "How is work going, anyway?" he asked, guessing his niece's willowy appearance resulted from long hours on her feet, waiting tables.

"It's going well," Sophia said over her shoulder from the kitchen. "I'm making decent tips and your friend pays me a reasonable salary."

Stepping back to the table, she handed her uncle a cup of coffee. "But I do miss Celine, though."

"Have you called her lately?"

"No, I'm not sure what to tell her," she said, biting her lower lip before taking a drink. "I mean, we had plans for later this summer to spend a week in Nice, just her and me." Sitting cross-legged in the chair, she looked at her uncle. "She knew I went to the hospital for you." Sophia lowered her head, waiting for the rebuke to come.

"Ok. I'm not surprised, Sophia," Gregory said. "I figured you needed to tell her something when you showed up with the uniform, right?" He raised her chin gently to gaze into her eyes, reassuring her. "It's all right."

Drying the tears from her cheek, she smiled at the gentleness her uncle could display. Her father's family traits were clear in his younger brother, as Gregory was much like him in so many ways. But she had also learned of the terror he could dispense when needed, since her mother had told her often the stories of men who had crossed his path.

"Do you want something to eat?" Sophia asked, getting up from her chair. "I can fix you breakfast or maybe a sandwich if you like."

"I'm fine," he said, finishing his coffee. "I should get back to Marseille; Louis and I have a few business dealings to handle."

"Louis is doing well, I take it?"

"Yes, his wounds are healing nicely according to Julien. Though he does have a slight limp nowadays," he chuckled. "And he's grown his hair out some and is sporting a beard."

Sophia shook her head. "I can't imagine him with a beard. And the others, they are doing ok too?" she asked, knowing her uncle had a handful of other men from his time as a Legionnaire working for him.

"Yes, they are," Gregory replied, placing his cup in the sink. "Your mother still worries about you too." He wrapped his arm around her shoulder while placing a kiss to her forehead. "You should call her, I'm sure she'd love to hear your voice. Even if it's just a few minutes, huh?" he suggested, hugging her shoulder just as his phone rang in his pocket.

Staring down at the number, his brow furrowed. Looking at Sophia, he placed his finger across his lips signaling her to be quiet while he answered the call. "Hello?"

"Gregory? It's Giuseppe Ricci, my friend," the Italian said over the crowd gathering inside the small eatery he and Benito were sitting in. "My manager said you stopped by. I'm sorry for not being available."

"No apologies are needed. I should have called first," Gregory said, sitting at the small table. "I was hoping we could get together for a discussion; when will you be able to meet me?"

Giuseppe looked at Benito whose eyes were glued to the small television mounted behind the order counter. On it, Benito saw a photo of himself on display as the announcer described the suspect in a police investigation.

"Giuseppe, are you there?"

"Yes, yes, I'm here," the Italian said. "If you'll excuse me, Greg, I've another call I must take. I'll get back to you my friend." He ended the call as hastily as it started. Turning to Benito, he spoke. "It's time to leave, now," he uttered, grabbing their drinks off the table.

Walking around the corner towards their car, both men moved hurriedly without looking around at the other patrons passing them on the street. Benito thumbed the remote, unlocking the doors as they slid into their seats.

"How did they get my photo?" Benito exclaimed.

"I'd say you were careless, but I'm also considering the police being very lucky," Giuseppe replied. How do I tell Alberto about this? he thought? Seeing his colleague's picture on display just jeopardized their plans to abduct Hector Dupont and trade him for Detective Genevieve Benoit.

Chapter Twenty-Five

The quiet murmur of six dispatchers speaking into headsets filled the room as the number of calls increased by the hour. The influx of sightings of the Italian suspect shown on local news broadcasts grew after each show. Inside the center, consoles lit up with each new caller, casting an eerie light display throughout the darkened space.

Looking on, Detective Lemieux shook his head, having cautioned Geneviève of the chaos she would create by insisting their suspect in her abduction investigation be televised throughout the city. But he was overruled by his captain, who sided with Geneviève.

"These calls are having an adverse impact on our operations, Captain Lemieux," the sergeant in charge pointed out. "We can't focus on the normal calls promptly enough." He couldn't help but notice the flashing lights for the emergency calls on hold at each operator's console.

"I recommend you assign two of the operators to handle the emergency number, and the rest can tackle the unofficial call-ins," Claude replied, finishing his coffee. "And I'll see someone comes in every hour to collect the tips you receive," walking out of the darkened room.

Starting his way to his office, Claude made a stop at the cafeteria for another coffee. Dodging the caution signs of a wet floor near the entrance, he stood in line for one of the staff to refill the grounds. A slight bump from behind caused him to turn.

"I'm so sorry, detective," the female officer said, looking up at Claude.

"That's ok, Sergeant...," he replied, glancing at her name tag. "Dubois is it," he finished, seeing the plastic emblem below her badge.

"Yes," Claire said, grabbing a to-go cup and lid from the counter. "If you'll excuse me, I'm here for some tea," she said, edging around the officer.

"Certainly," Claude said, letting the woman passed him. Hearing the kitchen worker had finished setting the coffee up, he side-stepped to the dispenser to fill his own cup. Splashing in the equivalent of three tablespoons of sugar, he capped the top and signaled the cashier before heading towards his office.

Catching a group of officers talking in hushed tones of a case, he soon came to the offices set aside for patrol sergeants and the detectives. Going in his office, he came across Berger and Masson discussing the outcome of the past evening's soccer match.

Lemieux placed his coffee down on his desk while pulling his chair back. "The two of you need to step into dispatch for a moment and observe the chaos posting the wanted picture on television created," the senior officer said.

"But if it produces results, isn't it a good thing?" Detective Berger asked.

"We'll know more after you two begin collecting and sifting through all those tips we're receiving," Claude said, reviewing a surveillance report on their mysterious shipping company. "Did the harbormaster ever find who helped move the freighter the other day?"

"No, seems the potential strike by the longshoremen has dampened his spirits," Detective Masson replied. "It is convenient for the strike to happen and the ship leaves the harbor at the same time though."

"And where is Benoit?" Claude asked, noting her absence.

"She was here a few minutes before you arrived, then left," Guy Masson said, reviewing the local updates on their surveillance request. "Seems the patrols are still coming up empty; no new sightings for Papillion Transport office workers," he informed them, tossing the report to his partner.

As the three officers discussed the report, Detective Benoit was providing a disposition to the investigating officers working the assault case from the police training facility. "And how did you come about locating the assailant?" one officer asked.

"The victim screamed, which woke me up," Geneviève said. "I literally heard it twice before running out of the villa," she answered, recalling the early morning events. She could sense her chest tighten as she relived the morning: visions of grabbing her gun, dashing out of the villa and spotting a flash of light in the distant shrubbery.

"And when you came across the cadet assaulting the woman, what did you discover?"

"I saw him straddling the woman, her arms were pinned down and he was trying to rip off her shirt," she said. Geneviève could feel beads of perspiration forming on her brow, snippets of her own struggle clouding her thoughts. "I confronted him, directing him to release the woman at gunpoint."

"You mentioned to the security supervisor you knew the cadet, is that right?"

"Yes, he was jogging in front of the Administration Building when he bumped into me," Geneviève said, wringing her hands. "Officer Cote was outside the building and saw it happen."

For another twenty minutes, the two members of the training security staff continued their questioning, more as a formality since no charges were being brought against Geneviève. Still, the session was conjuring up old memories she struggled to keep suppressed.

"We've just about covered everything, detective," one officer said. "If there's anything further, we'll contact your captain and you," he concluded, closing his file and getting up from the table.

"Thank you," she said, exiting the room. Walking into the busy hallway, Geneviève wandered back towards her office, oblivious of those around her. Passing the cafeteria, she noticed the small television broadcasting the news and the image of the Italian the police were trying to locate.

As she walked past the office used by Captain Georges and his SWAT team, someone called out to her from behind. Spinning around, she saw Francine stepping off the elevator, making her way through the crowd.

"Phew, I wasn't sure you heard me," the lab technician said. "How are things going for you? I found out someone broke into your apartment?"

"As well as can be expected, I guess," Geneviève said. "We've got a lead on the man, but it's still slow. So, tell me, how was your date with Nicolas?" she asked, wanting to discover more of her partner's evening with the young woman.

"It was nice," Francine said. "He took me to the new Asian place near the harbor. We had dinner, chatted for a ten, maybe twenty minutes, and then he took me home. Nothing to get too excited about," she said. "But he does dress much nicer than when he's here at the office. Maybe for the next outing, we can go on a double date. What do you say?"

"I'm not sure," Geneviève said with a touch of apprehension in her response. "Until I'm sure this stalker has been apprehended, I want to keep my social activities to a minimum. But after that, I'm sure we can make some arrangement."

Watching the two women in conversation, Detective Masson walked up behind Geneviève before saying anything. "Detective Benoit,

Captain Lemieux is waiting for you in the office," he said, causing her to jump. "Hello, Miss LeBeau," Guy continued, acknowledging the lab technician beside his colleague before continuing down the hall.

"And where are you headed?"

"Communications to see how much havoc you've wreaked," he said, continuing down the hallway.

"That was Nicolas's partner, wasn't it?" Francine asked.

"Yes, it was. His name is Guy Masson. And no, he's not married either," Geneviève said, answering the obvious question on her friends face before it was asked. "I'll call you about having lunch again, but I need to go."

"Ok, let Nicolas know I said hi," she said watching the detective walk away to her office.

Just as Geneviève was reaching the office, Guy had returned from Communications, this time with his hands full of dispatch notices from sightings of the Italian prowler. "I hope you're happy," he said, stepping past her to his desk. "According to the sergeant on duty, these are just for the first two hours," he explained, tapping his finger on the stack of paper.

"And now you can see why I was so reluctant to have your assailant's picture on television," Detective Lemieux said, tilting his coffee towards Geneviève. "I recommend you concentrate on the neighborhood near the bistro and your apartment. I'll be right back." He tossed his empty cup in the trash can before leaving the room.

"Let's get this done, shall we?" Detective Masson said, dividing the pile of dispatches. Each of the detectives began the laborious task of sifting through each printout, reviewing the descriptions the citizens gave; several had individuals with lean, muscular builds while others noted men with wiry features. Notices describing anyone with facial hair were soon discarded since the surveillance photo showed Benito Russo as clean shaven.

Making his way into the cafeteria, Detective Lemieux grabbed another large coffee, adding his copious volume of sugar before greeting the cashier. "How much am I up to today?"

"For today, it's 9.50," the cashier responded. "However, for the month you are close to 235.00 euros. And it's only the beginning of the second week of the month, detective," the woman reminded Claude. "You'll need to settle your bill by Friday evening if you expect anything on Monday."

"I'll see to it tomorrow," Claude said, exiting the eatery. Dodging the growing number of citizens entering the police department building, the newly promoted detective slipped past the SWAT team's office before hearing the hail by his superior.

"Captain Lemieux, I need a moment of your time," Captain Duval said.

"Yes, Captain? What can I do for you?"

Julien Duval looked over his subordinate officer, noting a slight tremor in his coffee cup before addressing him. "I've got an interesting bit of information from Officer LeBlanc's sergeant about the Italian," he said, holding a file folder in his hand. "How many cups does that make today?" he asked, nodding towards Claude's coffee.

"Oh... three or four, but who's counting?" Claude replied with a laugh. "So, what am I to learn from this report?"

Opening the folder, Captain Duval showed Claude the photo taken by the patrols near Geneviève's apartment. "This was taken four days ago at a park near Detective Benoit's residence." Removing a second photo from the folder, he placed it next to the first. "And this one is from your surveillance camera the other day."

Claude took both photos in his hand and fanned them out. "It's the same man."

"Yes, it's the same person," Captain Duval said. "We not only have these two images but also the sketch from the market owner from Officer LeBlanc's first encounter. So, what would your next step be, knowing what you do now?"

Claude leaned against the wall, letting other officers pass by as he contemplated his captain's question. "I'm curious as to why he's in the neighborhood of the bistro. Detective Benoit and I have never been in that section of the city, so why does he show up there? What's in that specific area related to her?"

"Let me know when you figure it out," Duval said. "And by the way, Benoit's account of the assault from the other morning is somewhat aligned with the victims," he noted, taking back the photos.

"Somewhat?"

"The victim couldn't scream as Detective Benoit claims," the captain said. "The cadet's attacker had placed tape across her mouth. So, at best, she might have cried out once. Which means Benoit heard a single scream, not the multiple ones she said she heard."

"It's not like her to boast of something that's not true though," Claude said, ready to defend his partner. "If she said she heard it, I believe she did."

"Claude, she might have heard multiple screams in her own mind before hearing the one that woke her," the captain said. "If she had thoughts of being attacked in her apartment by this prowler, who's to say she wasn't screaming herself because of it," he asked, painting a picture neither wanted to entertain.

"Should I talk to her about it?" Claude asked.

"She's not in any trouble, so I'll leave it up to you to decide if it's worth bringing up," Duval said. "Oh, and one more issue: you need to go see Captain Soucy in the Gang Task Force offices. He's got something of interest on your Algerian drug dealer. You should find him in the Annex."

Taking his leave of his friend and captain, Claude walked through the building towards the rear entrance. Going out through the security doors, he found himself walking down the loading dock ramp. Coming upon the first in a series of modular units, he entered the first.

"Can I help you?" the man at the first table asked, looking at the detective.

If not for the man's badge and ID hanging from his neck, Claude could have mistaken the officer for one of Marseille's growing number of transients. He looked haggard, his arms thin, almost like twisted lengths of rope as his tendons and muscles were visible under his skin.

"I'm looking for Captain Soucy?" Claude asked, showing his own ID to the man.

"Back there," was the reply as the man pointed to a makeshift office in the corner.

Making his way past several tables, each occupied by a member of the task force, the detective came upon the open door of the senior officer in charge. Rapping his knuckles on the door as he stuck his head in, he greeted its occupant. "Hello? Captain Soucy, I presume?"

Captain Soucy was short and squat sitting at the makeshift desk, piles of reports stacked to one side. On the wall behind him were several surveillance photos of known members of the more prominent gangs operating in the city.

"Correct on all accounts. You must be Lemieux?" he asked.

"Yes. Captain Duval mentioned you might have some information about our suspect being held at Chateau Il d'If," Claude answered.

"It seems this man is very important to many people," Soucy said, scratching his beard. "We've heard talk between the Unione Corse and Maghrebi gangs about a large sum of cash being used to gain information about his location."

"From what my partner learned when he was captured in Algiers, he's associated with a well-connected member of the Algerian crime syndicates," Claude said. "It turns out this person in Algiers had a sordid past during the fight for liberation. He killed two Army officers before turning against several local gang leaders."

"And yet your suspect is drawing interest amongst several groups. It does suggest he'd be worth 100,000 euros, doesn't it?"

Claude let out a low whistle. "Is that how much Khalid is paying someone for this information?"

"Khalid. Are you telling me this man is associated with Omar Khalid?" Captain Soucy asked, his sullen and bloodshot eyes lighting up at the name.

"Yes, we believe our suspect, his name is Talib, that he's related somehow to him."

Captain Soucy dug out a folder as thick as a paperback and opened it. "This is what we've been able to piece together on the drugs being supplied to the Maghrebi gang by Khalid," he said. "Every time I get an officer close enough to learn something important, he disappears for weeks. And when he returns, he's no longer welcome amongst the gangs and I need to re-assign him," he sighed, alluding to the dangers of undercover duty.

"You also mentioned the Unione Corse. What is their angle?" Claude asked.

"Our take is Khalid has an ally in the Italians," Soucy replied. "Which makes it even more tenuous to ask questions since the two groups control different portions of the city."

"That would explain the fool we caught several weeks ago conducting surveillance on my partner," Claude said. "And why there's a second Italian out there pursuing her."

"Turning on the Italians might be easier for you than going against the Maghrebi," Captain Soucy said. "If nothing else from a simple ethnic perspective. We've found they are very distrustful of anyone not having family originating in North Africa. I have to admit, putting the Italian's photo on the 6 o'clock news took balls on your part though," he chuckled.

"I told Geneviève it was a mistake, but Duval overruled me on it," Claude said, shrugging his shoulders. "And now she and her fellow detectives get to sift through the myriad of sightings of every tourist in the city."

"Captain Lemieux, I don't have to tell you or your detectives to watch your step on this one," Soucy said. "The sum of money being offered for this suspect of yours could lead to some drastic actions by the gangs trying to make a name for themselves."

Chapter Twenty-Six

The grandstand loomed over head as the former Legionnaire walked along the sidewalk. Roaming along the outskirts of Stade Weygand Pupilles, Julien LeBlanc knew the type of individual he was looking to meet. Members of the Corsican mafia frequented the soccer grounds to conduct business in the open without worrying about police activity being too close.

Two men approached him as he neared the gate. "What do you want?" the taller of the two asked.

"I'm looking for Claudio Carbone," the Legionnaire said. "I've got a message from Papillion Transport for him."

The second man stepped aside and talked into a miniature microphone inside his windbreaker, relaying Julien's request to the unseen recipient on the other end of the conversation.

In moments, the second man walked over to the Frenchman and gestured for him to raise his arms. He patted the man down, looking for potential weapons. With his training, Julien was adept at killing with his hands, so he never carried a pistol or knives when meeting an adversary in the open. When he was done, the taller man motioned towards the gate which was now open leading to the grass field.

Passing through the open fence, Julien saw a handful of men running on the field in a spirited game of soccer. In moments, the ball was sailing towards him, which he deftly stopped with his feet like a seasoned midfielder.

Jogging towards him, the erstwhile parrain or godfather of the Marseilles group of the Carbone mafia family slowed until he was a few meters from Julien. "You wished to pass along something from Papillion, I understand?" Claudio asked, catching his breath.

Booting the ball towards him, Julien stood looking over the fit and trim man before him. "My boss would appreciate some information about an effort to abduct a police officer," he said. "Seems this officer has information on one of the transactions we've completed, and we'd like to know how much of the effort has been compromised."

Claudio motioned Julien towards a small set of benches off to the side where they both sat. Grabbing a small towel, he wiped the sweat from his face. "I've heard an Algerian has offered a quarter-million euro for a female officer," he said. "Seems she embarrassed him and caused somewhat of a stir in his homeland. But he didn't ask for our involvement, so its success is in question," he explained, chuckling at what he knew of Alberto Scuderi.

"For that sum of money, I'd try kidnapping her myself," Julien replied. "But you said success isn't guaranteed, why?"

"The don who was approached has a soft spot for women," Claudio said. "His biggest problem would be transporting her out of the country, I'm sure. It might be an angle your employer might use if you wish to get your hands on her yourself," he continued before taking a drink from a water bottle.

"Is there anything else you can tell us?"

"Yes. Tell Gregory he owes us fifty-thousand euros for losing the warehouse to the police," the parrain said, alluding to the earlier arrangement with Julien's employer. "And he should be very careful who he aligns himself with." He quickly stood in front of Julien. "Not everyone is as innocent as they appear," the mean reminded him before jogging off to rejoin the match.

***

Across town, the two Italians were soon engaged with their bogus survey, a charade for abducting Hector Dupont. "Thank you for your information," Giuseppe Ricci said to the woman in unit 2-23. "Your information will go a long way in improving the area for everyone, I'm sure."

Angling away from the door, he saw Benito walking towards the car when he spied the red Peugeot being driven by the airport's security director. Whistling, he caught the attention of his colleague just as Hector parked nearby.

Benito heard the whistle and was able to spot their target as the driver's door swung open. Sauntering up to Hector, he soon was trying to engage him in cursory conversation. "Excuse me sir, but do you have a few moments?"

Hector glanced over his shoulder as he grabbed his briefcase from the backseat. Checking the parking area, he noticed no one else nearby, but his instincts told him something else. "How can I help you?" he asked.

"My associate and I are surveying local residence areas for a development firm in Milan," Benito said, gesturing to Giuseppe who was walking out from under the carports. "We are looking into how the area could improve by adding various amenities. It shouldn't take more than five minutes," he explained, reaching into his satchel.

"All right then, I'll give you five minutes," Hector replied, placing his briefcase on the trunk of his car.

No sooner had he replied, Benito was pulling the Taser from his bag, bringing it to bear on the security director. Taking the Frenchman by surprise, Benito tried engaging Hector with the Taser without aiming. But before he could pull the trigger releasing the electrode barbs, Hector struck the Italian with his briefcase. The impact of the briefcase striking Benito's shoulder before glancing off the side of his head caused the Italian's wig to fly off.

"What the hell?" Hector exclaimed, watching the hairpiece fly away.

Giuseppe was upon the two men when Benito made his attempt. Noticing the quick reaction of their intended victim, he froze for a moment, caught by surprise by the Frenchman's actions. Pulling his Taser out of his bag, he prepared to fire it but he soon found himself restrained in a bear hug which caused him to drop the weapon.

"And what do you think you were going to do with that?" the voice of Giuseppe's captor asked. "Are you ok, Hector?" The man looked at his neighbor, who'd drawn his handgun from its holster and was aiming it at Benito.

"Yes," he answered, his breathing steady and measured, as his Air Force training dictated. "Have you seen these two before, Viktor?" he asked, nodding towards the two Italians.

"They showed up yesterday outside the gates, then they were back today asking more questions," the shipyard worker replied. "It seems somewhat strange though... not the questions they asked, but the fact they're Italian."

"Is that true?" Hector asked, kicking Benito's shin while leveling the pistol at his chest. "You're both Italian?"

"What does it matter?" he answered, glancing at Giuseppe for a reaction. But the Italian was near passing out as the shipyard worker's grip held tight, squeezing the breath from his chest.

Before any more questions could be asked, the wail of sirens could be heard growing louder from the boulevard as several police cars were converging on the complex. In moments, the two cars squealed to a halt, the officers getting out and drawing their weapons as they saw Hector holding his.

"Put your weapon down," the lead officer commanded.

Following the officer's command, Hector placed it on the trunk of his car and stepped back. "My name is Hector Dupont. I'm head of airport security," he explained, pulling his ID badge from his shirt pocket. "This man tried to assault me with the Taser." He nodded to the weapon laying on the ground.

One officer walked up and took Hector's badge while another motioned for his friend Viktor to release his victim. As Giuseppe was let loose, the Italian collapsed, struggling to stay on his feet as blood rushed through his body.

After several questions, the police soon determined Hector as the victim and his neighbor and friend Viktor were providing aid, while Benito and Giuseppe were detained. "Both of you are under arrest for possession of an illegal device and assault," the lead officer said, placing the handcuffs on them. "Monsieur Dupont, we'll need to have you and your friend join us at the station to give written statements."

Word of the assault and capture of the Italians soon spread through the police channels, reaching Detective Lemieux in the headquarters building. As the two suspects were being processed at the local station, their pictures were soon compared with those taken during the surveillance activities near Geneviève's apartment.

Going in the office, he found his three junior officers pouring over the third bundle of notices from dispatch citing a citizen's report of the Italian prowler. "You can stop what you're doing everyone," he announced, putting his coffee down on the desk.

"And why is that?" Detective Berger asked.

"It seems your Italian prowler was apprehended just about an hour ago," Claude said. "Along with an accomplice. They tried to assault a local businessman." The lie was just until he could tell Geneviève in private that Hector had been the intended victim.

"Detective Benoit, you and I will be going to the substation to witness the interrogation," he continued, tapping her on the shoulder. "Masson, contact the communications sergeant; tell him to inform the television stations we've apprehended our suspect." Dropping his empty coffee cup in the trash, Claude turned to Berger. "I want you to gather the information on your missing freighter, it's time to get back to finding our mystery shipping firm."

As the two officers walked out to Claude's car, he broke the news to Geneviève. "I don't know any other way to say this, but the assault victim was meant to be Hector Dupont. He was able to subdue one man while a neighbor handled the other," he said softly, looking over the roof of the car at his female partner.

"Hector is ok, though?"

"From what I've been told, yes, he is," he assured her, getting behind the wheel. "He should still be at the station when we get there." He put the car into gear and pulled away from the parking lot.

"I guess my days of being a celebrity at the training facility are over," Geneviève said, staring out the window, her thoughts centering on Hector's well-being.

After thirty minutes of weaving through the city traffic, the two officers arrived at the station and were shown to the control booth for the interrogation room. Sitting in front of the computer recording the interview, the observer waited in silence for the suspects to be escorted into the room. Looking through the glass, they could see the interior, its stainless-steel table and chairs a stark contrast against the pale blue walls.

After a few minutes, a buzzer sounded. The observer reached over and released the electronic lock, allowing the officers and Benito Russo to enter the space. "And so, it begins," Claude whispered.

Geneviève didn't hear him. Her gaze was focused squarely on the Italian, Benito Russo. He had no distinguishing marks or facial features, but she could see where he had glued the prosthetic nose piece to his face. The outline of makeup and glue was a visible contrast to his normal skin color.

"So, Monsieur Russo, do you wish to explain the reason for the assault on Monsieur Dupont?" the officer asked, looking over the arrest report.

"I'll be happy to discuss things after the consulate has sent their lawyer," Benito said. "Until then, enjoy looking at my face." he said, leaning back in the chair.

"Such a pretty face, too. Very well," the officer said before nodding to the other officer who reached down grabbing Benito's arm and pulling him to his feet. "Bring in the next suspect," he ordered, switching folders.

In a moment, another officer was leading Giuseppe Ricci into the room before seating him in the chair. Looking at his reflection in the two-way mirror, he knew they would record everything he did and said during the interrogation session.

"Monsieur... Ricci is it?" the officer asked, reading the report. "Do you wish to offer your version of why you and your associate were assaulting Monsieur Dupont?"

"I'll wait for my lawyer," Giuseppe replied confidently.

"This is getting us nowhere," Geneviève said, turning away from the glass. "All they will do is trying to stall us and we'll never find out if it was Khalid who's paying them off."

Detective Lemieux stepped beside his frustrated partner. "Don't give up hope so easily, ma Cherie," he said, placing his hand on her shoulder. "We'll sort this out soon enough. Come along, let's see how your Monsieur Dupont is, shall we?"

Departing the room, the two detectives made their way to the senior officer's space where they met Hector providing his full statement to the assault from earlier. Turning, he glimpsed Geneviève and Claude in the doorway. "I didn't expect you to be here," he said.

"News travels fast sometimes," she replied, giving him a brief hug. Stepping back, she looked her companion over, searching for any sign of wounds. "You weren't hurt, were you?"

"No. I was lucky Viktor was busy doing his laundry or things could have been worse," he said, nodding to his neighbor sitting at the desk across the room. "So, Captain Lemieux, are these the men you've been looking for?"

"The one who was trying to subdue you with his Taser matches the description from the market," Claude replied. "But I'm not sure about the second one. Seems we've nothing on him, but there's something..." Snapping his fingers, Claude finally recalled seeing Giuseppe Ricci. "He's the one on the bench," he remembered, looking at Geneviève. "And I walked right past the sonofabitch."

"You mean he's the one in the park we saw after meeting with Officer LeBlanc?"

"Yes, but his hair is different," Claude replied.

"The one who came after me had a wig on, maybe the other one does as well," Hector said.

"And the first man, I could see where he had applied some form of makeup," Geneviève added.

"Excuse me," the mountainous man named Viktor said. "The officer is done with me and has offered a ride, Hector, so I'll be going back to the apartment."

"Thank you, my friend," Hector answered, shaking the man's hand. "We'll have dinner soon. It'll be my treat."

Viktor smiled because he knew Hector's offer meant a generous meal at one of Marseille's better restaurants of his choice. "I'll be looking forward to it, my friend."

The two detectives both looked at the man as he was escorted out of the station. "Now, where were we?" Claude asked, getting his focus back to the Italians.

"The men were wearing makeup," Geneviève said. "And I'd say it was because we provided the news stations with the photo of the first man. But we just gave them the photo the day before." She drummed her fingers against her folded arms in thought. "Which means he came to town with his plan to be in disguise for the abduction." She looked at Claude for validation of her theory.

"If that's the case, he's done this before," Claude pointed out. Stepping over to the coffee service, he poured himself a cup while adding three heaps of sugar. Taking a drink of the lukewarm caffeine, he promptly spat it out into the garbage. "Damn. So much for squad room cuisine."

Chapter Twenty-Seven

The news agencies throughout Marseille were broadcasting their story of the Italians, Russo and Ricci, being apprehended in their failed attempt to kidnap a member of airport security. Each station included a photo of the men from the booking process as part of the telecast, allowing the entire city to see the suspects, including Louis Clement.

Traveling back from Toulon, Gregory didn't have the aid of seeing the news, though he heard of the arrests. No sooner had the radio announcer provided information on the failed abduction, his cell phone rang.

As soon as he recognized the picture, Louis was on his phone, calling his partner. In moments, his call was answered. "Gregory, we've got a big problem."

"What is it? And when did you get back?"

"Last night. And that's not important," he replied. "I was just watching the news and it seems Geno Ricci has been arrested," Louis said, glancing up at the television. "The police provided his mugshot for the news to broadcast, and I'm positive it's him."

Gregory thought of his surprise visit to the Italian in Toulon, only to find he was not in town. And now the call from Louis about him being arrested added to his concerns. "I'm almost in town; we'll meet at the office in fifteen minutes," he said, ending the call while weaving his sedan in and out of the traffic.

Sitting behind the desk, Louis took stock of their plight as well, from their former member, Franco, and his girlfriend escaping the police which led to him being shot, to the need to move one of their ships from the harbor. Things are getting out of hand, and we've done nothing to bring attention to ourselves, he told himself.

While Louis sat reflecting on the past instances to Papillion Transport and their operations, Julien LeBlanc was returning from his meeting with Claudio Carbone. Stomping up the stairs two steps at a time, he entered the office catching his friend off guard. "You're back, I see," he said, hugging Louis.

Pivoting around in the chair, Louis greeted his colleague with an embrace. "Yes, I'm back and none too soon," he replied, pointing to a replay of the news broadcast. "Seems we've got another problem to negotiate." "I'm gone just four days and all hell breaks loose."

"And Hector and Pasqual, they're back too?" Julien asked.

"They'll be in today," Julien answered. "I had them take the train so they could unwind."

"And was their trip a success?"

Louis looked at the former medic and team member from his Legionnaire service. "Yes, Pasqual was able to dispatch the problem, but I'm not sure it will contribute to the Irish lawyer or the ship captains though," he sighed. "The older captain, Duncan, he's a proud man and I'm afraid his arrest will be the end of him."

Before he and Julien could continue their discussion, Gregory came through the door, catching the men by surprise. "And how was Scotland?" he asked, tossing his jacket aside.

"Pleasant," Louis said. "And Captain Duncan expressed his thanks for assisting him in his problem with the Scotsman. Now, can we try to figure out what to do about our current situation, please?" he asked, alluding to Giuseppe Ricci's arrest and its impact on their operations.

As if on cue, the television once again broadcasted a snippet of the arrest, displaying the pictures of the two Italians. Concentrating on the pictures, Gregory shook his head in dismay. "You're right; it's Geno."

"So, what are we going to do about him?"

"Right now, nothing," Gregory said. "Sure, he knows you and me, but he's never been to any of our offices. We've always conducted business over the phone." He twirled his cell phone in the air. "Which means we'll need some new ones by the end of the day."

"Do you think the Carbone family can do something about this?" Julien asked, entering the conversation. "Oh, by the way, speaking of Claudio... He says we owe him the fifty-thousand for losing the warehouse," he informed them, passing along the parrain's demand.

"That'll wait for the time being," Gregory said. Looking at Louis, he could see the concern on his partner's face. "We can use this as part of the ploy against Nazim," he added. Over the next ten minutes, he recalled the conversation he had with his sister-in-law, Claire, about Hakim Talib and where he was being held.

"So, let me get this straight," Louis started. "You want to do pass this information to Nazim, through the Italians, then tip off the police when he tries to free Talib?" Louis asked with a low whistle. "And how will we know when Nazim and the Algerians will make this attempt?"

"Easy," Gregory said. "We'll tell them he's being transported off the rock to another facility, which will be too tempting for them not to try and make a move. And we need to make sure our intentions at deceiving them are obscure enough to avoid being implicated, that's all."

"Gregory, we've been out of the game a long time," Louis pointed out. "What if they find out and come after us too?"

"It's why we need to get Romain and Elise to set up some training for us," Gregory answered. "Within a week, no more than two I'd say, we'll be back to our former selves. You'll need to figure out a new stance though," he noted, pointing down at Louis's leg.

"Don't worry about that," the diminutive Frenchman said. "When do we start planning?"

"Right after I visit our favorite banker," Gregory said. "Seems I need to make a withdrawal if I plan on discussing our things with the Carbone parrain."

***

With the summer sun beating down on the city, the crowds still made their way out along the promenade below Alberto Scuderi's villa. Sitting underneath the shade of an umbrella, his chilled wine nearby, Alberto was still bathed in sweat, reeling from the news about his two men in France.

"Bianca, did we get this communique validated?" Alberto asked the young woman.

"Yes, we did," she replied. "As soon as I saw who it was about, I contacted our representative at the consulate for confirmation." She dabbed her brow with a napkin. "Both men have asked for representation and have yet to say anything to the police."

"I would expect nothing less from them," he said. "Still, I'm not looking forward to the outcome of their arrests." He knew each man had an intimate knowledge of him and his operations in Naples.

"Bianca, please contact Antonio in Toulon," Alberto said. "Have him prepare a few men in the event we can free Giuseppe and Benito. And make sure he does so without alarming the Carbone family. They're the last ones I need finding out about this," he finished, gulping down his wine.

Taking up his cell phone, he scrolled through the names before settling on his friend and associate from Algeria. Pressing the call button, Alberto soon heard the familiar click of the telephone exchange.

On the second ring, a young woman's voice answered his call. "Bonjour? May I help you?" Ketifa, said answering the phone.

"Good day, this is Monsieur Scuderi. I'd like to speak with Monsieur Khalid if I may," Alberto replied. "It's most urgent."

"Just a moment," the young woman answered, padding across the hardwood floor to her master. "It's Monsieur Scuderi for you, your excellency," she said, handing over the phone.

"Good day, my friend," Omar said.

"I apologize for the intrusion, Omar," the Italian said. "I felt it important to let you know of a condition which came up in abducting the policewoman."

"Go on," the Algerian crime boss said.

Over the next twenty minutes, Scuderi related how his plan was compromised. First by the incompetence of Angelo who had undertaken his assignment more for his pleasure than the reward. And then, explaining to the Algerian about the botched attempt by Benito and Giuseppe to abduct the woman's lover.

"It seems I might have asked you to do something which was too difficult," Omar said, listening to the Italian. "Are you calling me to back out of our arrangement?"

"No, certainly not, Omar," Alberto exclaimed. "It's just with these men in custody, my options for taking action are limited. And with the freighter already in transit, I may need to arrange her delivery by other means."

The Algerian sat up in his chair, placing the empty cup on the end table. Rising to his feet, Omar paced across the veranda, considering his options. Getting his hands on the policewoman was more of an act to satisfy his bruised ego from their earlier encounter. The most important issue was finding his nephew Hakim safely.

"I'll give you three days to offer me with another solution Alberto," Omar said. "Afterwards, I'll turn to someone who is less concerned about appearances, do you understand?" he asked, alluding to his relationship with members of the Maghrebi gang in Marseille.

"Yes Omar, I understand," Alberto replied. "I'll let you know of my intentions later this evening."

"Don't delay, my friend. I'll be waiting for your call," the Algerian answered before ending the call.

Feeling the warmth of the breeze increase, Omar slipped out of his robe before stepping into the waters of his pool. Disappearing under the surface, he let his thoughts conjure up several ideas he would need to have before making his next call. The frigid water caused his skin to tighten as his body twitched, heat of the day washed away.

Coming to the surface, he spied Aisha standing dutifully near the edge, a towel in hand. Gliding gently towards the steps, he rose from the pool, his skin glistening as the water cascaded off him. As he was pulling his foot out of the water, the young woman wrapped the towel around him to begin drying off her consort.

Pulling on his robe, Omar picked up his cell phone and scrolled through a list of names. Soon he came across the name he only attempted calling on two other occasions. Pressing the select key, he was greeted by a ringtone.

Fourteen hundred miles across the Mediterranean Sea, Amed Gilles sat in a small back room of the mosque, surrounded by several of his devoted followers. As they discussed the dealings from the earlier evening, his phone vibrated with an incoming call. Looking at the number, he was cautious while answering.

"Bonjour?"

"Bonjour, Amed," Omar replied. "I apologize for the unscheduled call, but I was hoping to discuss a most urgent need with you."

"And what can I help you with, my esteemed brother?" Amed asked, dismissing the men in the room.

"I was hoping to have an acquaintance help with an abduction," the elder Algerian said. "But it turns out his men were too lax in their approach. All three of them have been arrested and I'm concerned they may talk."

"And what action do you wish for me to undertake for you?"

"For the sake of our operations, I need to have assurances they won't talk, of course," Omar said.

"This isn't Algiers; this is Marseille, and the police are more diligent," the younger one said. "If they were as careless as the ones you pay, I would have provided you with the information about your apprentice's cousin by now," he informed him, alluding to Hakim's location. "But I can see they are paid a visit by my lawyer and reminded of the circumstances if you wish."

Omar sat in the shade of his veranda, contemplating the consequences of an attempt to silence the Italians associated with Alberto Scuderi. Too quick a retaliation would bring attention to Amed and his men. No action would possibly jeopardize the ability for the Italians to help him in future events.

"Then please have your associate pay them a visit," he said. "Have your man remind them of their families and the cost of speaking against us."

"As you wish, Omar," Amed replied. "I'll let you know what was discussed as soon as my lawyer returns," he said, hanging up on the elder. Dialing another number, he was soon directing his lawyer to pay the Italians a visit, passing along what was said about their futures and that of their families.

***

Pulling his car into the parking spot for a market, Gregory noticed the Italian restaurant, with several men standing outside, smoking their cigarettes while scanning the thoroughfare in both directions. Shutting the car door, he walked across the street, approaching the entrance.

Stepping through the eatery doorway, he soon entered a small sitting area. Gregory's mouth felt dry and pasty, his stomach tightening as he knew being here on his own involved certain risks. As he glanced at the few patrons inside, a lean, slender young man stepped in front of him.

"Can I help you?"

"I'm here to see Monsieur Carbone," Gregory replied, keeping his gaze on the person.

Before anything else could be said, the parrain of the Carbone mafia family came through the back entrance, a fit, athletic-looking man in his late forties. Displaying a gold Rolex contrasted against his suntanned arms, Claudio Carbone didn't hide his wealthy position in society.

"Good evening Gregory," he said, extending his hand.

"Claudio," the Legionnaire replied, shaking the offered hand.

"Please, have a seat," Claudio offered, gesturing to the table and its two chairs.

Sitting, Gregory soon realized he and the Italian were the only ones left in the establishment. In a moment, the younger man from earlier brought out a tray with bottled water and glasses filled with ice.

Smiling, Claudio took a bottle and poured its contents into a glass before passing it to Gregory. "What do I owe for this visit?" he asked, pouring his own drink and sitting back in the chair.

"First, I apologize for losing your building," he began, placing a stack of one-hundred-euro bills on the table, paying the 50,000-euro fee

Julien mentioned earlier. "But the real reason for my visit today is to ask for help in passing along specific information to an Algerian," he continued picking up his glass and taking a drink.

"And why don't you do it yourself?"

"I'm apt to undertake something more drastic than talking if I came across him and his apprentice again," Gregory said of his growing disdain for Nazim and Khalid. "I'm hoping to have the police do the work for me."

"It sounds like you're trying to play one against the other," Claudio said. "And what is the payoff to the Carbone family? You and I have done little business since you took over my uncle's company," he reminded Gregory. "So, as the Americans would say, what's in it for me?"

Looking across the table, Gregory knew he'd be obligated to work closer with the criminal family by asking for his help. So, he thought for a moment, choosing his words with care. "We are moving away from our past business with the North African elements. But, we are still capable of moving most anything amongst the eastern ports," he assured him, knowing the Carbone family would trade in heroin through Turkey.

"I'm thrilled to hear that, Gregory," Claudio replied. "I was afraid you might try and become a legitimate corporation." He chuckled at the thought. "Tell me, what information do I need to pass and to whom?"

Without divulging his sister-in-law Claire as the source of information, Gregory provided the mafia godfather his intention of pitting the Algerians against the police. This would be done when they find out about Hakim Talib being held at Chateau Il d'If.

"And who is to receive the information?" Claudio asked.

"The man's name is Khalid. Omar Khalid of Algiers," Gregory replied, finishing his drink.

Chapter Twenty-Eight

The bus squealed as it stopped outside the vacant building, discharging its single passenger. Strolling along the sidewalk, a woman glanced over her shoulder as she approached the entrance, unlocked the door, and entered.

Watching the bus, patrol officers involved in conducting surveillance of Papillion Transport practically missed the driveway they had been parking in over the last five weeks. "Do you think this Captain Lemieux is trying to make a name for himself?" the driver asked his partner.

"I don't care if he is or not," the other said. "Just as long as I'm not getting assigned to patrol the neighborhood where the African gangs are growing. This might be mundane, but at least I can go home at night without worrying," the junior officer said.

"I was assigned one of the patrol areas for nine months," the driver said. "It was essentially like being in a war zone. We averaged at least one shooting or stabbing a week. It almost got to the point the medical crews refused to furnish aid," he explained, stopping the car.

"Look, we've got someone going in the building," the passenger said, pointing towards the vacant offices.

"Well, she's the first one in over three weeks of observing this place. Let's see what she's doing here," the senior officer said, getting out of the patrol car.

Claudette didn't detect the police car as she entered; she just knew Louis needed her to retrieve several computer discs from the office of the fictitious shipping firm. Unlocking the door, she made her way into the vacant office, walking towards the private bathroom.

Looking at the small vanity, Claudette opened the cabinet and reached underneath, feeling the small envelope. "Just like Louis described it," she said, tugging on the tape holding the packet in place. As it broke free, she heard the footsteps of someone coming along the hallway.

As the officers came upon the door, they checked it to see if it opened. Showing up to the former space of 'Papillion Transport, they found it to be unlocked. "Marseille Police. Show yourself," the senior officer ordered, a gun in a ready position.

Hearing the officers' voices, Claudette's heart raced, her brow moistening with perspiration. Slipping the packet into her purse, her legs shook as she stood, leaning against the sink. Stepping out of the bathroom, she was confronted by the two officers.

Claudette held her palms raised. "Please don't shoot," she said, her voice relating her nervousness.

"Put your hands down. What are you doing here?"

"I came to collect my paycheck," Claudette stammered, telling the lie she had concocted for this occasion. "The business let me go four weeks ago, but they didn't give me my check. I need to pay rent, but I can't do it on a promise," she pleaded, clutching the strap on her purse.

"And what were you doing in the back room?"

"I had to use the washroom," the woman replied.

"How did you get in this office?"

"I've still got my keys," Claudette said, holding up the lanyard with two keys attached.

"You'll need to speak with the detectives, I'm afraid," the senior officer, said gesturing Claudette towards the door.

After a short drive to the district building, Claudette was led into one of the vacant interrogation rooms where she was soon joined by Captain Lemieux and Detective Benoit.

"According to the officers, you were found in the former office space for Papillion Transport, is this true?" Claude asked.

"Yes. Like I told them, I was dismissed a month ago and I hadn't received my last paycheck," Claudette said.

"Last month? Are you saying you were let go after our interview on the thirteenth of last month?" Geneviève asked looking over her notes.

"Yes. Everyone was handed a letter the day after you showed up telling us our services were no longer needed," Claudette lied. "It was terribly sudden." She sat uneasily in the metal chair, her hands getting sweaty.

"And what are you doing for employment these days?" Claude asked.

"I'm still looking for a job. It's why I was going back to ask about my last check."

Claude looked down at his notes from their earlier investigation session into Papillion Transport with the inspectors from Scotland Yard. "If you'll excuse us for a moment," he said, gesturing to his partner towards the door.

After stepping outside, Claude turned to Geneviève. "I don't think she has anything to offer. Do you?"

"I'm not sure," she answered. "Waiting nearly a month before getting your money sounds like an awful long time, don't you think? I know I'd want to be paid as soon as I was released, but she waited a month."

"So, you think she is keeping something from us? But what is she hiding?" Claude asked.

"Maybe the company is still here in Marseille," Geneviève said. "But why send her to the office? Was she looking for something or just checking for mail service?"

Before Captain Lemieux could respond, Detective Masson came striding down the hallway towards him. "Captain, our Italian suspects have a visitor application," he told them, holding out a notice while catching his breath.

Turning to Geneviève, Claude waved his hands at the door. "Let her go for now. But inform the patrol officer's sergeant to make sure we have a good address for her. And tell him to keep tabs on her movements for the next 72 hours," he instructed, walking away with Detective Masson. "Then meet me in the office," he shouted over his shoulder.

Walking into the room, Detective Benoit told Claudette she would be released, but to make sure she provided a legitimate means of being contacted for future questioning.

"Thank you," Claudette said, getting up from the chair and leaving the room.

***

The messenger stopped his Moped outside the compound in Algiers under the scrutiny of several armed men standing at the gate. "I've a packet for his excellency Khalid," he said to the tallest one. Turning to one of the others, a few words were spoken before the tall one returned his attention to the messenger.

In moments, Omar Khalid's driver, Malik, appeared at the gate. "I'll accept the packet," he said, holding out his hand. Passing over the packet, the messenger stood, waiting and hoping for a modest tip for his services.

"Go with Allah's blessing," Malik said, closing the gate behind him, leaving the messenger alone with his guards.

Carrying the packet, Malik made his way to the veranda where Omar and Nazim Aziz were in conversation about their next drug shipment.

"A packet for you, your Excellency," the Algerian said, placing the envelope on the table before stepping back.

Omar stared at the envelope, inscribed with his name both in French and Arabic. Picking it up, he took the knife from the fruit plate nearby and slit the back open, pulling two pages from inside. His brow furrowed as he looked at the contents, each word providing an answer to a question, but further deepening the enigma of its origin.

Nazim sat quietly, showing his respect and not interrupting the elder Algerian as he read the notice. After several quiet and tense minutes, the elder man turned to him and waved the pages in front of him.

"Your cousin has been found," Omar said, breaking the silence between the two men.

"Where is he?" Nazim asked, struggling to contain his excitement of hearing the news.

"Oddly enough, he is still in Marseille," Omar replied. "The police have had him in seclusion it turns out," he explained, sliding the first page towards Nazim. "They've somehow found a new use for Chateau Il d'If and its dungeon."

Nazim read the first page and its description of how they held and interrogated his cousin. As Omar finished the second page, he too learned how the French police were using the former fortress. More importantly, he took note of the date near the bottom of the letter.

"If this information is correct, we've a means of liberating Hakim," Nazim said, handing back the letter to Omar. "Can your contact verify this? I mean, so far no one in Marseille noticed anything about him, but now we get this news," he noted, voicing his concerns to the elder Algerian.

"I understand your reluctance to accept this news as authentic," Omar said, looking at Nazim before turning his gaze to the waters of the Mediterranean Sea in the distance. "It looks somewhat suspicious to get this now, so soon after my call with an associate," he uttered.

Picking up the letter, he turned to the second page and gazed at the date written on the bottom. "What was the date the Irishman wanted our help in Tangiers?"

"He said it was the first week of September, why?"

"Your cousin's planned date to be moved is the end of next week," Omar said, pointing to the letter. "I'm not sure we can secure the right men for both instances. I'm only sure of a handful, not more than ten men, able of crossing borders. There are risks with having them travel back and forth so close together."

"And what of your associate in Marseille? Can he help us?"

"His help comes with a heavy fee, I'm afraid," Omar said. "I'm not one to be indebted with the likes of this particular associate. At least not by choice," he noted, finishing his water. "But that's not to say he couldn't at least entertain providing a few men for a small fee."

Nazim glanced at his mentor, while inside, he mentally noted Omar's reluctance while he only wanted to press forward. "With what we have here," Nazim began, laying his hand upon the letters, "I'll begin planning for Hakim's release. You can let your associate know I'll be the one to pay for his and his men's services."

Omar glanced at Nazim. Still trying to prove yourself. "You wish to risk reentering France after knowing the police have your passport on notice? And what contacts do you have in the city still?"

"I have the documents from the Italian I can use again," Nazim said. "All I need is one of your capable servants to change the photograph. The original shows me as clean-shaven, not with this," he smiled, rubbing his hand over the close-cropped beard.

Omar sat, thinking of his brother's son wanting to exact his vengeance against the French. Was I no different at his age? he thought. "I'll have Malik contact one of my other members to correct your documents. And while you prepare your plan, I'll see how many men I can gather to support you," he said. "But I want you to understand, Nazim... this may be your last time leaving the country."

"I understand," Nazim replied as he stood. "I'll be in the study if you need me."

Seeing him walk away, Omar finished his drink before looking up at Aisha. "I'll need a pen and paper," he said, directing the young woman. In a moment, she returned placing the items before him. Considering the letter's contents, the older Algerian listed the trusted followers of his organization he felt could go with Nazim back to France.

Dragging out the chair from behind the desk, Nazim too was writing various things he would need for their attempt to free his cousin. Turning on the computer, he was soon scanning the website for the tour company and ferry service to the former citadel. First service in the morning left Marseille at 0845 and made the transit to the fort in fifteen minutes. The last ferry departing was scheduled thirty minutes before sunset, depending on what time of year it was.

Almost thirteen hours when no boats should be near the docks, Nazim told himself. Unless it was the police, he realized. But if they were using the dungeon secretly, the police would need to arrive and depart just like the tourists would. If that's the case, the police change shifts midday to avoid arousing any suspicions. Nazim wrote his notes down as he dissected what most certainly was the routine being used by those holding Hakim hostage.

As he continued to plan for his cousin's release, Nazim wrote what he considered the possible issues he and Omar Khalid's men would encounter. A large group of men would raise suspicions with the police, he told himself. Not everyone could be businesspersons, and he didn't know of any women his mentor could consider assisting to help with disguising their activities.

After thirty minutes, Omar Khalid had his list prepared and sent his servant Malik into the city to pass the word to those he would need for the excursion. Unknown to Nazim, Omar had listed several women who would join the group, assisting in the ruse to liberate his nephew.

Chapter Twenty-Nine

Information on Hakim Talib's location in Marseille was passing from one person to the next, contained within the prayer room of the mosque. Nevertheless, in just an hour, word reached an undercover agent of the Gang Enforcement team, who relayed the information to Captain Soucy at the police's Annex compound.

Glancing over the handwritten note, the officer picked up the phone and dialed the number of his fellow captain, Claude Lemieux. On the second ring, an unfamiliar voice of a man answered, "Drug Interdiction; Officer Masson speaking."

"This is Captain Soucy. Can I speak with your captain?"

"Sorry, sir, he's down in interrogation. Can I pass along a message?"

"Yes. Have him come meet me. I've got a lead on one of the suspects being held at Il d'If," Soucy said.

"I'll let him know you called," Guy said, hanging up the phone. Leaving the office, he trampled down the stairs, making his way to the interrogation spaces in the basement. Rounding the corner, he caught his partner Detective Berger exiting one room. "Hey, Nicolas, have you seen Captain Lemieux?"

"He's in here," he answered, pointing his thumb towards the room he left.

As Guy Masson entered the control room, Captain Lemieux held up his hand. Staring through the glass, the detective looked at the suspect Giuseppe Ricci in conversation with another man, whose back was to the window.

"Captain Soucy called," Masson said in a hushed tone.

Claude turned. "What did he want?"

"He said for you to come meet him. Something about a suspect being held at Il d'If," Guy answered. "He sounded somewhat animated about wanting to discuss it with you, if you ask me."

"All right," the captain said. "Was Benoit back in the office?"

"No, I haven't seen her since this morning's discussion with the woman."

Claude glanced back at the two men engaged in conversation, though he heard nothing of what they said. Tossing his coffee cup in the wastebasket, he looked down at the technician. "If the lawyer wishes to discuss anything, tell him to call the arresting officer for an appointment. And then contact me afterwards," he instructed, stepping past his fellow detective before entering the hallway.

"Guy, I want you to find Benoit and have her join me at the Annex, at trailer number three as soon as possible," Claude said, striding towards the elevators. "Likewise, what do we have on the shipping firm? Anything so far?"

"Still nothing," Masson answered. "The harbormaster hasn't been notified of any sightings of the freighter which left without permission yet. "According to their records, the De Gaulle still needed to offload twenty-one containers of cargo here in Marseille."

"Then let's look at other harbors where they can offload those containers," Claude said, stepping into the elevator. After he pressed the button, the doors closed and the car ascended to the main lobby. "And get with the patrol who picked up this woman earlier has anything else on her. Where she's living at, her known acquaintances, where she banks..."

Rushing through the crowd as soon as the doors opened, Captain Lemieux made his way to the Annex where he found his counterpart, Captain Soucy, discussing future surveillance activities with several of his undercover agents. Waiting for a pause, Claude stood away from the group.

As he noticed Claude approaching the group, the officer for Gang Enforcement finished his brief and stepped away from his officers, waving Claude towards him. "Captain Lemieux, I received some interesting information," he said, escorting him to his makeshift office.

Resting behind the table, Soucy unfolded the message from his subordinate working within the Maghrebi contingent. "It implies word has gotten around about a former suspect which was handed over to you for drug smuggling," he explained, reading the note. "One of my officers has found out your suspect's location was leaked to the head of an Algerian gang."

"Omar Khalid," Claude muttered quietly.

"Yes, so it appears. Shows he's reaching out to one of the local gangs here in Marseille to help liberate him," Soucy said. "We've had trouble getting close to this particular gang leader in the past, so getting this information is very helpful."

"But who leaked the information?" Claude asked. "How did it get to Khalid?"

"Each a very good question, Claude," Soucy replied. "Even with my resources, I knew nothing about your suspect until this came up and its link to your detective."

Examining the note, he tossed it back to his counterpart. "I don't read Arabic," Claude said.

"Sorry about that," the captain said, taking back the note and reading the contents aloud for Claude to hear. "It's obvious Detective Benoit was likewise being targeted by the Algerian, Khalid."

"And with the current events, it suggests he's been seeking help from the Italians as well." Claude replied, filling the captain in on the latest developments with the arrests of Angelo Mazza, Giuseppe Ricci, and Benito Russo.

"To the best of my knowledge, none of the Italian or Corsican families here in the city are involved," Captain Soucy said. "But that's not to say we don't have our own issues with officers being corrupted by money or coerced through some other means. The information could have come from inside just as easily."

"If this information is correct, it's only leaving out one detail," Claude said.

"What's that?"

"A date the Algerians will take action. It doesn't give us any room to prepare," he said, scratching his chin. "I'll need to discuss this with Captain Duval. And possibly even get Captain Georges' team involved as well. Can you translate the note for me?"

"Give me five minutes," Soucy said, pulling out a pen.

***

Claudette's gut told her something was wrong. Watching the woman walk into the small bistro, the police officer lost sight of her suspect for the briefest of moments. As Detective Benoit stepped closer to the entrance, she saw Claudette standing in line, preparing to give her order to the clerk.

Scanning the eatery, Geneviève could detect nothing out of place, or anyone that would appear to cause her to take any actions. Walking past, she stopped outside a boutique window, glancing at the apparel on display. Utilizing the reflection off the window, she kept her eye on the secretary. In a moment, a man who walked up behind her obscured her vision.

Feeling the nudge from behind, Claudette glanced over her shoulder, noticing Louis standing to the side of her. Just as she had practiced, Claudette dropped her purse on the floor.

"I'm so sorry, let me get that for you," Louis said.

"Thank you, but I'll manage," she said as she and Louis bent down to retrieve it. In mere seconds, she passed along the computer discs to him while pushing her make-up case back in to the bag.

"Thank you," she said with a look of relief on her face.

"You're welcome," Louis said, smiling as he slid the discs in his jacket. "It looks like your order is ready," he noted, pointing to the counter.

Picking up the tray, Claudette moved to the side where she found a table and sat down. Glancing out the window, she noticed Louis's friend Julien sitting in a car parked across the street. Watching him gave her a reason to calm down, knowing they wouldn't let anything happen to her.

Detective Benoit noticed the brief exchange between Claudette and the man as he handed her purse back. The distortion of the glass didn't allow Geneviève to gain a clear view of the man, but she couldn't shake the thought she'd seen him before. Concentrating on the man allowed her original suspect to slip unnoticed from the bistro and away from the detective.

Wandering out of the eatery, Louis walked around the front of Julien's car before sliding into the passenger seat. "Let's go," he said.

Geneviève watched the bearded man walk across the street and get into the car. As the driver pulled the vehicle into traffic, she realized the man behind the wheel was the same one she encountered at the market near her apartment. Moreover, his companion had the same build and mannerisms as the one she had shot a month earlier.

As the car disappeared amongst the traffic, Geneviève's cell phone rang. Glancing at the number, she knew it was from the office. "Hello?" she barked, answering it after the third ring.

"Benoit, where in the hell are you?" the familiar voice of Guy Masson asked her.

"I went for a walk. What do you need?" she asked, looking back into the bistro for the woman she was tailing. "Damn it, she's gone.".

"What did you say?"

Hearing Guy ask his question, Geneviève stammered, "Nothing... it's nothing, Guy. Why are you calling me again?"

"Captain Lemieux wants you to meet him and Captain Soucy at trailer three in the Annex," the detective said. "Something to do about the suspect being held on Il d'If."

"All right, I'll be there in five minutes," she said, striding down the boulevard towards the police station under the watchful stare of Claudette Minot from the alley. Genevieve conjured up the various issues, which could relate to their suspect, Talib.

"What does the Gang Task force know about him?" she asked herself as she entered the police compound. Scanning the dingy white units, she could see a tangled mess of power lines connecting the trailers as she noted the faded numbers on each corner. Arriving at the one the task force occupied, she pulled open the door, its protest a loud screech as it swung on the hinges.

"Can I help you?" the hoarse and raspy voice of a woman asked.

The sight of the person asking the question surprised Detective Benoit. What was once a stunning young woman sat someone portraying an image of self-abuse and overindulgence of alcohol and drugs. Or so it looked to Geneviève. The officer sat hunched over on the tables, her hands holding several folders. Her hair, matted and oily, was parted in the middle, partially obscuring her face, but the skeletal look of her was obvious. The skin drew tight across her nose and chin, the cheeks sunken like pits.

"I'm sorry. But I'm Detective Benoit; where can I find Captain Soucy?" she stammered, embarrassed to be caught staring at the woman.

"It's ok, officer," the woman replied. "I'm Officer Patrice Galant," showing her badge. "I've just got two more weeks before my transfer to Nice," the woman continued, knowing her outer features belied her position and true worth within the police force. "You'll find the captain over in the office," she said, pointing to the closed door in the corner.

"Thank you." Walking past the sorted tables and chairs, Geneviève knocked on the door.

"Come on in," a man's voice said from the other side.

Entering the office, she noticed Captain Lemieux sitting at the makeshift desk with his counterpart sitting opposite him. "You wanted to see me?" she asked, closing the door behind her.

"Yes. This is Captain Soucy," Lemieux introduced, motioning to the other officer. "One of his men has come across information about Hakim Talib and where we have him detained.". Giving the note to

Geneviève, he continued. "The note provides clarification Omar Khalid is behind the Italian's effort to abduct you as well."

"How do we use this information to our advantage?" she asked, wishing the nightmare of being stalked to an end.

"Good question. The best way is to set up a sting operation to arrest the men trying to free Talib," Captain Soucy said. "But it likewise puts my agents at risk of being found out."

"I don't want to risk the work you and your people have put in," Claude said. "It may be time to return our suspect back to the general populace of prison. Which one is the problem. We don't want him going to Fleury-Mérogis Prison; the Muslims there won't take to getting a drug dealer sent to them."

"What about Clairvaux Prison?" Geneviève asked.

"His crime doesn't call for that form of treatment," Claude said. "I'm not sure we could convince Monsieur Chevallier to sign the petition and forward it to Paris anyway," he explained, wringing his hands together.

"That just leaves Fresnes, since La Santé is still going through its modernization," Captain Soucy said. "Either facility you send him to will be a resort compared to the dungeon he's in now."

The three officers sat in silence, each one struggling with the potential need to move the prisoner from his current location. Captain Lemieux's mind raced with possibilities of what could go wrong in moving Talib from the cell at Il d'If. "When was the last usable bit of information we got from the suspect?"

Geneviève looked at her partner before speaking. "It was the location of the warehouse."

"And nothing more useful from him since then?"

"No. I mean, we've never been made aware of more than that. Why?"

"What are you thinking, Claude?" Captain Soucy asked, seeing the detective's forehead wrinkled in thought.

"If we've milked him dry for everything he possibly knew of the drug operations," Claude began, getting up from the chair, "and all we've got was the location of a warehouse, it might be the only thing he knew."

"So, you don't think his value is in what he knew of the operation?" Soucy asked.

"No. I'm thinking it's more about his relationship with Khalid," Claude answered.

"He's family," Geneviève blurted out.

"Exactly. He's related to Khalid; presumably a nephew, right?"

"Of course," Geneviève said. "When I was with Inspector Haddad, we reviewed the file on Khalid. It showed he had a brother." She closed her eyes to concentrate. "The brother was killed during the uprising for liberation by the Algerians. The report said a Legionnaire was responsible for slaying him. Then it's possible Hakim Talib is his nephew. But what about Louis Remesy? Who is he to Khalid?" she asked.

"Who is this Remesy you mentioned?" Soucy asked.

"He's a suspect wanted by Scotland Yard for drug trafficking," Claude said. "Detective Benoit tracked him to a meeting with Khalid in Algiers after he left Marseille." He proceeded to give the Gang Enforcement captain a brief synopsis of Geneviève's encounter in Algiers.

"You kicked three assailants' asses by yourself?" Soucy asked. "I've heard the stories about a female officer ruining several officers' ego with their hand-to-hand combat skills. That was you?"

"I took several self-defense classes when I was young," Geneviève said, embarrassed to admit her accomplishments.

"Going back to the Algerian's note," Claude said, breaking the awkward silence building between Soucy and Benoit, "we've an opportunity to act against Khalid if we play our cards right."

"What are you thinking about?" Geneviève asked. "From what I gathered in Algiers, he won't leave his compound unless under heavy guard."

"You said it yourself. Remesy is probably related somehow, too," Claude said. "I can't think he'd stand idle if he knew he had a chance at freeing a family member from custody. All we have to do is set a date and offer them with the proper incentive to act. But, before we do anything else, I need a cup of coffee."

Chapter Thirty

The computer hummed as the turntable spun the compact disc inside. Louis ran his fingers across the keyboard, typing in the security code to open the files he'd accumulated on the Carbone family over the years. As the computer screen flashed, his chair was squealed in protest while he leaned back. The opening of a soda can jerked him back to the present as Julien handed over the drink.

"Does Gregory know you've kept separate files on the Carbone contingent?" Julien asked, nodding towards the screen.

"He knows I was gathering information on all the organizations here in Marseille," Louis said, watching the images of papers slide from one folder to another on the screen. "I just gathered more on Claudio, that's all. I started these files when we were still in Toulon," he explained, tapping his finger on the second disc.

"So, you don't trust Claudio?"

"Let's just say he wasn't happy to lose the shipping firm to Gregory and me from his uncle," Louis said. "But he still didn't have it in him to rid the family of his brother either when they found out he was gay." Tapping out a new command on the keyboard, Louis had the computer humming again, this time saving the data from the first disc.

"I've got a feeling Greg's desire for information on the Italian's attempted abduction of the policewoman will drag us into something worse," he said, sipping the cola. "And I'm inclined to have something to negotiate with before it gets out of hand."

"Do you think we can get the Algerians and Italians working against each other?"

"I'm not concerned about that," Louis said. "I don't want have to glance over my shoulder wondering who's coming after me if I can help it. If it means getting information to the police so they can apprehend the Algerians, then so be it."

The low tone of the security device attached to the front door echoed through the office, causing each man to turn his attention to the CCTV monitor. In the screen, the image of their friend Gregory heading to the stairway was recorded.

Entering the office, the head of Papillion Transport had the expression of a man preparing to attack at a moment's notice. "Who the hell does that little prick think he is?" he stammered as he grabbed a seat near Louis.

"You're talking about Claudio, right?"

"Of course, I am, damn it," he snapped back. "I'm sorry, yes, it's Claudio. He demanded we commit to moving 1,000 kilos of heroin a month for him," Gregory replied. "He said it was a small price to pay for passing along the information to Khalid." He closed his eyes and took a deep breath to calm himself down. "However, he likewise mentioned he would help us in the event Giuseppe talks about our operations."

"How did he know about Geno?" Louis asked.

"Because I told him," Gregory sighed. "With him getting arrested, I wanted to find out who he was working for besides us." Pointing to the flashing prompt on the screen, he changed the subject. "What are you copying there on the computer?"

"I was reading over some older files I gathered on Carbone when we moved here from Toulon," Louis replied, sliding the cursor over the "next" button and clicking the mouse.

"How did Claudette look?"

"She looked a bit rattled, but other than that, she held her own," Julien answered before Louis could. "But when we met her, a female police officer was following her. Come to think of it, she might have been the same one from the market I saw last month."

"She's the one who shot me," Louis added.

"How sure are you?" Gregory asked. "Did she recognize you?"

"Longer hair, scraggly beard and almost no limb to speak of," Louis answered. "What's to recognize from eight weeks ago?" he asked, moving his chair back. "Plus, I've kept in the shadows most days and stayed away from our usual haunts."

Just as Gregory stood up, Louis's cell phone played a popular ringtone announcing an incoming call. Snagging it, he answered the call. "Hello, Hector."

"I wonder if Hector knows the ringtone Louis chose for him is about letting the dogs out," Julien chuckled, catching snippets of the conversation.

Even Gregory had to smile at the thought. His amusement didn't last long as he returned to the task at hand. Getting Nazim and Omar Khalid to act on the information of Hakim's location and knowing the police were using experimental drugs for interrogation weighed heavy on his mind.

"Hector and Pasqual are wondering where you want to meet up," Louis said, holding his hand over the phone.

"Romain and Elise said they'll meet us near the equestrian academy in the Palama district tomorrow at eight o'clock," Gregory replied. "They'll have everything we need for the day."

Louis passed along the information to the two other members before hanging up. Finishing his soda, he tossed the can into the trash before turning back to Gregory. "I hate to ask, but when does Claudio expect us to begin this drug trafficking for him?"

"He said they'll have a shipment ready by mid-September," he replied. "But the departure point is Izmir, not Istanbul. It suggests Claudio's former associates aren't as welcome in the capital when it comes to the smuggling business."

"And what are we going to do about our contacts in Istanbul?" Louis asked. "You don't expect them to move 500 kilometers just to help us with a sleight of hand with our documents, do you?"

"We'll need to ask Ahmet for some recommendations, I suppose," Gregory replied. "Until then, we'll focus on what we can control ourselves. Have we gotten any word from Sebastian and the *De Gaulle*?".

"They'll be done off-loading by midnight," Julien replied after grabbing a clipboard from the table. "We just need to give them a destination and cargo manifest to create a loading plan."

"Then let's get busy, shall we?" Gregory said sitting behind his desk. "The *Joan of Arc* will arrive the day after tomorrow from Alexandria and I'll want to get her back out to sea as quickly as possible."

***

With fresh cups of coffee, Captain Lemieux and Detective Benoit sat outside Captain Duval's office waiting for his return. "After we brief the captain, I'll go and discuss things with Captain Georges so he's not caught by surprise," Claude said.

"And what do you want me to do?" Geneviève asked.

"You're going to contact the detention supervisor and make arrangements for us to return to the island," he said. "Once we're there, we'll prepare our guest for his return to the mainland and a proper prison cell."

"Won't we be risking someone spotting him and getting word back to Khalid?"

194

Tossing the now empty cup in the trash, Claude turned to Geneviève. "That's part of the plan. If we can tease Khalid with our suspect, we just might get him to do something rash. Or we'll see if this Remesy character is related by drawing him out." He paused as the outer door opened to Captain Duval entering the office.

"Captain Lemieux, are you here to brief me on your Italian suspects?" he asked, walking past the two officers. "Or is it about the news from Captain Soucy?"

"A little of both," Lemieux said, following Duval into the office with Geneviève following close behind. "It suggests the two Italians were part of a ploy to find out about our Algerian's location." Sitting across from his friend, Claude continued. "Looks as if an Algerian, Omar Khalid…"

"The one Detective Benoit confronted in Algiers," Duval interrupted.

"Yes, sir. As I was saying," he continued, "it appears Khalid contacted the Italians first to abduct Benoit, and when they failed, he reached out to a Maghrebi faction here in Marseille."

"But what does the attempt on Detective Benoit have to do with the suspect from the drug smuggling?" Duval asked, nodding towards Geneviève.

"We believe Hakim Talib is related to Khalid," Geneviève added to the discussion.

"I think now would be the best time to move Talib off the island and place him into the general populace at one of the mainland prisons," Claude added.

"But Captain Soucy can't say how this gang got their information on your suspect on Il d'If, can he?" Duval asked.

"No, he can't," Claude said. "We both believe there might be someone on the force either being paid to furnish the information or they are being blackmailed for some other reason."

"And why I've turned the information over to Internal Affairs," the senior officer said. "I want you and your detectives focused on finding out about the drug smuggling and this missing freighter associated with Papillion Transport. A vessel that size doesn't set sail and disappear without a reason," he continued. "And since the British have tied it to smuggling, I want to show we haven't given up on them, do you both understand?"

Each of the detectives looked to blink in unison at the statement made by their superior. Finally, Geneviève cleared her throat and spoke ahead of her partner. "But what about Talib, sir? If we can, shouldn't we seize the opportunity to flush out who's responsible for leaking the information about him?" she asked. "And maybe, just maybe, catch Khalid and Remesy in the process as well?"

Captain Duval leaned back in his chair. Observing the detective, he could see the reason in her argument. Nonetheless, he knew better than to trade someone's life, even one of a suspect, to catch others of wrongdoing. "You would make a fine lawyer, Detective Benoit," he said. "But we don't want to tip our hand about the suspect and lose everything prematurely."

"What are you suggesting, Julien...? I'm sorry... Captain Duval." Claude asked.

"Right after I was briefed on the situation, I requested a second security detail be dispatched to the island," he explained, getting up from his desk. "They've been in place since last night. And it sounds none too soon either.,

"Why do you say that?"

He glanced out the window towards the harbor. "Dispatch received a call from the tour office this morning about a group asking for passage on the first vessel this morning," the captain said. "This group consisted of fourteen men and six women. The same number making up our regular security detail for the facility."

A gentle knock on the door interrupted the conversation as Captain Duval's clerk entered. "I'm sorry, sir, but you asked for this information be brought to you as soon as we got it from Paris," she said, handing over a folder.

"Thank you, Patrice," Duval said, taking the documents from her.

Examining the contents for a few minutes, his outer expression changed from being in control to confusion as his brow furrowed and his lower lip curled inward. Holding the folder out, he handed it over to Claude. "Well, it appears your owners are not who they say they are," he confirmed, grabbing a bottle water from his desk.

"What do you..." Geneviève asked, only to be stopped by Claude's raised hand.

After several awkward minutes, Claude looked up at his friend and captain before he spoke. "Is Paris sure about this?" he asked. "If what's in here is true, we may never know the truth," he muttered, closing the file.

"What is it, Claude?"

Tossing the folder on the desk, he turned to his partner. "According to what was found in central records, it would appear the two owners of Papillion Transport were declared dead ten years ago."

"How though? We've records of their ownership in the company," she asked.

"What the detectives in Paris found were accounts of the two men making a business trip to South America, but never returning," Claude said.

"The more disturbing part: one of them, Emilio Carbone, was a close relative of Paul Carbone. It might be someone in the family still running the business."

"That would explain their involvement with drug smuggling," Geneviève said. "It all makes perfect sense now."

"How do you explain their disappearance, then?" Claude asked.

"They left the country and had their features altered," the detective said. "And after they recovered, they returned after assuming new appearances under the same name. All that would be needed would be an altered birth certificate, I'm sure."

Captain Duval sat listening, his hands set under his chin in a manner exhibiting the act of praying as he listened. "You make a compelling argument, detective. However, the archives in Paris further held copies of death certificates in the files. Which means someone has assumed their identities to facilitate running the business."

"So, what's our...." Claude asked before being interrupted by Captain Duval's desk phone.

Stabbing the speaker button, Duval answered. "What is it Patrice?"

"We just received a call from the detail on Il d'If. There appears to be an altercation amongst a group of tourists near the docks," the clerk declared.

"Very well. Have Captain Georges and his team alerted and prepare a motor launch for their use," Duval said, ending the call. Turning to Lemieux and Benoit he added, "It suggests the Algerians are possibly acting on their information."

Chapter Thirty-One

A group of tourists, led by two women, walked amongst the ruins of the crumbling citadel, taking in the remnants of the past conquerors' lives from the fifteenth century. As each member strolled through the various passages, they each looked at the location of security cameras and sensors.

Shielding his eyes from the sun, Nazim Aziz stared at one of the three towers, its exterior surface showing the ravages of weather and time upon it. Peering at his wristwatch, he knew from the information Omar Khalid was providing that the police would change personnel in the next thirty minutes, if not sooner. Off in the distance, he could hear the shrill sound of a vessel's horn as another ferry approached the island.

Amongst the crowd of tourists, several couples broke off and took their place near a few of the entrances to the fortress as the ferry neared the docks. Nazim spun around, hearing the boat operator announcing its arrival, watching several men gathering on the deck, backpacks slung over shoulders in the same fashion soldiers would carry them.

Standing near Nazim was Malik, Omar Khalid's trusted servant and leader of the men and women assembled to liberate Hakim from his imprisonment. As the latest wave of tourists made their way from the docks to the fortress courtyard, several of Malik's men proceeded down the path towards the boat.

"Remember, they need to control the vessel without destroying the radio equipment," Nazim reminded the Algerian criminal.

"They know what to do, Nazim." Malik said, moving off to the main entrance to the citadel.

As the last of the police detail exited the boat, Malik's men jumped aboard, quickly subduing the crew members near the exit door. In minutes, Nazim spotted two of the men enter the bridge and assume control of the boat. "It is time," he told himself as he followed the crowd towards the inner court of the fortress.

Four members of the police detail had earlier gone into the entrance to the dungeon when they were confronted by several of Malik's men, pistols at the ready. "Cooperate peacefully or die quickly," one gunman said. Gesturing the lead officer towards the security door, he added, "Your code please," he ordered pointing to the exposed keypad.

The officer knew he and his men would die if he hesitated, so he entered the correct code, and then stepped aside. As the door swung silently on the well-oiled hinges, a narrow rock hewn passageway appeared. This happened in two other areas of the fortress as Malik's men forced their way into the hidden passages behind the police.

Walking through the courtyard, Nazim, Malik, and Ketifa were soon behind the last group of three officers as they approached the entrance. "Do as I say and you won't be harmed," Nazim said, nudging the silenced pistol against the policeman's ribcage.

"Do you know who I am?"

"I'm more interested in what you can do," the drug smuggler said.

"You'll die before you make it to the docks, you know," the officer said, trying to stall the inevitable outcome. "I've twenty officers waiting for you when you exit."

"We can't let them ruin our timetable," Malik said, his frustration evident with his curt expression and tone.

Nazim knew the timing would be precarious if he didn't free Hakim soon. The transport Omar had arranged for would not be stopping to loiter while he and Malik's men negotiated with the police. Pushing himself and the gun closer towards the officer, he once again emphasized his position. "Open the door, now," he ordered, bringing the pistol up to the officer's head.

Without hesitation, the officer's fingers stabbed out the entry code, releasing the locks.

Hearing the faint click of the latch, Malik used his foot, pushing it open to allow six members to escape the heat of summer accumulating within the courtyard.

Snaking through the labyrinth of corridors, they soon came upon the control room where they were met by the others. "Where did you secure the other police?" Malik quickly asked.

"Follow me; I'll show you," one of the supposed clerics said, leading him down a hallway.

Nazim turned his attention to the medical technician sitting in front of the computer. "Where is your captive?" he asked, leveling the pistol to the woman's head. "Where is Hakim?" His voice cracked under the pressure.

The woman looked over at the senior officer before speaking. "He's in cell number eight," she said, pointing to the video screen, its image a contrast of green and black showing a figure curled up in the corner.

Nazim glanced at the monitor and saw the grainy image of his cousin huddled under the ragged burlap blanket. On a secondary monitor, he saw a group of officers gathering in a hallway. "Where are those men?" he demanded.

"The fourth level. Just below the holding cells," the woman said, the hesitation in her voice belying the vulnerability she was feeling.

Pointing to two of Malik's men, Nazim barked his orders. "Secure the stairs leading to the fourth level and hurry."

Holding one guard by the collar, Nazim pushed him towards the passageway, pressing the gun to his temple. "Show me where this cell is or you'll die." He quickly turned to Ketifa, who'd tossed her robe aside to expose a submachine gun. "Guard the woman. And shoot her if she tries anything. You two follow me," Nazim instructed two other men of Malik's contingent.

The officer stepped out of the control room and slid his hand along the wall until it met the light switch. Flicking it upward, the once darkened abyss of the dungeon was now bathed in fluorescent brilliance. Nazim pushed the officer along, his pistol digging deep against the guard's kidney. As they trudged along, Malik's men followed, occasionally turning to see if they were being followed.

After descending one of the narrow set of stairs, the four men came upon the cell holding Hakim Talib. "Open the door," Nazim commanded.

Slipping the key into the lock, the guard did as he was told, and soon the dungeon cell was awash with the light from the corridor, temporarily blinding Hakim. "Who's there?' he asked.

"Kill him if he tries anything," Nazim told Malik's men as he stepped away from the guard and entered the cell. "It's me, Hakim. It's Nazim; we're here to take you home," he said, reaching out to his cousin. Aiding the young man to his feet. Nazim could see the extent of his cousin's condition.

Hakim's image was one of malnourishment and isolation. Being fed soup and bread had taken its toll as the skin showing on his arms and around his face was sagging noticeably. His hair, once thick and well-kept, was now a matted and greasy mess. While he sat in isolation for the last six weeks, Hakim's complexion had become pale for one living in the desert.

Nazim struggled to contain his emotion. The sight of his cousin, a sickly character struggling to keep his balance while he stood, drove his anger to a new level. The once proud young Algerian would need a great deal of care to regain his strength. As he helped steady Hakim, the young man forced himself to smile as he realized the person before him was not a delusion created by the drugs.

"Nazim, we must hurry," a voice came from behind the drug smuggler. Twisting, he saw Malik standing in the cell's doorway, rivulets of sweat cascading down his forehead. "The boat will pass soon and we need to be ready for it," he reminded him, urging the older man to move.

"Come, Hakim. It's time to go," he said softly, wrapping his arm around his cousin and helping him into the corridor.

***

Across the harbor, the police motor launch sped across the water, its speed highlighted by the rooster-tail display of water that followed them. The operator and engineer were given orders to transport the SWAT team to the island as quickly as possible, and they were making every effort to do so.

"We'll split up as soon as the boat touches the dock," Captain Georges shouted over the engine as he was looking over the teams and pointing out the places on the map they were to cover. "Team Two, you'll move against the ferry and secure it; I'll lead Team One towards the courtyard. Captain Picard and his teams will come in by helicopter and be dropped into the courtyard after we secure it."

"What rules of engagement are we using for this action, Captain?" Officer Cormier, the explosives technician on the team, queried.

"We've got some civilians already on the island, so hold your fire unless you have a clear sign an assailant has a weapon in hand," Captain Georges ordered. "Does everyone understand? What about you Benoit?" he asked Geneviève. "You have any issues with our approach?"

Standing amongst the team, all Geneviève felt was the excitement building as they approached their target. "I'm fine with everything, Captain," she replied, fidgeting with the MP5 submachine pistol slung around her neck. Staring past the officer and the boat operator, her eyes grew larger as the single stone dock loomed ahead.

"Captain Lemieux, you'll stay onboard with Officer Dupre' until we give the all clear signal," the SWAT commander said, staring at his counterpart. "I mean it, Claude."

"Understood, Pierre. I'll wait here with the boat," Claude responded, not wanting to cause a scene in front of the team.

"Captain, the ferry is secured to the northwest berth so we'll be landing on the eastern section," Officer Dupre' shouted over the engine's roar. "Have your men stand by the port side," he added as he swung the launch around, its bow pointing towards the ferry.

The SWAT team took its position along the rail of the boat as it lost speed and came alongside the stone landing, scraping its hull against the sandstone buttress. In moments, four members had jumped from the boat and took up defensive positions.

Standing on the bridge, two of Malik's men saw the approaching police boat and contacted the Algerian criminal for instructions. "Do not let them gain access to the stairway," came the call. "They must not reach the main building." One man made his way to the ferry's main deck, where he took up a position unleashing a stream of bullets in the SWAT team's direction.

"Anton, take the gun out!" Captain Georges screamed, directing his sniper to action. The officer leapt upon the roof of the launch with his rifle, taking aim at the lone gunman on the ferry and fired at his target. The Algerian criminal never expected the lethal round as his world ended in a flash, the sniper's bullet impacting his exposed forehead.

Just as the gunman was silenced, the other members of the SWAT team made their way across the landing towards the stone path leading to the upper levels. Proceeding cautiously but with purpose, each member swung their weapons back and forth, preparing to take any necessary action in a moment's notice.

Over the two-way radio, Captain Georges heard the alert come from the helicopter pilot stating a second vessel was placed on the south jetty below the main buildings. "Pierre, this is Jean-Luc. I can see at least three people guarding the boat," the second SWAT commander said, looking down from the helicopter.

Coming to the landing at the top of the stairs, Captain Georges waved his team closer to him. "There's a second landing on the south side," he said. "Cormier, Lavigne, and Benoit, secure that boat. The rest of you, fan out and secure the exits. Don't let any group exit the areas. Once the second team is in place, we'll whittle the numbers down, understood?"

Acknowledging the order, Officer Cormier turned to his fellow members. "Ready to move, Milo? How about you, Benoit?"

"I'm ready to go," Geneviève said, subconsciously thrusting her breasts forward in an act of bravado, her face flush with excitement.

The three officers began the quick jog across the open courtyard, their weapons held low, but ready. Dodging past the corner of the main house, they soon found themselves in a narrow passage between the building and a walled off garden. Staring up at the building for any movement, Geneviève saw the top edge of the stone wall towering several meters over her head.

Coming to a dead end in the passage, Corporal Cormier spun around. "We need to go back," he said, nodding to the wall behind him.

"Give me a boost," Benoit said, slinging her weapon across her back. "I'll secure a rope on the other side." There was a pause as she looked at the other officers. "Come on, we don't have any time for a debate," she demanded, lifting her foot off the ground.

Cormier pulled the rope from around his neck and placed it over Geneviève's before leaning against the stonewall. "Come on, Lavigne, it'll be simpler than lifting me," he promised, reaching his arm out to his partner.

Lifting Geneviève to the top of the wall was simple for the two men trained for the task. As they positioned themselves under the detective, they pushed the woman easily to the point she could throw her leg over the wall and straddle the top. Looping the rope, Geneviève secured it to an outcropping of stone and let it fall to her companions.

Glancing over the edge, she found several spaces allowing her to descend from the wall back onto the ground, where she took up a position to defend the others. Stepping forward, she spotted a pathway which would lead them down to the small jetty and the waiting boat.

"Wait for us," Cormier said in a hoarse whisper as he dropped to his feet next to her. Lavigne was next to shimmy down the rope, joining the other two members. "Ok, let's go," the corporal said, leading the way down the path.

Before the officers could make their way to steps traversing the wall of the fortress toward the jetty, five people emerged from a secluded entrance in the main building ahead of them.

"Hakim," Benoit said to her companions, recognizing one of the men in the group. "He was our suspect being held here." She brought her weapon to bear on the five walking into the open.

Taking his hand and pushing the barrel downward, Cormier reminded Geneviève of their engagement rules. "They don't have any weapons," he said. "Lavigne, you take the right side while I come up from the left. And Benoit, you maintain cover for us."

As the officers laid out their plans, the Algerians continued down the granite steps toward the landing. Seeing the group nearing the bottom of the steps, the operator started the boat's engine, its roar echoing off the fortress walls.

"Move, now," Cormier said, getting up and making his way towards the steps, the others in tow behind him.

Striding ahead of the other two officers, Geneviève was now able to lead them down the steps, her determination to recapture Hakim Talib overpowering her sense of justice. In a few brief steps, she was within twenty meters of the group when the lead person turned and looked in her direction.

"Remesy!" she shouted, bringing her weapon to her face. "Stop right there; you're under arrest," she ordered, not hearing the rev of the boat's engines in anticipation of being unleashed. In her blinded sense of revenge, Geneviève further failed to notice Ketifa raising her rifle to bear on her.

Hearing his alias being yelled out, Nazim Aziz turned towards the three officers. "Keep them at bay until we're at the boat," he yelled as he helped the struggling Hakim towards the landing.

As the female officer pushed past, Cormier brought his weapon to bear on the last person in the group. As Benoit made her presence known, he caught sight of an AK47 being held by one member who dropped their robe, leveling the weapon at the pursuing officer. In a split second, the Algerian woman was showering the trio with a hail of bullets.

Chapter Thirty-Two

Ricocheting bullets careened off the stonewall, one striking Geneviève's Kevlar helmet, emphasized the severity of the scene she'd created. Caught in the open, she dropped to the ground, pinned down by crossfire unleashed by Algerians on the boat and her fellow officers, Cormier and Lavigne, from behind her.

Dragging herself to the edge, she caught sight of Talib followed closely by the man known as Remesy, the drug smuggler wanted by Scotland Yard. Working to gauge the timing of the surrounding gunfight, she came to a knee and let loose a flurry of shots toward the boat's stern.

Showing skills honed after long hours on the shooting range, Geneviève was able to pepper the pleasure craft from bow to stern. With the volume of bullets suddenly increasing, the occupants on the boat ceased firing their weapons for a brief moment. This allowed the three officers to make their move closer to the landing.

"Get us out of here," Nazim yelled to the front of the boat as he turned away from the gunfight.

With little encouragement needed, the second man scrambled onto the forward deck to cut the line holding the boat in place. While slicing the rope, he was struck with several shots from Lavigne, who had stopped his descent in favor of providing more accurate shots at the suspects. The impact of the bullets striking the deckhand led to him dropping his knife as he rolled overboard and into the water.

Ketifa lay upon several cushions as she sighted in on the officer and let loose a volley of machine gun fire at the steps leading to the jetty. This momentarily halted the hail of bullets from above, but it also took her attention away from the other two officers who'd made it to the jetty.

Staring back at Nazim, she noticed terror in his eyes, his expression telling her he'd spotted the imposing figure of Cormier taking aim and pulling his trigger. In a brief instance, the life of the once beautiful desert flower who'd been plucked from poverty in Algiers was soon snuffed out in a hail of gunfire. Nazim could see the bullets ripping through her shoulders and neck, blood spewing across the deck.

As the drug-induced haze faded, Hakim saw the crumbled body of Ketifa on the deck, blood oozing from her wounds, gathering on the surrounding deck. Seizing the weapon, she'd dropped on the deck, the Algerian blindly swung it over the boat's edge, pulling the trigger.

With shots flying across the water, Benoit, Cormier, and Lavigne soon encountered other gunfire as Malik and two of his men came rushing out the main building towards them. Looking at the French police officer kneeling on the steps, Malik opened fire with his machine gun, spraying bullets across the wall above the officer.

Instinctively, Officer Lavigne ducked, flattening himself on the ground in a vain effort to make himself as small a target as he could. Raising his head, he caught the three gunmen moving towards him, guns raised and pointing in his direction.

As one of Malik's men closed to within twenty meters of Lavigne, a volley of gunfire rained down from above, catching the gunmen by surprise. As Malik and the other gunman looked skyward, they encountered more police officers lining the parapet firing down upon them. In an act of self-preservation, the gunman standing next to Malik tossed his machine gun aside and threw his hands above his head.

"You coward," Malik spat, pulling the trigger on his own machine gun. Bullets ripped open the man's chest, spewing flesh and blood across the gravel. A cruel smile crossed Malik's face as the SWAT sniper for Captain Picard placed a well-aimed round through Malik's forehead, killing him in an instant.

The scene taking place before him was not what Nazim expected. Bodies of Omar Khalid's men lay crumpled on the ground, as did the lifeless form of his consort Ketifa, lie upon the deck of the boat. As the gunfight between the police and Khalid's henchmen began subsiding each passing second, Nazim made his way to the bow to finish slicing the mooring line. "Get us out of here," he shouted up to the helmsman as he trotted towards the boats stern.

Noticing the sudden movement from her prey, Geneviève jumped up and ran towards the boat, leveling her pistol at Hakim as she kept screaming above the engines roar. Pausing, she dropped to one knee and took aim at the Algerian prisoner as he turned, a wicked smile of satisfaction edged across his face.

Feeling her face grow flush with anger, Geneviève was pulling the trigger as swiftly as she could until the slide locked open, signaling her magazine had emptied. Through her rage, she remained focused, seeing twelve of her fifteen bullets impacting their target. With grim satisfaction, she watched three of the first four bullets strike the Algerian, dropping him to the deck.

Benoit's joy was short lived as the launch surged away from the jetty, heading out to sea, to be lost among freighters and pleasure craft sailing the open waters.

The helmsman gunned the engine as he heard the bullets impact the boat. Peering back, he looked at the prone figure of Nazim tugging on the pants of his cousin as several rounds hit Hakim across his torso.

Howling in pain, Hakim fell to the deck, his shirt a growing mass of crimson where the bullets had torn through his fragile body. He looked over to Nazim who was trying to say something, but couldn't be heard over the roaring engines, as the helmsman pushed the throttles against the stops. As the distance between the island citadel and the pleasure craft grew, the danger decreased, allowing Hakim to prop himself against the rail.

"Hold this here," Nazim shouted over the wind, stuffing a wad of cloth against one of the entry points on his cousin's stomach. Grabbing the cloth, Hakim tried to pressed it hard against the hole, but the blood continued to ooze out, its color growing darker.

Standing next to the helmsman, the Algerian peered out to sea. "Where are we going?"

"We are to meet a freighter according to his excellency, Khalid," the man said, shifting his eyes between the compass and the horizon. "We should make contact in an hour."

Nazim stepped back to the stern, only to look at the ashen face of his cousin staring back at him. Kneeling next to Hakim, he pulled the cloth from the most serious wound, watching the slow ooze of blood, its color now a deepening mix of burgundy and black. From previous altercations, Nazim knew this was a clear sign of a mortal wound to Hakim's liver, and he was gradually dying before his eyes.

Death's shroud was beginning to envelope the wounded Algerian. "Cousin, how much further to the freighter?" Hakim asked in a voice that was but a raspy whisper.

"It won't be long," Nazim replied as he pulled a large beach towel around Hakim, cradling him close to his body.

* * *

On the opposite side of the archipelago, Geneviève's partner was busy assisting in subduing gunmen who'd taken the ferry crew hostage.

207

On the radio, reports could be heard as the SWAT team was completing their action.

Soon, the two SWAT teams began making their coordinate sweep of the fortress, rounding up the few remaining members of Malik's gang of criminals dispatched by Omar Khalid. In the distance, two more police boats were escorting a commandeered car ferry, which was loaded with emergency vehicles, making their way to the embattled fortress.

While SWAT officers conducted interrogations of staff and civilians left on the island, Captain Georges radioed for Captain Lemieux to meet him in the courtyard for a debriefing of the squad.

As he lumbered up the stone steps, the heat of the summer sun forced Claude to shed his jacket before he cleared the last step. Walking towards the group, his arms itched as sweat formed on his skin, the slight breeze failing to offer relief. Nearing the officers, one tossed him a bottle of water, sensing the captain's need for a drink.

"Merci," Claude said, gulping the liquid down. "Well Captain, what's your assessment?" he asked, as he looked at the SWAT commander.

"We were fortunate today," Pierre said, his face bathed in perspiration. "None of the officers were hurt, and no civilians were harmed in the melee either."

"And the assailants?"

"Four dead, three wounded, seven apprehended," Captain Georges said, reading off his notes. "But it still leaves six unaccounted. We are assuming they made their way out to sea on the launch."

Captain Lemieux noticed his partner walking up to the group from the opposite direction, her image displaying no emotions. As she grew closer, Claude noticed the telltale sign on her helmet of a missed shot getting dangerously close to ending her life.

Standing at the edge of the assembled officers, Geneviève exhibited the signs of an officer who encounters a hostile foe. After the echoes of bullets flying and screams of the wounded and dying subsided, the officer's own adrenaline began to ease up, returning her to the present. Even now, she was processing her actions and of those around her, trying to best learn what she could have done to improve the outcome.

"Detective Benoit, would you care to add anything?" Captain Georges asked, looking at her sweaty and dirty face.

"I'm sorry, Captain. What were you saying?"

"I asked if you had anything to add for the debrief," the SWAT commander replied.

"Yes, I do," Geneviève said, looking over to Officers Cormier and Lavigne. "I want to apologize to Cormier and Lavigne for placing them at risk for my own gain," she muttered, nodding towards the officers. "I needlessly discounted their safety in my attempt to subdue the suspects."

"And as for those unaccounted for, Captain," Cormier said, giving Geneviève a chance to gather her composure, "we've pulled one from the water, but he didn't make it."

"I'm reasonably sure of two... if not three, missing assailants are dead or severely wounded," Geneviève added, recalling the deckhand falling overboard and Cormier's gunfire killing Ketifa. "And I'm positive at least two of my shots hit the prisoner Talib," she stated with renewed confidence.

"Unfortunately, the helicopter couldn't be dispatched in time to shadow the boat carrying your suspects," Captain Georges said. "According to reports from the harbormaster, there was too much clutter with vessel traffic for them to make out their destination."

"With that said, we've lost our chance at catching Khalid," Captain Lemieux muttered to himself as he scanned the horizon. Turning back to the SWAT commander, Claude broached the problem of an informant. "Captain Georges, where are the seven you detained being held?"

"We left them where they were: in the catacombs," Georges replied. "I couldn't think of a better place to begin our questioning, wouldn't you agree?" A wry smile crossed his tired and beleaguered face.

"My feelings precisely," Claude replied, heading towards the entrance to the interrogation facility.

"Captain Lemieux, what are you going to do?"

It was the tired voice of his partner asking the question. Turning to her, he looked at the strain of the day etched across her face: the shoulders slumped, hair a tousled mess from her helmet.

"I want answers to several questions. It's better I ask them now while I have the means," Claude replied, walking through the solitary door below the towers buttress. Leaving the heat, he could sense the coolness of the air-conditioned space chilling his skin. With each of his strides crossing the stone steps, they were leading the officer deeper into the fortress.

Opening the control room, Captain Lemieux found the senior medical technician and pulled him aside. "Can you introduce the serum without having the suspects eating or drinking?" he asked, citing what he and Geneviève observed weeks earlier.

"Yes, but why?"

"I have a few questions I want to ask and I need answers right away," Claude said. Pointing to one of the security officers, he gave his order. "Come with me," he said, exiting the control room and heading down the brightly lit corridor.

Reaching the first holding cell, Claude glanced in one of the miniscule chambers to find Malik's followers huddled with three other men in the corner. "You, step to the center of the room!" he ordered, pointing at the Algerian. "The rest of you take a seat on the floor," he told the four remaining occupants. "Open the cell," he said, directing the officer who'd accompanied him.

With the cell opened, Captain Lemieux stepped in and grabbed the Algerian's robe and dragged him into the corridor, allowing the officer to secure the door. "You appear to be the type who likes to talk. We'll discover how much you have to say in a few moments," he warned, pushing the criminal towards the interrogation room.

Finding him outside the room was Geneviève. Relieved of her SWAT gear, she stood by the doorway with only her pistol in its holster. "What are you going to do, Claude?" she asked her partner as he pushed the member of Malik's group past her.

"We've a rat in the cupboard, and I want to know how it got there," he said, his face flush with anger. "I'm in no mood to wait six weeks for some half-ass report on how information is leaked." He pushed the criminal toward the empty gurney in the room.

"You can't do this to me," the suspect stammered. Seeing the medical technician preparing the syringe, he realized they would use drugs in an attempt to have him talk. "This is inhumane treatment," he continued to say, his voice growing louder. "I've rights. Even under your Vichy government." The man struggled as two guards placed him onto the stretcher.

"Claude, this method isn't right. It isn't who we are," Geneviève pleaded. "You're better than this and you know it. We already know its Khalid behind all this; we don't need to hear it from one of his henchmen."

All eyes were on Claude as he turned from his partner to the technician holding the syringe. Taking a deep breath, he fought the urge to grab the narcotic and plunge it into the criminal. "Take him back to the cell," he directed the officers. "How do we learn who's leaking the information now, huh?" he asked, turning away from Geneviève and heading to the courtyard.

Chapter Thirty-Three

As the pleasure craft came alongside the freighter, several crew members threw a rope ladder over the rail, hitting the water between the two vessels. Grabbing one of mooring lines, Nazim tied off the boat to the ladder rungs while the helmsman killed the engines.

Looking over the side, the freighter's captain, Adem Coetzee, could detect the obvious forms of two bodies laid side-by-side on the stern, a blood-stained tarp covering them. The pleasure craft looked like someone had used it for target practice as most of the visible surfaces bore signs of damage from gunfire. He noticed one man pull open the engine space covers and place a small package against the hull. "Make sure you set the timer for at least five minutes," he shouted to the two men.

Nazim looked skyward, shielding his eyes from the glare of the sun. "It's set for ten minutes; that's enough isn't it?" he asked, the silhouetted figure hanging over the rail.

The captain of the Southern Warrior nodded before answering. "That's plenty. Do you need any help?" he asked, pointing to the bodies. He'd previously dealt with having corpses onboard his ship, but this was different. He was being paid a handsome fee to transport three Algerians to Tunis, but he wasn't aware two of those were the bodies being lifted onboard.

"Be respectful, please," Nazim mentioned to the two merchantmen who'd made their way to the deck of the pleasure craft.

Each man nodded in silence as they removed the tarp, exposing the body of a man and woman to those looking on from the freighter. Lifting the woman onto the pallet, they draped her lifeless form with an Algerian flag Captain Coetzee had provided. Next, they lifted the body of Hakim and placed him along the side of Ketifa before signaling the crane operator to lift them off the boat.

"Are we sure the charges are set?" Nazim asked the lone survivor of the morning's gunfight with the police and their narrow escape from Il d'If.

"It is ready, Nazim," he replied, reaching down to begin the sequence to scuttle the craft.

As he watched the man reach down to the explosives, Captain Coetzee ordered the freighter to get underway, relaying his commands to the engine room via radio. In moments, the ship shuddered, the senior engineer bringing the dual diesel engines up to speed, causing the sizeable bronze propellers to churn the water behind the ship.

The helmsman watched the freighter creeping ahead and jumped from the deck, grabbing ahold of the rope ladder. Glancing back, he looked at Nazim stealing a glance around the luxury boat before leaping across the water and on to the ladder. Taking out a knife from his waist, he reached down and severed the line keeping the two vessels together.

In less than a minute, the boats already drifted apart, a hundred meters at first, then the distance growing with each passing moment. Swinging his leg over the rail, Nazim stood wearily before the South African merchantmen. "I wish to thank you, Captain," he said, extending his hand.

Accepting the show of gratitude, Adem Coetzee shook the young man's hand. "I'm sorry for your loss," he said softly, acknowledging the death of Hakim and Ketifa. "We'll be in Tunis by tomorrow afternoon. Until then, I'll see you and your associate are made comfortable."

"And what will become of my companions?" Nazim asked, noting the absence of his cousin and Omar's consort from the empty pallet on the deck.

"They've been moved to our refrigerated section," the captain said solemnly. "They need to be kept cold until we can arrange for their transfer off the ship," he explained, stepping out of the sunlight and into the cooler confines of the ship.

"And how will that be done?"

"I'd rather not explain those details to you. Rest assured, it will be done with dignity so we can return them to Monsieur Khalid," the captain said, opening the door to one of several spare cabins onboard the freighter. "You'll find toiletries and towels in the bathroom. I suggest you clean up; then, we'll look at to getting you fed," he added. "Mister Walls, my first officer, will return to escort you to the galley in an hour."

"I'm uncomfortable, Nazim. What are we to do if they don't allow us off the ship?" the helmsman said.

"Let's accept their generosity for the moment and refresh ourselves," Nazim replied. "Then we'll worry about what comes next." He pointed to the cabin next to the one he would use. Going in, he found the spartan-surroundings of the cabin clean and well kept. Closing the door behind him, he found fresh clothing in the dresser drawers.

Hanging in the small closet were several clean overalls and a pair of deck shoes.

Removing his sweat-drenched and bloody clothing, Nazim walked into the small bathroom and noticed the fatigue etched on his face. I should have taken my time and planned properly, he told himself. Omar had provided eight of his most trusted members from Algiers to help him and now they were either dead like his cousin or apprehended. Things were going well until the police woman interfered again. Getting into the shower, he spun the handle, letting the water run until the room was filled with steam.

Standing under the stream of hot water, Nazim felt the tension subside, but not the anger. Reflecting on the loss, his thoughts turned to Omar, and his need to explain the failure of his attempt to him. Not only did he risk his people, but Omar also had to accept an alliance with the Maghrebi gang leader, Amed Gilles. Nazim knew that appeasing him for the loss of his people may take a greater effort.

As his mind cleared, seemingly with the passage of water over his body, loud knocking from the cabin door interrupted Nazim's thoughts. Turning the spigot closed, he grabbed a towel and stepped to the door. "Yes, who is it?"

"Mister Walls, sir," the first officer replied. "The evening meal will be ready shortly. I'll be standing by at the end of the passage to your left when you are ready," he said before stepping away from the cabin door.

***

Detective Benoit sat silent in the patrol car. The lights of the city flickered as the daylight surrendered to the night and its citizens gathered to socialize amongst the tourists, like bees to a flower.

Geneviève saw none of it. Her thoughts were still on the island, replaying her actions during the infiltration to free Hakim Talib. How could I act so foolishly, she thought? Cormier and Lavigne knew exactly how to manage the plight we were in, yet I didn't let them do their job because of my own desires for justice.

While the patrol car was stopping for some pedestrians, Geneviève looked out the window, staring at the faces walking past the car. In the men, she noticed her suspects, Hakim Talib and the drug smuggler Louis Remesy, who was actually Nazim Aziz. The reflection of the men smiling back was a sign mocking her ineptitude and failure as an officer.

"Officer Benoit, we're here," the driver said, nudging her shoulder.

"I'm sorry, officer. Thank you for the ride," Geneviève replied, grabbing her gear before getting out and heading towards the armory. Slowly trudging towards the police facility, it was clear by her stature and gait what the day had taken from her physically.

As Detective Benoit was heading towards the armory, her partner was standing in the office of his friend and senior officer, Captain Duval. Awkward silence grew as Captain Duval read the preliminary report of Hakim Talib's escape from Il d'If.

"Tell me, Claude. Do you think Detective Benoit's actions were justified?"

Claude blinked and drew in a deep breath. "I'm not sure, Captain. I wasn't present at the time she took those actions against gang liberating our suspect," he replied. "It would be unfair for me to speculate on whether her actions were justified or not." His hands twitched by his side.

"And, what of your actions at the detention center, huh, Claude? Do you wish to explain just how you would account for drugging a suspect to gain information?" Duval asked. "The senior medical technician is preparing to file a grievance against you."

The officer's shoulders sank perceptively at the reprimand from his friend. Claude knew Julien couldn't condone his conduct at the citadel earlier in the day. But he also felt the captain would accept his actions to try to gain some information on how the suspects learned of their operations.

"Damn it, Julien, someone told those people what was going on out at the facility," Claude exclaimed. "They identified how many security and medical members there were on the shift. Hell, they even learned the exact number of men versus women."

"Calm down, Claude," the senior officer replied. "I'm well aware we've got someone supplying information to the gangs outside this building," he sighed, collapsing into his chair. "We started looking closer at the problem when you and Benoit caught the drug dealer with the surveillance photo. Since then, we've narrowed it down to three possible suspects."

Claude pulled the chair away from the desk before sitting down. "I'm sorry, Julien. I'm just so… frustrated I guess at not making any headway. It's all coming to a head and I'm afraid it's going to get out of hand."

"You mean with Benoit?"

"It's not just Geneviève. It's the drug trafficking, the abduction attempts, everything. But yes, her conduct too. Something's going on in her head she's not telling me," Claude said. "It's something from her past; I'm just not sure what's triggered her current state of mind that's all."

"And aren't you doing the same thing? You're suppressing your emotions of losing Nadine in every bottle of wine you drink," Julien said, confirming what he already perceived of his friend. "You need to finish grieving and then move on, for your own good."

"Are you telling me to forget her?"

"No, I'm not," Julien said. "You'll never be able to forget the life you had with her. But you do need to realize she's gone and move on yourself. You'll find another woman to spend your days with; and trust me, you would not be tarnishing the memory of Nadine if you did."

"Enough about my personal life, Julien. What about…?" Claude said before being interrupted by the buzzing of the intercom.

"Yes, Patrice, what is it?"

"Detective Benoit is here to meet you and Captain Lemieux."

"Send her in, please," Captain Duval replied.

Geneviève made her way into the office, her once confident stride now a slow shuffle. "I understand you wanted to see me, sir."

"Have a seat, Detective," he replied, gesturing to the empty chair next to Captain Lemieux. "The two of you have had a very busy day, haven't you?" He hoped his smile didn't come across as forced as he felt it.

"It wasn't my most memorable one," Geneviève replied, looking towards the officer but not making eye contact with him. "I allowed my desire to see the suspect punished to overcome my judgement." She absentmindedly swept a few strands of hair from her face. "It almost cost the department two fine officers in the process."

Claude sat quietly. He realized it was important for his partner to confess to her poor performance if she ever wanted to become better. Peeking at his friend Julien, he could see the senior officer sitting patiently as Geneviève recounted her actions.

"For the record, Captain Georges said your actions, though unorthodox, did not differ from those of any new team member," Captain Duval said. "He was also pleased with your ability to function under fire."

"Nonetheless, what you did today also tampered with his plans to incorporate other departments into his team activities. However, you must remember, Detective Benoit, Cormier and Lavigne underwent months of training together. They learned through sheer repetition to trust each other and respond to the others' actions. Another officer, even with the best intentions, might jeopardize their roles."

"I'm not sure I understand, Captain," she said.

"Between the increases in drug trafficking and the activities by several of the gangs, Captain Georges had submitted a proposal," the captain said. "It wanted greater participation of Drug Intervention Team and Gang Enforcement Task Force members when the SWAT teams were called in," Duval said. "But your… shall we say... enthusiasm during today's action has him questioning his proposal.".

"I don't think today could be used as the sole reason to discount his proposal, Captain," Claude said, defending his partner. "You recognize sometimes it's impulsive action getting the results we want in various instances."

"Yes, I do, Captain Lemieux. But Detective Benoit's example today didn't net those results, did they?" the senior officer answered back. "The suspect was freed and we're left with only an empty warehouse for the effort."

"Where does that leave me?"

Both of the senior officers exchanged a glance before Captain Duval spoke. "It leaves you with two days of administrative leave," he said softly, sliding a slip of paper towards Geneviève. "And I expect you to take every minute of it away from the station. With the arrest of the two Italians, you should be safe returning to your apartment."

"I'll give you a ride when you're ready," Claude said, leaving the office.

Taking the paper from the desk, Geneviève stood before answering. "I understand your concerns, Captain Duval. I'll do my best to return with a clearer focus for the task at hand." Closing the door behind her, she swiped her hand across her face, wiping away the tears from her cheek.

Chapter Thirty-Four

The ride to her apartment was done in silence. Geneviève sat in the front seat, stone-like, her body succumbing to the lack of adrenaline and willingness to act as it should. Navigating through traffic, Claude stole a glance towards his partner every few seconds, knowing what she'd been exposed to, but afraid to broach the subject lest he cause more anguish and despair.

"Stop!" Geneviève screamed.

The sudden and abrupt show of emotion scared the detective enough he slammed on the brakes, nearly causing a collision with the driver behind him. "What the hell?" Claude stammered. "Are you trying to give me a heart attack?"

"I need a few things," she said, jumping out of the car.

Claude looked around and recognized her scream had him stopping in front of the small market near her apartment. He deftly pulled the police strobe from its holder, affixing it to the hood while the drivers behind him showed their displeasure through honking horns and colorful language.

As her partner dealt with the motorists, Geneviève snatched a small basket and roamed the aisles, selecting various food items from the shelves. As she turned the corner, she stumbled into a handsome gentleman who was also shopping, nearly causing the pair to fall to the floor.

"I'm so sorry," she said, grasping the man's arm. Looking at his face, Geneviève realized she'd seen the man recently. "Excuse me, but don't I know you?"

Julien LeBlanc stared at the officer, working hard to suppress his emotions at coming face-to-face with the woman responsible for shooting his friend Louis Clement. The woman he'd seen in the store from a month ago was now gone. The one before him today appeared tired and disheveled, her hair a matted down tussle, and her black fatigues dirtied and stained.

"If you did, it must have been from another life," he quipped. "But we met a month or so ago while shopping, I believe.".

"That's right," she said. "You were picking up a few things to tend to your friend's wound from an accident. How is your friend doing these days?"

"He's doing better," the former Legionnaire replied. "At least well enough to get back to work." He struggled to keep his outer demeanor neutral as he peered into his basket. "If you don't mind, I need to finish getting a few things. I'm having a guest over for dinner and I don't want to keep her waiting."

"Oh, of course," Geneviève said, dismissing Julien while noticing Claude enter the market.

"Are you almost done?" he asked, letting Julien slide past him in the aisle.

"Just a few more items," she said, following the young man at the checkout counter. "You don't have to stay. I'm just around the corner, you know?"

"I know, but I want to make sure you're ok," Claude replied, seeing her check out the other man. "Do you know him from somewhere, Geneviève?"

"Just from around here. I've seen him once or twice before," she answered, walking towards the cooler for some milk. I never told Claude this was the man I suspected might have been connected to Louis Clement when I first met him, she told herself.

Having made her purchases, Geneviève and Claude were soon trudging up the stairs to her apartment, Claude dutifully carrying the groceries while she thumbed through the mail she'd collected upon entering the building. Unlocking the door, she led Claude to the kitchen so he could unburden himself from the bags.

"Thank you, Claude," she said, giving her partner a brief hug.

"Are you going to be all right?" he asked, looking around the apartment.

"I'll be fine. I just need a few days to figure things out that's all," Geneviève said, putting away the items she bought. "The two Italians are detained. So, I've no need to worry about being abducted, do I?"

"Only if we go on the assumption they were the only ones making an attempt," Claude said. "And Captain Soucy hasn't been able to confirm if the Corsican families are involved or not."

"Are you concerned Khalid may try something more drastic?" she asked, taking a bottle of wine from the cupboard. "Today certainly wasn't what he intended to see done, don't you agree?" she asked between struggling with the bottle and the opener.

"Give me that before you ruin it," Claude said, taking the wine and corkscrew from her. With a deft touch, he skillfully removed the cork and poured out two glasses. "He's still a concern. If what you said about the woman dying along with several of his men, Khalid will no doubt want some form of revenge."

"It wouldn't surprise me if he did," Geneviève said, sitting at the small table. "But if today was any indication, it would appear he is rather haphazard in doing anything."

Claude sipped the wine, letting it swirl in his mouth as he savored the sweetness of the grapes. "Where did you find this?" he asked, holding the glass up.

"Jules, the market owner has a brother in the Rhone Valley who produces several varieties each season," she replied, holding the glass to the light. "He's becoming well known for his Viognier blends like this one."

Setting his glass down, Claude looked at the young woman. "Where do we go from here?"

"What do you mean?"

"You and me. We can't keep secrets from each other, not if I need to trust you with my life at some point," Claude said. "You've mentioned being concerned about me and the same holds true for you, Geneviève," the detective added. "I'm as concerned for you and the things haunting you from your past, too."

Geneviève sat silent, knowing Claude was asking her to divulge things she fought hard to suppress. "If there were things you need to know, I would tell you," she lied. "And if I wasn't mentally able to handle the job, I wouldn't be assigned to your team, now would I?"

"No, I guess you wouldn't," Claude said. He could see in her expression she wasn't ready to let him in on her past. "Get some rest these next two days. I'll expect you to be ready to tackle the ship owners when you return," he added as he stood from the table. Walking to the door, he glanced over his shoulder at her. "Don't forget to lock the door." He winked, exiting the apartment.

***

Moments after entering his apartment, Julien grabbed his cell phone, dialing the number for the office of Papillion Transport and his friend Louis. "Come on, answer the damn phone," he stammered, pacing the front room. After the fifth ring, he heard a familiar voice, but it wasn't Louis.

"Bonjour, mon ami," Hector Pichon answered in his typical jovialness.

"Hector? Where's Louis?"

"He's busy at the moment," Hector replied. "Speaking of which, where are you right now?"

"I'm at my apartment."

"Hold on, here's Louis for you," he said, passing the phone to its owner. "It's Julien for you."

"Julien, what's the problem?" Louis asked.

"I just came across the police woman again. In the market near my apartment," he said.

"Do you think she recognized you?"

"Yes, she mentioned meeting me when I was buying supplies to fix your wounds," Julien said. "Nonetheless, she was also the one following Claudette from the other day too." He circled his lounge chair as he spoke. "But I don't believe she put the two encounters together."

Louis sat at his desk recounting the other day. He noticed the detective following the receptionist and recognized her as the same officer who placed two bullets into him two months ago. "So, she didn't mention seeing you on the street? Some police detective she is not recalling you from your last run in with her."

"Louis, according to Carbone, the Algerians are offering 250,000 euros for her abduction," Julien said. "It wouldn't take much to try grabbing her ourselves, and we could use the money."

"It's tempting," he said. "But Gregory doesn't want to bring attention to our activity so soon after the incident with the British. And I know he doesn't want to exchange pleasantries with Khalid."

Hector sat opposite Louis, listening to half the conversation using the tip of his knife to scrape the underside of his fingernails. "Who is Khalid?" he asked, flipping the knife in his hands.

Louis shook his head at Hector while trying to listen to Julien's rant about kidnapping the officer. Preparing to reply, Louis was interrupted by Gregory entering the office along with the fourth member of Papillion in Pasqual Sequin.

"Who is this guy Khalid everyone is talking about?" Hector asked, turning to Gregory.

"Why do you ask?"

"Louis was mentioning to Julien you don't want to do business with him, that's all."

"Is Julien the one Louis is talking with," Gregory said, sitting at the table.

"Yes. They're discussing some detective Julien wants to kidnap and turn over to the Algerians," Hector answered. "There's a hefty fee for her too. What's the deal with this Khalid, anyway?"

"He's the drug supplier Nazim made arrangements with working out of Algiers," Gregory said. "And he's connected with a Moroccan who arranged for the chemist to alter the hashish for Nazim as well. I found out this Moroccan is known for public executions when his people make mistakes."

"Sounds like the folks in the rain forests," Pasqual said, joining the conversation.

"He's a lot worse from what I've learned," Gregory said as Louis finished his call with Julien.

"Julien's on his way over. Who are we talking about now?" Louis asked.

"Khalid's source in Morocco," Gregory replied. "I was just mentioning to Hector how he's known to execute members of his syndicate in public. And he went so far as to boil one unfortunate soul in oil when he found out he talked with the police."

Before continuing the discussion, Gregory's phone chirped with a text message. Opening the file, he saw it was from Claire. 'Important you contact me, altercation at center,' it read. Letting out a sigh, he went to his desk, pulling out a separate cell phone and selecting a number on the screen. "Suggests our information got to Khalid quicker than I thought," he said.

Getting out his cell phone, Gregory scrolled through the list of numbers until he found Claire's and selected it. Standing by for her to answer, he walked over to the window facing the harbor. Off in the distance, the outcropping which held Chateau Il d'If created a void in the glistening water. Without the aid of binoculars, Gregory had no way of seeing the number of boats surrounding the citadel.

"Bonjour, how can I help you, messier?"

Hearing his sister-in-law come on the line, Gregory asked if she could talk freely.

"The reception is not great here; let me call you back in a minute or so," Claire replied. "Julia, I'll be back in a few minutes." She left their office in the police station and stepped outside the building in the rear. Claire pulled a cigarette and lighter from her coat before redialing Gregory's number.

"Hello?"

"Gregory, there was an attempt to free your colleague from Il d'If today," she said. "Both SWAT teams were deployed to subdue the group. They somehow were able to gain access and free him," she said, lighting her cigarette.

"Did they detain any of the kidnappers?"

"Yes, several were arrested, and at least three were killed," she said, taking a drag on her cigarette. Looking about, she was wary of someone overhearing their conversation. Stepping away from the building, she strolled between several police cars.

"When do you think you'll learn names of those arrested?"

"Tomorrow at the latest," Claire replied, stubbing out the cigarette on a car's bumper. "Why do you want to know?"

Gregory turned away from the window and saw the four men staring at him, all of them wanting to hear what he was learning. "My business may be at risk depending on who the officers detained," he answered. "I specifically need to know if a man by the name of Nazim Aziz or Louis Remesy is amongst those arrested. But Claire," he cautioned, "be careful. Do nothing that'll put you at risk, understand?"

"All right, I can look at the preliminary reports," she said. "I'll send you a text with what I learn, will that be ok?"

"That will do," Gregory replied. "Au revoir, Claire."

"Well?" It was Louis asking what all the men wanted answered.

Julien LeBlanc came into the office just as Gregory was preparing to answer Louis. "What did I miss?" he asked, dropping into a vacant seat at the table.

"Claire mentioned there was an attempt to free Hakim Talib from Chateau Il d'If earlier today," the head of Papillion Transport announced. "She mentioned there were several casualties and several members who were arrested."

"It sounds like we got what we wanted, right?" Julien asked. "We wanted Aziz to try something foolish and for the police to act on it."

"My concern is how promptly the information got from Carbone to the Algerian and for them to assemble and act," Gregory said.

"You think they had information already?"

"Someone did," Gregory replied. "Since moving here to Marseille, we've avoided the Maghrebi elements. It might be time we consider them an adversary to our operations."

"You think Khalid has an allegiance with them?" Hector Pichon asked.

"I'm not going to discount it after today," Gregory replied. "From today on, we retain a means of protecting ourselves, understand?" He looked at each member of his group. "Louis, call Romain and see when he'll be ready for us."

"Are we operating as a squad again?" Pasqual asked, twirling his knife.

"Until we get a better handle on who to trust, yes, we are," Gregory said. "At least traveling in pairs when we're outside the building."

"And what of Phillip? How do we get word to him?" Julien asked, concerned for his cousin.

"With Giuseppe being arrested, I'll be going back to Toulon and getting both him and Sophia," Gregory said. "I'll see if Romain and Elise can help with keeping her safe for the time being."

As the discussion wound down, the office phone rang. Louis looked at Gregory for a sign if he wanted the call answered. Receiving a nod, he reached over and picked up the receiver. "Bonjour. Papillion Transport; how can I help you?"

Amed Gilles sat in the small office of the mosque close to where Louis and the office of Papillion Transport was located. Looking at the photos laid out across his desk, he cleared his throat before speaking. "I'd like to speak with Monsieur Richelieu, please."

"One moment, please," Louis replied, putting the caller on hold. "It's for you," he said, handing Gregory the phone. "They want to talk with Richelieu."

Punching the flashing 'HOLD' button, Gregory answered. "This is Monsieur Richelieu; how can I help you?"

"Yes, messier, I was wondering if you and I could meet and have a face-to-face discussion?" Amed asked.

"And may I ask what your name is? I don't wish to be rude when addressing you," Gregory asked.

"My name isn't important for the moment. But I'm sure Mademoiselle Dubois is," he said.

The color of Gregory's face changed as fear and rage overwhelmed him. "I'm not sure I understand."

"Come now, such a beautiful woman can't elude your thoughts, messier," Amed said. "I'm sure you thought she was safe supplying your fictitious organization with information. I can assure you the world can be a particularly dangerous place," he warned, insinuating harm could be done to Gregory's sister-in-law. "And all this was done in plain view of the authorities... highly ambitious on your part."

"Where and when do you wish to meet?" Gregory asked.

Chapter Thirty-Five

Omar Khalid sat silent on his home's veranda in Algiers. Still shaken by the news, he was still trying to understand how his nephew, Hakim, had been killed in Marseille. His associate, Amed Gilles, was wasting no time in passing the information about the gunfight at Il d'If and the attempt to free his brother's son.

Along with the news of Hakim's demise, he also had the task of letting Aisha know her sister's life had been taken from her. Even as he sat alone, their bodies were being returned to Algiers from Tunis. Once he'd found out from Amed that Nazim was safe on the Southern Warrior, Omar contacted the freighter, beginning the solemn task of returning the bodies.

Contacting his counselor, Mister Alvaro, the necessary documents were soon prepared and sent with the two vehicles needed to make the journey to Tunis. Here, members of Khalid's criminal syndicate took possession of the bodies and meeting Nazim and the lone survivor of Amed Gilles's contingent.

Opening up his phone, Omar selected the number of his associate in Casablanca, Youssef Raif, who'd arranged for the freighter's services. After the second ring, a man's voice answered. "Alu?"

"Ssalamū 'lekum," Omar responded. "I'm calling for Monsieur Raif. Is he available?"

"Who may I say is calling?" the man asked.

"It's Monsieur Khalid, from Algiers."

An awkward silence fell as Omar waited for his call to be passed along to Youssef. Sipping the mineral water next to him, it did little to cleanse the bitter reality that two of the closest members of his family were now gone.

"My dear friend," Youssef said, accepting the phone from his servant. "I'm sorry to learn of your loss. Is there anything I can do for you?"

"First, I'm grateful for your assistance," Khalid said. "And I appreciate your condolences. Considering my losses, I want to exact swift and merciless revenge on the Marseille police. But I'm not so foolish to think doing so would lift me of my pain and suffering."

Youssef could gather in his associate's voice the level of anguish and despair in having lost those close to him. It wasn't long after Omar had come to Youssef to set up his drug trade that the Moroccan had learned of the Algerian's past accounts. He had learned of Omar Khalid's brother and his only son Hakim. With his death, it was only natural the elder would want to see those responsible being held accountable for taking the young man's life.

"Omar," the Moroccan said, "there may be something I can offer. I've learned one the partners of your apprentice may have had a hand in action against your nephew."

"How did you learn of this?" Khalid asked.

"For the moment, it's unnecessary for you to learn how I obtained it," Youssef said. "What is important, however, is the manner we use this against Papillion though." Straightening himself in the chair, Youssef continued. "I've already taken steps towards exacting revenge against the infidels who are responsible for the loss of my associates. In time, it would not take much to discredit them in our line of work."

"That won't bring our people back," Khalid said.

"No, it won't. But those responsible will not be around to meddle in our future affairs either," Youssef said. "Plus, with our swift reprisal against this group, it'll help establish our brothers in Marseille against the Corsicans as well."

Khalid stood up from the table, pacing the veranda while considering the ramifications of Youssef's actions against him and his organization in Algiers. Without the insight from Nazim, he was unsure how his former French partner Gregory Arsenault would react. More importantly, how far he would go to protect himself and his associates.

"And what do you plan to do if the French retaliate?"

"I have faith in my associates, my friend," Youssef said. "They'll do what is necessary to protect you and I when the time comes."

***

Geneviève Benoit walked out of her apartment, making her way towards the marina. Passing the various shops, she caught her reflection in the windows. Her shoulders were slumped while her chin drooped as if she was pouting. Others walking past her would only see the image of someone who was lacking confidence. Inside, her struggle was with her own frailty and inexperience as an officer.

"How did I not see the foolishness in my actions?" she murmured, walking through the intersection near the beach. Shifting through the evening crowds, Geneviève soon found herself walking the promenade, a gentle breeze tossing her hair. Pausing outside a local restaurant, she took in the aroma of the food being served. As she was about to enter, her cell phone rang. Not recognizing the number, she cautiously answered the call. "Hello?"

"Geneviève? It's Francine LeBeau," the forensic technician said. "I hate bothering you, but I didn't know who else to turn to." There was a tone of panic in her voice. "I was supposed to meet a friend near the mall off of Avenue Rellys and she didn't show up."

"Is it uncommon for your friend to be late?"

"Yes. She's very particular about meeting at a specific place and time," Francine said. "I'm worried, Geneviève," she whispered, the growing concern clear in her voice.

"Can't you call her to see why she's running late?"

"She doesn't carry a cell phone," the technician said.

"Where are you at the moment?" Geneviève asked, looking at her watch.

"I'm just outside the coffee shop on the south end of the mall."

"See if you can contact Nicolas and I'll meet you in fifteen minutes or so," the detective said, walking towards a row of waiting taxis.

"Ok, please hurry," Francine said, ending the call.

Striding to the first taxi, Geneviève opened the door and slid behind the driver, announcing her destination. "Oui, mademoiselle," came his response putting the car in motion.

While navigating the boulevard, Geneviève made a call to Claude.

"Good evening, Geneviève," the senior detective said.

"Claude, I just had a call from Francine LeBeau," she said. "It sounds like she might be in some sort of trouble. Can you meet me at the mall off of Avenue Rellys?"

"I'm not any condition to drive," he said, alluding to his drinking. "Have you tried calling Nicolas or Guy?"

"I told Francine to call Nicolas," she said, watching the driver navigate around a caravan of tourist buses. "Claude, she was talking as if she were in a panic, almost. It didn't sound right, you know?"

"I'll call the local office for a patrol to meet you at the mall," Claude said. "Let me know how things are as soon as you can." He hung up on her, then dialed the police dispatcher.

Moments after her partner finished talking, the taxi pulled up to the sprawling mall, its array of neon lights flickering in the evening. "That'll be eight euros, if you please," the driver said, looking back at Geneviève.

Pulling a ten euro note from her wallet, she handed the money over as she exited the car, "Merci," she muttered, making her way towards the entrance. Walking into the expansive atrium-like interior, she soon caught sight of her friend. "Francine!" she exclaimed, waving her hand to get her attention.

"Thank God you're here," the woman said. "Nicolas is on his way too. Patrice is never late like this."

"Where were you to meet her?"

"On the other side of the roundabout behind the mall, near the bus stop."

Geneviève looked at the young woman with a quizzical expression on her face. "Why are you meeting there?"

"She's part of a commune," Francine lied. "She doesn't like being seen in public, you know crowds and such. Especially if she hasn't had a chance wash up or change her clothes."

"So, she's homeless? Is that what you're trying to tell me Francine?"

The forensic technician looked aside before answering. "Yes. I mean, she promised me not to divulge how she lives or where. Every few weeks I bring her a couple pairs of clean pants and tops, some snacks. I'm just helping while she gets herself settled."

"How long has she been on the street?"

"About three months now," Francine said. Looking passed Geneviève, she noticed Nicolas walking towards them. "Over here, Nic," she said with a wave.

"Hey Geneviève, Francine; what's going on?" Nicolas asked, joining the two women.

"My friend was supposed to me and she hasn't shown up."

"This is why you didn't want to go out tonight?" Berger asked.

"Meeting Patrice had nothing to do with not seeing you tonight, Nic," Francine said, a touch of defiance in her voice. "We had this planned for the last three weeks; I just remembered when you asked about dinner, that's all."

"Let's solve one problem at a time, shall we?" Geneviève offered, getting the couple to focus on the missing friend. "First off, what does she look like?"

"Oh, maybe five and a half foot tall," Francine replied. "Wavy brown hair, brown eyes and average complexion I suppose." She struggled to contain her emotions while she described her friend.

"Do you have a picture of her by chance?" Berger asked.

"Sure," Francine said, pulling out her phone. Scrolling through the gallery, she soon came upon a series of her and her friend. "Here you go - she's on the left," she said, handing the phone to the two detectives.

Geneviève and Nicolas squeezed together to view the images on Francine's phone.

"I've seen this woman before," Geneviève said, looking at Francine.

"Oh really? Where?" Francine asked, feigning a look of surprise.

"Yeah, where?" Nicolas asked.

"She was sitting in Annex Three where Captain Soucy and his Gang Enforcement officers gather," Geneviève said. "She mentioned she had two weeks before being reassigned oddly enough." As the two detectives stood looking at Francine, two patrol officers walked up and introduced themselves while asking for identification.

"Captain Lemieux asked we aid you," the first officer said, handing back their IDs to each of the officers. "He mentioned we're trying to find a single woman, is that correct?"

"She's actually…" Nicolas said before being stopped by Geneviève.

"Officer, she's homeless and was befriended by Miss LeBeau," Geneviève said. "Her health is questionable and we want to make sure she's able to make it through the rest of the summer."

"Where were you supposed to meet?" the second officer asked, looking at Francine.

"Near the traffic circle, behind the bus stop," Francine said.

"Then I recommend we start there," the first officer replied, heading towards the exit.

After making their way through the expansive parking lot, the four officers and Francine soon walked along a dirt path towards the kiosk for the local bus service. Stepping to the right and into some brush, Francine pointed out a clearing in the grass. "This is where we would meet," she explained, turning towards the officers.

The two patrol officers shone their flashlights towards the bare patch amongst the bushes. As they swept the field, Geneviève noticed a small envelope caught in the brush at knee level to where they stood. "Shine your light over there," she directed one officer.

Swinging the light back, they all saw what she had spotted.

"Do you have gloves?" Nicolas asked, turning to Francine.

"Yeah, here are some," the technician said, pulling a pair of surgical gloves from her purse. Turning to the patrol officers she shrugged. "Can't leave home without them you know," she said, forcing a laugh.

Pulling the gloves on, Nicolas reached into the brush and pulled the envelope free. Turning it over, he found nothing written on the outside, but could feel there was something inside the envelope.

Sliding the flap out, he pulled the single folded piece of paper out, along with a single photo of a woman. Spreading it open for the both of them to read, each of them took turns glancing at the image. On one side they found writing in Arabic script, flipping it over, they saw what appeared to be the same message written in French.

As the two officers read the note, they exchanged glances. "Are you reading what I am?" Nicolas asked.

"It's a ransom note," Geneviève said. "It suggests the Maghrebi gang in this part of town have added kidnapping to go along with their extortion and drug selling activities. Because now, if we are to take this seriously, they've abducted Officer Patrice Galant."

"What are you saying?" Francine asked

"We're looking at a note and photographic evidence that she might have been kidnapped," Nicolas said. "This is now a crime scene. Officer, contact your station and let's get more officers out here to search. One of our own is missing."

*** THE END ***

Discover other titles by Anthony J. Harrison:
(all titles are available at most online retail outlets)

The Irishman's Deception – A Conor McDermott Novel

Betrayed by a Scot – A Conor McDermott Novel

Suspicious by Design – A Geneviève Benoit Novel

Thank you for reading my book. If you enjoyed it, won't you please take a moment to leave me a review at your favorite retailer?

Thanks!
Anthony

<u>Acknowledgements</u>

First and foremost, I'd like to thank my wife, Mary, for letting me scratch this itch called writing and for supporting me with her comments and encouragement, even after I locked myself away for hours at a time. Also, a big thank you to my daughter's Rebekah and Jennifer for letting 'Dad' to his thing without the need to keep asking "why'd you write that?"

Next, to my good friend and co-worker, Doretta Burgess, for providing the first level of sanity checks, grammar checks and being that punctuation pundit on all the many pages of my random thoughts and ramblings. Also, to the members of the Ventura Fiction Writers Group; Dru, Wendy, and Ron for helping me understand the difference between 'showing' and 'telling' in my writing and Robin for encouraging me to 'just keep writing'.

<u>About the Author</u>

Anthony is a first generation American and native Californian, the son of Scottish immigrants, and who's fraternal grandparents hailed from Ireland, while his maternal grandparents hailed from Scotland. A product of a mixed education (part parochial and part public schools), he developed a thirst for reading early in his childhood and took to writing fiction as an escape from his work as an Instructional Systems Designer. When not working on improving his writing, Anthony can be found on the local golf course, honing his game invented by his ancestors.

Comments or feedback are welcome at;
<u>mailto:fairwayscribe@gmail.com</u>